ISALEER HORUS
AND THE MAKER OF GUILLOTINES

D. K. ROCKWELL

Vol. I

BRIEF STORY OVERVIEW

This story was established over a four - year period, just before the wrath of God, in the times known in Revelation as
"Apocalypse..."
"Armageddon..."
"The Great Tribulation..."
It goes as follows.

As the age of darkness approaches, evil has begun to arise like never before. Martial law has been declared, and the Elite Occult Orders have unified under the Illuminati flag, sending forth soldiers to go door to door apprehending anyone without the mark of the beast. The masses are fearing an all-out holocaust; riots begin to form a global resistance army called the Rebellion. The mainstream media's head adviser Isaleer Horus has been taken to the Black Forest, thinking this was just a luxurious vacation retreat for the world's elite.

NO ONE SAID ANYTHING ABOUT DEMONIC OCCULT RITUALS!

Plunging the world into utter darkness, the Illuminati are driving themselves to madness as they séance and sacrifice in demonic occult rituals harkening for the Dark Lord to show them a way to use black magic to turn all of Earth into a prison planet. The story thickens when Isaleer discovers he is only part human. His birth father is the Dark Lord Satan himself. Isaleer Horus is a demonic gargoyle prince. As he has true Satanic blood flowing through his veins, the Elite Occult Orders hold him in the highest regard. Isaleer Horus will soon learn what he is capable of conjuring as the son of Satan.

Meanwhile, hundreds of millions of people just vanished off the face of the Earth. Where did they go? Who took them? Those who remain are left to face the terrors told about in the Book of Revelations.

WARNING

**This is book is not suitable for
children thirteen and under**

Any child under the age of thirteen should seek parents' permission before reading this book. It is strongly recommended that parents pre-read this book to assess appropriately the suitable nature of this text and its contents. With regards to discrepancy, this book contains occult rituals, brutality, gore, drugs, alcohol, minor sex scenes, demonic possession re-enactments, and other topics not suitable for children. It is strongly suggested by the author that if young children read this, they read this together with their parents. This is a book written by an adult for adult entertainment purposes.

For The Optimal Reading

EXPERIENCE

**This story was made to be enjoyed in the
darkness of night, So Turn off Every Single Light.
Say your prayers, and face your fright.**

HOW TO
CORRECTLY EXPERIENCE

Isaleer Horus
and the Maker of Guillotines

For the best reading experience, you will need the following:
1. A handheld light source
2. A Holy Bible
3. A gasmask
4. A hazmat suit
5. Anointing oil (for the religious)
6. A catalyst to enter spirit realm

BEFORE READING

This book must be prayed over before reading. The story contained within these pages is black magic exposed and unveiled.

ALL IN THE ROOM WHILST THE BOOK IS OPEN MUST PROCLAIM ALOUD BEFORE READING, WHILE HOLDING HANDS IN UNISON, "I COVER MYSELF IN THE BLOOD OF JESUS CHRIST."

Without covering yourself in Christ's blood, you will be unprotected and exposed to a large demonic presence, which has in some cases led to full demonic possession. In several instances, those who have read this book and partaken in its read-along have had violent vomiting spells. Others have experienced extreme anxiety attacks. High-ranking witches and warlocks have blessed this book. The author has taken the time to contact both the Church of Satan and the Satanic Temple to request to speak with the highest ranking Lord in charge of these international religious organizations. Without being contacted directly by their highest ranking Lord, the representatives of both organizations wished the best of luck to this series, therefore blessing this series and deeming it an open portal in which both angelic and demonic hierarchy may pass through at any time while the book is open. Be wise when reading this novel. It is not a simple story, as it contains the names of the highest ranking demonic hierarchy. If read carelessly, this book has been given the power to summon the names spoken aloud into the reader's presence. The knowledge imparted by way of this book of the Occult is not to be reenacted, practiced, or performed. This book in brief moments subjects its readers to black magic, the Occult, and witchcraft. Do not dabble! You have been warned.

MIND FRAME

THOU MUST ENTER WITH HUMILITY AND RESPECT AMIDST
The Royal Hierarchy before Entering the Book

"What fear do I face while the sunlight is out? But tremble underneath the night terrors, as they come forth from the night. If you truly wish to experience this story, you should turn off the light."

-D. K. Rockwell

HIDING IN PLAIN SIGHT

ince the beginning of time, men have desired to know firsthand what it's like to hold and harness the power of God.

Since the Beginning of time, the age of Adam and Eve, man has desired to be as like unto God.

And unto curious man t'was, by a serpent's whisper into her ear, that the Fall of Mankind from Paradise came when both man and woman were brought to lust and desire as they passionately sought to clutch the forbidden knowledge of good and evil, just as Almighty God.

Since the early ages, throughout all nations and tribes, certain men have dabbled in witchcraft, sorcery, and the Occult, searching the universe for knowledge on major topics and guidance in making decisions.

The dark sorcerers who practice black magic have delved into séance with Ouija Boards and awoken dark places, using the boards as portals in the center of pentagrams, just to feel the rush of even the fantasy that would accompany controlling all of mankind in world domination.

Evil, corrupted, and twisted men have daydreamed their lives away, pondering on how it must feel being worshipped and glorified as God Almighty before an audience that they fully controlled. As they relaxed their souls, they took complete control. These same evil men have carried the torch into our generation, and they, too, desire world domination, just as their forefathers did. They have longed to experience the power of global control.

To most, this is only a thought. However, to the global elite, this is their everyday battle as the entire Earth, every man, woman, and child, is affected by the choices and decisions these global CEOs and bankers make on behalf of the planet's inhabitants.

To the most elite of the elite, this is not just a thought. To a man who controls all the currency of Earth, this is a reality he must rebuke. Each day he must revoke all those desires from his mind, for if he actually truly has the power to abuse his authority and bring this evil fantasy to life, then eventually man would become curious and desire to taste of this forbidden power. "But once you have tasted, there's no going back…"

For in order that you may taste, first you had tasted
The mark of the beast upon thy soul.
As The Devil, Satan, Lucifer,
That Old Serpent takes control…

They gathered in secret, devising a plan to rule the nations. These men and women have carefully guarded their agendas and, based on their position, power, influence, bloodline, and wealth, have entered into an Order, all the while being selected by Lucifer to carry out certain major and minor roles in bringing forth Satan's return as the Antichrist. These are very dangerous men, willing to do anything in their pursuit of power. They will stop at nothing and no one to reach the New World Order. They seek only the destruction of the Earth. These men hide in plain sight. They are the leaders of the world in society, government, agriculture, and technology, along with the global mogul titans over the marketplace. These are the global elite who have sold their souls to Lucifer for a chance to rule by his side as gods over the Earth. In theology circles, we have unveiled these men as the ones who are to welcome in the end times. This time is more commonly known as the day of Apocalypse. We here in the twenty-first century know it better as the New World Order and its imprisoned planet. It is on this day when all of Revelations chapter six will begin. These days have been prophesied in the book of Matthew in chapter twenty-four. As believers in Christ, we will be killed because we get in the way. Before God Almighty returns in the clouds to bring forth what is known as the wrath of God, first there must come the disappearance of nations. Then must come the great tribulation, and then the age when the sun, moon, and stars no longer shine—the age of the Apocalypse.

Our story begins at the tail-end of the era known as the Age of Man, just before the start of the disappearance of nations.

Table of Contents

Chapter ⃝

WHAT EYE CAN OFFER YOU

Our story begins at an aristocratic mansion on a wonderfully bright sunny day in a city called Boca Raton…

As the limo driver pulled up to the Morgan estate, he quickly put the vehicle in park, jumped out of the car, and began making his way across the driveway, which was shaded by a luxurious Coliseum-style stone pavilion. Weaving to and fro through the cars already lined up there for some sort of celebration, Mr. George continued to straighten himself up, continuing to make his way to the main entrance. The Morgan family were having the front door guarded, and thus Mr. George had to pass through security in order to ring the doorbell. Adjusting his tie and correcting his collar, making sure he looked presentable, Mr. George the limo driver began knocking on the door, occasionally peering around, expecting someone to possibly come flying out of one of the many entranceways in a raging fit of hysteria, being that there was an elegant celebration going on throughout the Morgan estate. The limo driver kept his eyes on a swivel, mostly because of all of the hot chicks that were there, but mainly because with all of these entrances, one must avoid the element of surprise. He suffered from Tourette's syndrome. Being startled or put under extreme pressure caused horrible words to project out of his mouth beyond his control. As he looked around, he noticed ten limos including his own parked comfortably under the mansion's massive overlook, which doubled as a gigantic shaded entranceway for VIP parking guests. Continuing to ring the doorbell, he checked his watch periodically. He rang the doorbell several times, but no one answered. As he stood waiting for a butler to answer the door, he frantically went over his lines again. "H-Hello, Mr. Morgan! I'm sorry for being…balls…late! I was stuck on I-95 during rush hour. You know how the highway is in West Palm and $@&#. Aha. How are you doing today? Oh! Do you want me to get those bags for you, sir? Ahhh, $@&#!"

After mumbling this ditty almost ten times, he shook his head and squared his shoulders, remembering to stand up straight.

Taking a deep breath, the limo driver said to himself, "And no matter what, DO NOT LET ANY CURSE WORDS SLIP OUT OF YOUR MOUTH!"

He couldn't help but brace himself for whatever reprimand was to come. Undoubtedly, the reprimand was coming. That was a fact. He then rolled his head and neck in a singular circle around his shoulders and took another deep breath. Mr. George began to collect himself as he mumbled quickly again, "Mr. Morgan, it's George, the limo driver. How are you tonight? Might I take those bags for you, sir?"

After nailing his line, he quickly scrounged up some advice for himself. "Stay positive… That's the key. Stay positive. He might be in such a festive mood that he doesn't even care. Think about it. Straighten up."

Mr. George gulped and blurted out, "#%$#!"

He was having a hard time letting go of the anxiety he felt over being late. Hopefully Mr. Morgan wouldn't even notice, or, being so delighted by his celebration, he wouldn't care if he did. Beads of sweat fell down George's face. Each falling sweat bead reminded him why he hated wearing a suit in Florida, especially in July. His handkerchief was the only thing that seemed to hide his loss of composure. No sooner did the limo driver put away his handkerchief than the intercom next to the door began to ring. *BEEP!*

A voice from the intercom asked, "Who's that at my door?"

The limo driver replied with confidence, "It's George, the limo driver."

Mr. Morgan yelled back, sarcastically remarking, "Oh, wow!"

The only thing the limo driver could reply with was, "I'm sorry, sir, the traffic on I-95 was…"

Instantly, Mr. Morgan fired back, interrupting Mr. George and shouting, "Shut up! Just shut up! Don't even bother starting with your stupid excuses. Right now I can't stand you. Now, my butler is collecting all my suitcases; he will bring them down to you in a moment. Be prepared to move quickly. Do you understand me?"

"Yes, sir, I won't let you down again." The limo driver had hoped he was overreacting to this whole situation, but after the conversation over the intercom, the evidence to the contrary was piling up quickly. Perhaps he had understood only a smidgen of the extremity of this situation. Mr. George removed his finger from the intercom and placed his hands on his head. In a panic, he gasped and exhaled, saying, "Ah, $@&#!"

As he continued to draw the sweat away from his face, he finally regained his wit just as the full gravity set in. He had really screwed up this time. This time, he was not late to some high school prom pickup or some special dinner date. This was a famous political figure who was accustomed to excellence and prestige. Showing up late was dishonorable and disrespectful, no matter the excuse.

As Mr. George stepped back from the intercom and put away his handkerchief, he stopped to admire the view. He had never seen wealth like this before in his life. This was the first time he had ever seen such an extensive collection of cars all in one driveway. It didn't stop there, though. Yes, the car collection was extensive and well worth over ten million dollars, but the car collection was not the only breathtaking sight this courtyard had to offer.

The view to the left of the Morgan estate was even more appealing to the eyes. Turning his attention to the helicopter pad, Mr. George noticed a large black executive helicopter, complete with gold cursive writing on the side reading, "Morgan International."

As Mr. George continued to take in the wondrous view of this sixty acres of prime real estate, he retraced his steps all the way to the front gate. It was time to recap on where he was. Starting from the entrance and working his way to the Morgan family's mansion, he saw shrubbery, which guarded the view of the home from paparazzi, and two large stone pillars standing twenty feet tall, which held the automatic gate system in place. At the top of the pillars were horses carved out of marble. The gate opened to a stone driveway wide enough to be a two-lane highway. Winding around several bends, each corner was marked by a new set of sights to behold. The whole yard was a wondrous display of expert landscaping craftsmanship. The gardeners had designed a checkerboard flower display, and the men in charge of trimming the hedges had made them look like sculptures. As magnificent as this yard's landscaping was, it gave way to the view overlooking the Atlantic Ocean from the ballroom-style gazebo.

The Morgan family's personal yacht was docked in the harbor no more than five miles away, but this week had called for celebration, so the yacht was anchored about one thousand feet offshore.

The Morgan family loved to golf, so all the grass was made fit for golfing, complete with a driving range and a putting green.

Mr. George continued to stare at all the magnificent things this mansion had to offer, daydreaming and pretending all of this was his.

Just then, Isaleer pulled in the driveway of the Morgan estate in an executive limo. Isaleer had overbooked himself again. All last night and this afternoon, he had been in business meetings. Exhausted, he figured he would take a nap while his limo driver drove him to Haley's house. After noticing the limo approaching at full tilt, Mr. George was quickly brought back to reality and poised himself. Isaleer's limo driver stepped out limo and came around to open the door for his passenger. Isaleer's driver waited a few seconds; when he heard nothing, he looked inside to make sure Isaleer was ok. He began chuckling to himself. He was used to seeing Isaleer like this. Isaleer was of new money, so he was still learning the ins and outs of this lifestyle. Rule number one: One should always check his calendar and never overbook himself, or exhaustion will be his best friend.

Fascinated, Mr. George walked over to the executive limo and peered inside to see for himself. There Isaleer was, lying bizarrely on the floor of the vehicle. Isaleer was so tired he had forgotten to take off his black leather-studded jacket. He opened his eyes only to see both his personal limo driver and this other random limo guy staring at him from the doorway. Normally a person might be frightened by the thought of waking up to people just watching him, but Isaleer was used to being watched. He blinked his eyes a couple of times, trying to wake up. No doubt, Isaleer had little eye buggies that needed to be wiped away. Looking around, he saw that he had a bottle of water right next to him, so he poured some on his face. WHAM! He began putting the scene together and came to realize he was lying on the floor, awake and alive. Isaleer looked up at the limo driver here to pick up Mr. Morgan and said, "Yo, um, are you alright, bro? Why aren't you standing by your limo or doing something for your master, bro? Have you never seen someone take a nap in a limo before? Haha. Who are you?"

Surprised by this sight and the rude words that had just come so easily from this young man's mouth, Mr. George's words just shot out. "Yes! I'm Mr. Morgan. I mean—I'm not Mr. Morgan. I'm…I'm the limo driver. I'm George. I'm here to take…uh, uh, uh…Mr. Morgan to the executive airport."

Taking a deep breath, Mr. George began again. "I'm here to take the limo and Mr. Morgan to the executive airport, and I'm ready. I am just waiting for his butler to come down with all his luggage. Master."

Isaleer smiled, laughing, and said, "Ah-ha… So the rumor is that you're late for your scheduled arrival. Haha. Cool story, bro. Haha. I'm excited to see him go off on you. Hahaha. Please forgive me, servant…"

Collecting himself, Isaleer continued, "Listen, George, you need to step away from my limo right now. I literally rolled the dice today, and I rolled zero and ^%*$ every time. If you don't quit being so damn nosey as to who I am, you're gonna have much bigger problems than being late. I want to be here when he goes off on you. I bet you look stupid when you get yelled at, coward. Don't you? Ahahahaha!"

In any argument, Isaleer definitely got his strength from taking the hope away from his victims, by cornering them. He did so as if to say, "Not only do I want to watch you suffer, but I want it to be slow and painful and at my pace because you have nothing over me, and I have everything over you. Because you ever tried me, I will end you right now. I have my facts straight, and you've still got nothing." It could be said that Isaleer liked to play with his food.

After Isaleer's remark, Mr. George became much more self-conscious. He mustered up enough strength to smile through his emotional conflict "Will you be accompanying Mr. Morgan to the airport? If so, do you have any bags for me to go get, sir?"

Of course, Isaleer was not going to miss this opportunity to take advantage of some poor soul. "Uh, no. I'm not going with him. Mr. Morgan did, however, want me to give him this one suitcase. Don't put it in the trunk. This suitcase goes in the back seat with him. Here, enjoy! The rest of Mr. Morgan's suitcases are sitting up at the front door. They must have been put out while we were getting to know one another for what the $#@! ever purpose. Seriously, I just wish you would shut the actual $#@! up. While your long-talking @$$ mouth wouldn't shut up, the butler came out and dropped all the luggage for you. 'K. Bye, bro. Servant."

Mr. George walked briskly to the trunk of Mr. Morgan's limo and began loading the suitcases. After all was said and done, Mr. George closed the trunk and waited for Mr. Morgan to make his way to the limo. After waiting about two minutes, Mr. George walked back to Isaleer, who was now texting from outside of his limo. Mr. George attempted to begin small talk. "What was your name?"

Isaleer, tired of talking to this dude, said, "$#@! off, servant!" Pissed, Isaleer couldn't help but say under his breath, "You're a &^%$ing idiot. You're about to be chewed up and spit out. Kill yourself, fool."

Some time passed. The silence signified to Mr. George that Isaleer did not want to talk.

After another five minutes, Mr. Morgan made his way out the front door of his home. He took a deep breath of the crisp ocean air and said his goodbyes to all his guests, assuring them that they must carry on without him.

Mr. Morgan then smiled at Isaleer and said, "Security notified me that this limo driver has been pissing you off. Don't worry, son. I'm going to make this %$#@er wish he was never born."

Walking down the steps to the executive limo, he took each step like a rock star, smiling the entire way. Not one of his guests knew anything was wrong. His armed security team escorted him to Mr. George, who stood waiting at the back door to seat Mr. Morgan for his ride to the airport. Mr. Morgan said to his security team leader, "I was given a summons from the Order of the Thirteen to bring forth my son. I don't have a son. I only have my beautiful daughter, Haley. With Isaleer's new arrival to the top of the charts, I think now is perfect. I'll ask him tonight as we are pulling out. Make sure security knows there will be another with us."

Mr. Morgan looked at Isaleer as he approached Mr. George and said with a smile, "Watch this."

Mr. Morgan then turned to Mr. George and shouted across the entire pavillion, "'Sup, %$#@er! Get my door, boy! Security, this man can't even show up on time for a politician. Pay him no mind; he is just a low-life servant…and not even a good one at that. He's a fool."

Mr. George walked quickly over to the back passenger door of the limo and opened it for Mr. Morgan. Mr. Morgan sat gently in the limousine. Before Mr. George shut the door, Mr. Morgan had some more words to say to the limo driver. "Now, why'd you run me late? I put full confidence in your company's punctuality. I was very clear when I told you to be here at a specific time, and you're still gonna %$#@ing run me late? Now you gotta race me like a wild, crazy lunatic all the way to where I need to go. You better be a safe and fast driver, and I do mean both—safe and fast! Now, you can shut my door, and go ahead and get me where I need to go. Oh…and I will be contacting your superior about your tardiness."

The limo driver replied shamefully with his head down, "Yes, sir, I am sincerely sorry."

Mr. Morgan replied, "Yeah, yeah, yeah. I don't really care about all that. Just shut my door, and let's get me where I need to go."

They began to pull out of the pavilion and up the driveway. As planned, Mr. Morgan urged his driver to stop the limo and roll down the back seat window so that he may speak to Isaleer. "You got a lot of potential, kid. Why don't you come with me tonight and uh…show off some of your talents to some of my important friends? Let's see what Eye can offer you."

Isaleer smiled curiously. "I mean, I appreciate your extending that beautiful offer to me. However, your daughter has requested that I go to church with her tonight."

Mr. Morgan had never really taken Isaleer to be the Bible-thumping type. "I didn't know that you were a church boy, Isaleer?" Curiously, he waited for a response.

Isaleer decided to be honest "I… Well, actually I'm not, but she's requesting for me to go to church with her, so… I mean, whatever, I will go for her."

Mr. Morgan couldn't have cared less, though. "Yeah, well… I had actually expected for you to make bigger moves. Like, if you had gotten in the car with me, I could've seen you being a politician in a few years, making a good kind of money—money that would allow you to take care of my daughter the way I expect a man to be able to take care of my daughter." That could not have been any more truthful. Mr. Morgan was a business-minded human being, and in his mind, all the Christians wanted was to beg and bum off the wealthy such as himself. In his mind, they only wanted him in the church for his money.

Isaleer couldn't help but feel a certain type of way after realizing Mr. Morgan found his line of work to be unsatisfactory for dating his daughter. Perhaps he had forgotten Isaleer was numbers one, two, and three on the Billboard Top 100. "Was that your way of insinuating that I am not able to take care of your daughter financially in the position that I am currently in…sir? No disrespect, Mr. Morgan, but I just won eight awards at last week's music award ceremony out in Hollywood. My accountant said I'm worth an estimated twenty-five million dollars, and that number is growing daily. I'm pretty positive I'm able to take care of your daughter. That is, if you're saying you're concerned."

Mr. Morgan replied, "That is precisely what I am saying, son! Not just that though, but see, you're young, so you… You're focused on the financial part of this, but what you've failed to realize is that I already know you are signed to a major record label. I know you have plenty of money to provide for my daughter, but my question is about the moral part of this. See, what you're doing at your age is ok, but will you be ok with looking at yourself at fifty years old and being known as a musician? Or would you like to be a politician? Son, I'm offering you a once-in-a-lifetime chance to come with me to a place where I can turn you into one of the most prestigious men in the world. I suggest you really juggle because I'm only going to ask you this once. Which is more important, this church thing, or coming with me and seeing what Eye can offer?"

All Isaleer's life he had wanted to lead his nation. He loved America! This was his home. He hated seeing idiots get into office without any clue how to hear the citizens' pleas for help. In this moment, Isaleer was literally being offered a political opportunity by a leading government official. Mr. Morgan wanted him to get into politics; this meant one phone call, and he was in. This seemed like the chance of a lifetime for young Isaleer; he seized this moment like a lion pouncing on a baby elephant. There were no games involved; he ripped this baby's throat out instantly and without hesitation.

"Well, sir. BOOM! You literally just made a believer out of me. If you think I can do better, then show me the way. I will not question your advice again. If you would just scoot over, I'm gonna go ahead and text Haley and tell her that you're kidnapping me to go better my life."

In perfect timing, Isaleer's phone rang. The caller I.D. said it was Haley; she was in a wonderfully good mood. This was nothing new when it came to church days. These seemed to be her favorite days of the week. She got to do two of her favorite things: get dressed up all cute and worship God. Reaching for his phone, Isaleer said to Mr. Morgan, "Actually, that's her calling right now."

Isaleer put the phone to his ear, remembering that he was about to talk to his girlfriend. He had to quickly find the boyfriend-voice, which was hidden behind all the business-voices. He thought the best way to start was by trying not to be so serious; he jumped off a cliff and hoped he packed his parachute right. Clearing his throat, he greeted Haley. "Well, hello, beautiful."

Gasping, excited to hear Isaleer's voice, she replied, "Hi, baby!"

Isaleer smiled and gained his composure, remembering he was sitting right next to her father. Biting his bottom lip, he said, "Oh, God. Well, how are you doing, Haley?"

"Guess what, baby? I'm not wearing any pa…"

In a panic, Isaleer began coughing and quickly interrupted her, remarking, "No, no, no, no, no, no, no, no! Babe, do you need to say anything to your dad? I'm sitting right next to him."

Haley replied, "Just put the conversation on speaker phone really fast."

As Isaleer began pulling the phone away from his ear to put the conversation on speaker phone for Mr. Morgan to hear, Haley said, "No! Baby, all I was saying is that I love you. I just wanted Daddy to know that I would do anything for my sexy man."

Haley always had a way of shocking the world with the things she would say. She was one of those chicks who never really thought before she spoke, essentially just saying whatever to whomever, whenever. This instance was merely a prime example.

Isaleer collected himself and replied, "Oh yeah, babe? Well, if he didn't know that, he does now. Ah-ha. Silly girl." He forgot to say "I love you" back, probably because he was too busy rolling with the punches Haley found amusing. Most likely, she was just awaiting his reply, armed with another statement just as bold. If that's what she was waiting for, then this was going to be a very long conversation because Isaleer said nothing… Isaleer was a young man sitting in a limousine with the father of his girlfriend, and she just announced she would do anything for him. It's awkward enough for a young man to sit next to his girlfriend's father, but it's downright terrifying when her father is a powerful politician. Mr. Morgan was regularly seen on TV discussing foreign and domestic affairs. This man had a security team waiting at the entrance of his home, ready to escort him anywhere he went, and they all carried submachine guns. It would be incredibly easy for a man like Mr. Morgan to make anyone go missing.

Isaleer had two thoughts, the first of which being, *Haley, think with your head. Quit pissing your dad off while my name is being used.* The second thought was, *Thank God I'm a famous celebrity. At least if I go missing, it will be in the news.*

After a few moments, Haley said in frustration, "Well, do you love me?"

Isaleer sighed, reminding himself to lighten up. This was that business-mind Isaleer had such a hard time shaking off. "Babe, you're breaking my heart. Of course I love you. Just bear with me. I'm with your father, and we're discussing business matters."

Haley was getting distracted. Bored of talking business, she changed the subject to the one that had originally been her reason for calling. "Aw! I'm so proud of you. You are such a champion, baby. Definitely my bright and morning star! Well, babe, if you don't mind, could you find a halting point in your conversation with Daddy? It's time for us to get to church. Can you please bring the car over so that we can go to church? I'm wearing your favorite perfume."

After an awkward silence, Isaleer just spit it out. "Um… Yeah, about that, babe. I was just about to text you. Um, your father is kidnapping me. We're going to, I guess, do man-things. Uh… I don't know how long I'll be gone, but, um, I guess I'll see you when I get back. Love you?"

Isaleer awaited her response. Surprisingly, all she snapped back with was, "Wait, what? Is that something you want to do, or is it something he's making you do? Just don't let Daddy push you around, 'k?"

Without hesitation, Isaleer assured her that this was a choice he was making on his own. "Oh! No, no, no, no, no, no, he's not pushing me around. He's definitely—actually, it sounds like he's extending quite the offer to me, and I'm actually excited to see where this could go. I'm choosing to go with him and see where this goes and then to, uh, go to church and see where that goes. Um, but I do have that book in my back pocket, and I'm… Uh, I'll be reading it on the way there. Ok?"

All at once, it was settled, and she was perfectly ok with everything. All she truly wanted was for Isaleer to get closer to God. "Yes! Please, please, please read it, and start with Psalms. You're a Psalms kind of guy."

That was such an unusual thing to say. How does one even respond to that? "Haha. I'm a Psalms kind of guy? What does that mean?

Mr. Morgan, growing tired of sitting in his driveway waiting for Isaleer and his daughter to wrap up the conversation, looked at Isaleer. He pointed to his watch and cleared his throat, saying, "Wrap it up kid. We've got places to be and people to see."

"Oh, oh, babe—babe. No, I gotta go. Your dad is giving me the death-stare. Hold on. I gotta go, babe, but I love you so much. I'll see you when I get back. Ok?"

If Isaleer had known these were the last words he would hear Haley say, he would have cherished them much more. "Ok. I'm gonna miss you so much. I'll be praying for you, babe. I love you, Mr. Isaleer Horus!"

Isaleer was at the front of the driveway, close enough that he could see Haley popping wheelies in her custom wheelchair but too far away for them to talk without using their cell phones. Haley was paralyzed from the waist down, but that never stopped Isaleer from loving her with all of his heart. Haley always found ways to use her disadvantage to her advantage. One of the many ways she did this was by always hopping up on Isaleer's lap when they were sitting anywhere for too long. Haley sat on his lap more than she sat in her own wheelchair. Most of the time, she didn't even carry her wheelchair. Isaleer was just expected to piggyback her everywhere, though he didn't mind this one bit. It made him feel like a prince carrying his princess, and he loved it.

As Isaleer rolled up the window to Mr. Morgan's limousine, he waved goodbye to Haley. Mr. Morgan began preparing him for how to act around the people to whom he was about to be introduced.

As Mr. Morgan talked, Isaleer zoned out and reached with his left hand to his back pocket, feeling the Bible and thinking of Haley. For a moment, Isaleer wished he had just gone to church with her.

Soon enough this will be a thought that haunts his every dream…

Chapter 1

"RED ON YELLOW, KILL A FELLOW."

r. Morgan and Isaleer drove over the bridge of Boca Raton in silence…

All of a sudden, Mr. Morgan ordered Mr. George to raise the privacy wall. As soon as he had raised the wall, Mr. Morgan put the limousine's noise-canceling speakers on full blast. With the noise-canceling speakers on at their highest volume, it seemed as though Isaleer could hear his own heartbeat. Mr. Morgan looked Isaleer dead in the eyes with all seriousness and said, "There is no turning back now."

Isaleer wasn't afraid; he grew up a rather dark child. The thought of no turning back seemed to make this adventure much more appetizing.

When the light turned green, the limo turned right, and they were in the city of West Palm Beach. Isaleer looked to his right and saw the bay overlooking Boca Raton. From here, all kinds of major buildings were to the left. It was nothing to see multiple exotic luxury cars parked beside these buildings. In some aspects, it was the luxury of the well accomplished to truly park wherever they wanted about the city streets, for, truly, who is going to tell the owner of a half-a-million-dollar car that he can't park in front of their store? Who is going to tell the luxury class that the parallel parking zone is only good for thirty minutes? In a way, with that kind of wealth, you were respected as a titan among men. He was the man that actually could get that million-dollar car that you dreamed about. He made that dream become reality.

Isaleer snapped out of his thoughts. He could feel the limo pulling into the turning lane. He, along with Mr. Morgan, Mr. George, and Mr. Morgan's security team, pulled into the parking lot of Mr. Morgan's building. The front entrance, past the face of the building overlooking the West Palm Beach coast, read "Morgan International." It was a fifty-story building. Isaleer never truly knew what Mr. Morgan had done to acquire his fortune. Mr. Morgan always said he was in real estate, but that just never added up in Isaleer's mind. How can a man be in real estate in an economy like this and be a billionaire in a market that isn't flourishing? Something wasn't adding up in this picture. Of course, Isaleer wasn't questioning Mr. Morgan's income or how he acquired his revenue. Isaleer was too busy trying to wrap his mind around the fact that Mr. Morgan was a government official who almost weekly flew to the UN building or some far off country to deal with foreign affairs or promote some insane policy. Honestly, who could call out a political and business titan like this? A man of that kind of stature stays left alone to deal with his own business.

A random thought occurred to Isaleer. When trying to identify the difference between a king snake and a coral snake, one just need remember that old rhyme, "Red on yellow kill a fellow..."

No doubt Mr. Morgan was into something extremely corrupt, so Isaleer could see the red lining his scaly mind. The thing that kept his mouth closed was how Mr. Morgan's immense wealth could literally build pyramids out of gold. Isaleer's new money net worth was estimated at around twenty-five million, but that was pocket change compared to Mr. Morgan's mighty mogul money. His numbers were staggering to both him and Isaleer. If you were him, you were drunk on celebratory champagne glasses. If you were Isaleer or anyone else below him right about when Mr. Morgan's net worth was officially declared, you took a double shot of humility. Why in the world would someone need that much money?

Mr. Morgan had billions of dollars in assets…just assets! He had hundreds of millions in personal and leisure assets alone. He owned a yacht that had an executive helicopter pad on the top deck. He owned a yacht that had a garage he could pull his hybrid car into, and that was just his boat! His homes were even more outrageous—seven fifty-million-dollar mansions set up on seven continents. He didn't have businesses; he had kingdoms. Morgan International controlled two major empires, both locations chosen out of conscientious knowledge that his audience of elite clientele were very exclusive and expensive buyers. This being so, he only needed two major locations to cover the globe. He chose to have his permanent home in West Palm Beach and to have his second location for his build-sites in Dubai. The West Palm Beach building Isaleer and Mr. Morgan at which were currently located had its own exclusive parking garage. The other building was his two-hundred-floor architectural monument set up in Dubai.

Again, Isaleer saw the red rings on the snake…but all that red was sitting comfortably on a lot of yellow. All that yellow symbolized all the gold he had made thus far from all the corrupt business moves. That red, bloodthirsty soul sitting on gold let Isaleer know that Mr. Morgan was a coral snake—and he was, in fact, deadly.

As a political figure with assets accruing a sum of nearly eighty-five billion dollars, Mr. Morgan was capable of pushing major bills with purposeful loopholes, giving the stamp of approval on corrupt policies for lobbyists who wanted political control based on their wealth, as well as control of the business world. This also meant Mr. Morgan, as a representative of the United States Foreign Ambassadorship, had been arranging under-the-table agreements with foreign leaders of nations, misrepresenting of his country. He knew full well this was an act of tyranny and treason, but he knew his government personally and knew they would never call him out for what he did for them under the table—out of the sight of the masses. He traded lies and deception to the American people in exchange for money, power, and trust among the multinationals and global elite. Again, "Red on yellow kill a fellow." So who's to say he didn't know all along?

As Mr. George, Isaleer, and Mr. Morgan pulled into Morgan International's parking garage, they were greeted by a host of Secret Service members who escorted the limo through the parking garage to the second highest level. After several minutes, or the time it would take for twelve armored SUVs and a limousine to climb to the top of an eight-story parking garage, the head of Morgan International's security team came and tapped on the glass. This signified that the perimeter was safe. Mr. Morgan notified Mr. George to stay in his seat until he was given orders to get out of the car. Mr. Morgan would have the passenger door opened by his head of security. This was where Mr. George, Isaleer, and Mr. Morgan were to do a vehicle exchange. This was unplanned to all but Mr. Morgan and his security team. According to Mr. Morgan, a man worth billions is a fool not to be escorted around in something armored and to make a few exchanges now and again.

As Mr. Morgan prestigiously stepped out of the limo and snapped his blazer into place, his head of security said, "Follow me, sir. Your ride is waiting for you."

Mr. Morgan and Isaleer followed the fifteen armed security team members from the limousine and through the dark parking garage. The blue lights flashing from the black armored SUVs blocking the entrances and exits of all the parking garage ramps assured Isaleer that whatever they were about to do was extremely political. As both Isaleer and Mr. Morgan reached the armored SUV which was to take them to the airport for transportation to California, Isaleer realized something: He had no clue what he was doing or where he was going. Mr. Morgan and himself were flying to California; that's all he knew. At this point, there really was nothing Isaleer could do. He had nearly fifty submachine guns around him. If he refused to follow Mr. Morgan at this point, things were going to get real very fast. At this point, with what little information Isaleer knew, he already knew too much. He was a part of this crazy ride, whether he wanted to be or not.

As they stepped into the back of the armored SUV, there was a wall that separated them from the security team who drove the vehicle. After they closed the door to this SUV, the cabin was sealed airtight, and then the oxygen began to be administered.

Mr. Morgan said to Isaleer one last time, this time making it crystal clear, "There is no turning back. Everything you're about to see is absolutely confidential, and if you hint a single word of anything you're about to witness and take part in, you will no longer exist, and everything you say will be counted as a lie. You are nothing compared to these men. In fact, it would be easily swept under the rug when you were considered schizophrenic from the pressure of Hollywood, and the music industry drove you to heavy drug usage and overdose… or worse, suicide. So don't try to be an Alex Jones. That'll just get you killed out here. Since there's no turning back for you now, this which I take you too is the level where your wealth, success, and fame have elevated you immensely. Now, you go a place where the Hierarchy are vastly interested with working with you. This is something the spiritual Hierarchy does for the powerful and wealthy. Spirits care not for the poor. It is the rich who can move the chess pieces in place for the all-seeing Eye who sits in his secret chambers, speaking to the Dark Lord and discussing King Lucifer's rise as the Antichrist—alone. These men have power far beyond the brinks of this mortal Earth. These men have kings and mighty emperors as they're concierges to do dealings with the spirit realm upon their behalf and declare for them what will and will not be done upon the Earth, all in the name of Satan. You do not mess with these men, Isaleer. They séance and summon demons. Brother, you don't mess with these men. These men are fourteen trillion dollars in and more. These are men who control entire nations and have major funding in everything. If they summon for something, most likely it will come, and more will follow. At these séances, you will be standing among the elite, and when or if they get pissed and hate you, you will be harnessed and sacrificed. You cannot enter these meetings without a special mark. With what is to come, I want my daughter to be safe. With you among the secret societies, she will be safe. I have made the call in advance to the Brethren. Your black initiation robe is awaiting you in the grove. You will sell your soul to Satan, or you will be sacrificed. Get used to hearing the chants of thousands shouting, "Six-six-six," and "Hail, Satan." Get used to orgies and blood sacrifice. Get used to it, boy, because soon you will, through your music and influence over Hollywood, be able to move chess pieces just like us. Comprehend?" The first time Mr. Morgan said that, his point was already clear: Keep your mouth closed about what you see. However, the second time, with all these security teams and armored SUVs present, had Isaleer thinking this was possibly a very bad decision. Now, all of a sudden, life and death were brought into the equation. Given no real choice, Isaleer played along, trying to feel out the vibe, but how are you supposed to feel out a vibe when you're sitting inside of an oxygen-fed, armored military transport vehicle? Isaleer wasn't even breathing in natural air anymore. Suddenly, Isaleer began wondering if he was about to be involved in Mr. Morgan's secret life of crime. Mr. Morgan came over the radio and said, "Ready the box and its contents for travel."

The head of Morgan International's security team said, "Yes, sir! Give me five minutes, as I do the gift -wrapping." The head of Morgan International's security walked over to the limo where Mr. George was sitting, awaiting his orders and nervously sweating up a storm of anxiety. The security lead tapped on the glass and said, "Step out of the car quickly, and follow me. Your payment is inside the building."

Mr. George didn't really have a choice; his entrances and exits from the garage were blocked by armored military vehicles, and his immediate exits from the limousine were blocked by six heavily armed men who were standing outside the limousine in an attack formation.

The Formation of the Soldiers surrounding Mr. George

MAP KEY:

---

x = mr. george ▷= heavily armed

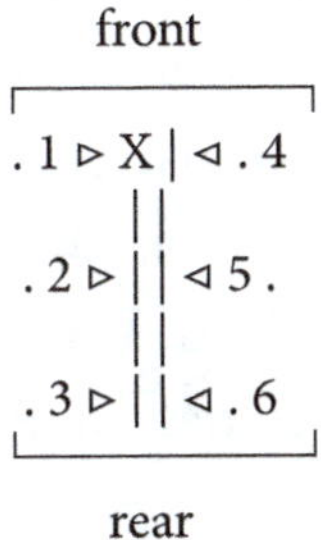

Mr. George feared something was up. This was too unfriendly an approach. Why did they need six men to surround him just so he could collect a paycheck? Confused, Mr. George mumbled inaudibly to himself, "I understand Mr. Morgan being rushed and retrieved by secret security, but I'm of no value to them. Why are they surrounding my ca… I was late! Oh my God. These men think I have a bomb in the car, or I'm an Islamic terrorist. They had me go through the motions of picking up Mr. Morgan, so I wouldn't suspect they were on to me. Now they are ready to strike."

Backed into a corner, Mr. George thought about what he should do. There are two ways to die: as a man or as a coward. Collecting his thoughts and coming back to the moment, Mr. George tried to remain calm. He hoped he was overthinking this whole thing. Mr. George got out of the limousine quickly and complied with orders of the security team.

The head of Morgan International's security team shouted, "Let's go! To the double doors, let's move! Let's move!"

Walking briskly through the double doors, Mr. George instantly realized this wasn't where he was going to get paid, but by then it was too late. He could see a six-by-six wooden box, a body bag, and even more heavily armed men standing with their submachine gun laser-scopes pointed at Mr. George's body.

The choices where, presumably, either go in the box willingly, or go in the box unwillingly. If he went willingly, he might stand a chance to live. If he tried to resist, he most assuredly would die.

Mr. George halted in his tracks about five feet from the wooden box and said, "I don't understand. You want me to get in the box?"

The head of Morgan International's security team said, "That is correct."

Mr. George said, "What?! No! Why? No!"

The head of Morgan International's security team said, "Because Isaleer Horus was chosen to join the Illuminati, and you are his sacrifice. That's why." The head of security's facial expression changed, making him look like a drill sergeant. "GET IN THE &^*%$#@ BOX, SACRIFICE! LET'S GO! I'M NOT GONNA STAND HERE AND WAIT FOR A SACRIFICE TO MAKE UP ITS MIND."

Mr. George put up a fight until they hit him with an almost-lethal dose of tranquilizer. In seconds, his begging and pleading ended with him unconscious on the ground, drooling.

The head of Morgan International's security team said, "Alright, team, giftwrap the contents, and ready the box for travel. We've got two minutes before departure. Let's move."

Within a minute and a half, all six heavily armed men walked out through the double doors, carrying the box with Mr. George inside to the transport Hummer. As they strapped the box down for travel in the rear trailer, the escort unit began its departure from the Morgan International building to the West Palm Beach Executive Airport.

There was no stopping in this convoy. This convoy blocked traffic and halted movement of highways and roads. On these kind of trips, Mr. Morgan always got the right-of-way and never saw red lights. His forward teams went ahead of him and blocked intersections so that he didn't have to wait at traffic lights. Stopping at traffic lights meant possible attacks, so aggression from the Secret Service was strictly enforced. Quick, fast, and in a hurry, the security team lined up in formation and led Mr. Morgan out of the parking garage and out onto I-95, making their way to the executive airport.

"First off, Isaleer, I'm telling you right now: What you are about to see, you cannot tell anyone about. I MEAN NO ONE! This is an upper-level gathering of people who have the ability to get away with murder. If they find out that you are talking about what's going on in secret, you will end up dead. Have you ever heard of the Occult or any Occultist Orders, like the Illuminati?"

Clearly, the cat was out of the bag now. It seemed like Isaleer was about to go to a billionaire gathering of the world's elite. At this séance, they summoned demons and made sacrifices, all the while worshipping Lucifer and hailing Satan at an elite masquerade. They harkened for the Dark Lord to point them in the direction they should go. Chess pieces now must be moved in order to bring about the rise of Satan.

Chapter 2

THE INITIATION CEREMONY

"I could hear them just as clear as day. This is why you don't play with magic. You either go all the way, or you close it and leave, but you never dabble in the spirit realm blindly without regard. All spirits, holy and wicked, white and black, reside in the spirit realm. If you dabble blindly, you have no control over what you will encounter."

-Dexter Rockwell 777

To the lower-level Illuminati members' surprise, the Order of the Thirteen had sent out a summons letter earlier that month to all the families of the world's elite. Every single witch and warlock was made to be present for tonight's special ceremony, which this year celebrated the Order of the Thirteen by selecting two new members to join them at the top of the pyramid scheme in the practice of black magic. These two young, lucky recruits would be replacing two original members who had passed away from old age. These two new recruits would go from low-ranking puppets to two of the thirteen highest-ranking Illuminati members.

Did You Know?

Men who practice in the magical arts are defined as warlocks.

Women who practiced magical arts are categorized as witches.

According to The Book of Crowley, however, respectable sorcerers never use either of these titles but rather refer to themselves as simply philosophers.

Above the Order of the Thirteen, in the Illuminati ranking system was only the Highest Wizard Lord, Lord Navari, and the one whom the Order called the Eye. The Eye spoke directly to Satan. Once his presence had been evoked by the Order of the Thirteen, it was then manifested in a private room so that only the Eye could see him face to face. No one else was worthy.

It could only be done within an all-black home, which was only home to full-black things. Inside the Black Mansion shined no natural sunlight, for its windows had been painted black. The walls were black. The floors were black. The doors and the boarders were black. The decorations and the clothes were black. The yard's natural grass was ripped out and replaced with a concrete foundation and then top-layered with black AstroTurf. All of this was done in compliance with the rules that governed the interior of the home.

During Séance, only high-powered laser lights and neon LED boards could be used to generate the various light displays throughout the home's many rooms. The room in which the Devil was to meet with the Eye was to be pitch black, for Satan would be in attendance to this meeting as well.

The Eye would be chained to a throne and then locked inside a bulletproof, fire-resistant, noise-canceling room. After the airlock doors sealed the Eye inside the pitch black cell, he was then released into what seemed to be a black, two thousand square-foot one-level room.

The walls of the room amplified the corruption inside of an evil man's mind. It was the honor of the Order of the Thirteen and the Highest Wizard Lord to summon forth Lucifer's presence and wait for the Eye to receive orders from the chamber.

The Eye would speak to Lucifer, asking questions such as, "How do we get the masses to see things from your point of view?" or "If we release this spirit, how will it affect the world, or will it affect at all?"

or "How can we take them to the Mark of the Beast?" or "In what direction should we take the world?"

The Eye was going to be the Antichrist for the end of days, during the time spoken of in the Book of Revelations, in the time of the Apocalypse and the wrath of God, during the days when the sun and moon would no longer shine. It was his job to take the throne in the temple of Jerusalem. It was also his job to proclaim he was the Christ Savior, but that day had not come, so for now the Eye's only job was to move these plans in that direction.

Each member of the Elite Occult Order was valuable to the scheme of things. Where one was located on the Earth in some ways determined one's level of superiority. The highest-level members stayed located very close to Israel. The main focus was to train for the day that they would infiltrate the city of Jerusalem and claim the Temple as their castle. The Holy of Holies resided within the temple grounds; this was the most anointed place on planet Earth. If the occult could get into the Temple, they could bring forth all kinds of creatures and demonic animals, simply because of the spiritual concentration of the ground. Those in charge of infiltrating the Temple of Jerusalem were none other than The Order of the Thirteen. When it came time, they would escort the Eye, now the Antichrist, to his throne. This was the reason these members were so much higher-ranked than the rest of the Elite Occult Orders members within the Illuminati.

The Order of the Thirteen and the Highest Wizard Lord were the only people to have ever seen the Eye's face. No one knew where he lived or resided. He was never to be seen or known.

For the first time in seventy years, the Order of the Thirteen had sent out a summons to all the elite members who had studied under the order. The summons said, "Bring forth thy sons for the choosing of two new recruits who must join the Order of the Thirteen."

The original members of the Order of the Thirteen were men who had extensive Occultist bloodlines. They were children who had grown up in the Occult and had been dedicated to Satan since their conception.

As children, the original Thirteen had been removed from society and placed in Occultist Order Academies, where they were trained in the art of Latin pronunciation, being that Latin was the original language of the Goetia. Being able to read these Occultist books would allow them to be able to summon demons and command the demonic presence to do their bidding. Additionally, schools trained these men in the art of black magic.

When the original members of the Order of the Thirteen became young men, they were assigned to specific colleges to join certain societies and orders. The life of a member of the Order of the Thirteen consisted of everyday séances and ritual sacrifices. It was not uncommon for the members to live on farms. This made animal sacrificing an everyday event. In fact, one member of the Order of the Thirteen actually went on to own a chain of slaughterhouses, and he did his séances from within the factory walls. Obviously, it should go without saying that this was a life of extreme silence and secrecy.

Consecration before a ceremony amongst the Brethren required each member to create a list of desires they expected to be fulfilled in exchange for a sacrifice that pleased the demons that these men were planning to summon. These parchment paper documents were then signed with blood and sealed with a wax crest, only to be opened during the time of séance.

It was a known fact within spiritualist circles that certain demons require certain sacrifices. Not every sacrifice requires blood upon an altar. In fact, some demons required sex acts to be performed in their presence. Depending on the demon, it could require a certain sex act, such as an act of homosexuality or an act of rape. In some instances, this could also require bestiality or an orgy. In other less severe instances, certain herbs were to be burned as a sufficient sacrifice. However, there were demons such as Baphomet, Moloch, and Beliel who demanded that blood be drained from a living sacrifice until that sacrifice was dead. Baphomet accepted ram's blood. Moloch accepted the blood of a child. However, all of these, including Beliel, truly desired the blood of the innocent. Unless one was in the Order of the Thirteen, by delving in this deep with no prior experience, one could expect to be overtaken and killed for mocking the demons' presence with an unworthy ritual. It was not enough to evoke the demonic presence from a line that may be read in the lesser keys; it was essential to know for oneself which demons coexisted with one's own personality type. Calling the wrong demonic presence into the room could result in the conjurer realizing what they have summoned is not a demon at all but rather a Principality, or even worse...one could accidently summon for a king among Principalities. This was the rite of passage for the Order of the Thirteen. They didn't do dealings with dukes or knights or courts men among the demonology system of hierarchy ranks. It was their honor to deal directly with the highest of demonic kings and even call for principalities.

Before these men were endowed into the Black Forest Society to stand in command over all the members, they were required to travel to a third-world country and perform a human sacrifice, séance, and ritual. The Order of the Thirteen had to be comprised of men who were willing to do whatever was required of them. When being given this much power, they had to have human blood on their hands. These were the men who would deal directly with the Eye and who would summon for the Dark Lord Satan. The Dark Lord would always require a human sacrifice to be killed before even considering answering a call. In some cases, he would even require cannibalism. Satan was acknowledged by two other obvious names (Lucifer and The Devil). However, Occult members referred to him by a large number of names which all evoked a personality side of the Dark Lord. Only the Eye himself ever got to conjure Satan's full presence

As the new recruit summons was received in each member of the society's household, each and every member made his way to the Black Forest, sometimes called the Bohemian Grove, for the initiation ceremony.

Like always in The Black Forest, it was a hot July afternoon. The humidity in the air made this range of woodland feel like a rainforest somewhere in a remote part of the tropics.

Men would often walk around the timberland pathways in little or no clothing. The heat was exasperating. Standing underneath these five hundred-foot-tall sequoia trees had a way of making one feel lost in a world where one should expect dinosaurs to roam about the Earth. It brought one's mind back to a time thousands of years ago when the Earth was much younger. This massive forest helped one achieve a complete liberation from the modern-day civilization.

The man-made pathways and trails leading from the lakes and campsites to the lodges and clubhouses also led through the surrounding mountains and to the club's lakes. Any roads surrounding the Black Forest were at all times under surveillance. Watch posts were filled with armed garrison ready to shoot intruders on site. It was so secretive that the Black Forest/Bohemian Club Society had their two thousand five hundred-acre span of woodland removed from every GPS aerial map system on the World Wide Web.

Though this two thousand five hundred-acre forest resort was intended to be an escape for the world's elite, it was not all vacations, retreats, fun, and games. Make no mistake; this place was a gathering ground for the world's elite to summon forth all the powers of Hell. This place was among the most Occultist grounds in North America. Though relaxation from society was the original idea behind this camp, it was not the main focus. The main focus was always getting all the major CEOs of the world in one location and unifying their agendas to always revolve around the New World Order.

For most of the year, the Black Forest remained desolate and almost without life until spring gave way to summer. Right around mid-June, the forest began to come to life. Today was the start of the mid-summer encampment, which would last two weeks.

The limos and armored military transports began to fill the Black Forest. Outside the Bohemian Grove's gated entryway stood thousands of rioters and protesters who protested against these secret gatherings of the world's elite. Many of these men and women who stood rioting and protesting were arrested as they began to take action, throwing smoke grenades, trying to cause a scene so they could slip into the forest without being captured.

There was speculation about the many evil agendas that were conspired under these gigantic trees. The goal of these protesters was to record live from inside of the Black Forest and tap into the national television news feed, exposing the Occult for the whole world to see.

These brave men and women called themselves "the righteous journalists." Later, these men and women would be executed for treason and acts of terrorism. The execution of frontline journalists for exposing the locations, agendas and secret rituals would start the civil war in North America. People took up weapons and tore down government buildings on the way to the White House. The goal of the American people was to kill all the politicians and governmental leaders, including the President. If the mark of the beast and the Antichrist's promotion, coming right from the Oval Office, no amount of arguing or negotiation was going to solve anything. The American people knew what had to be done. It was time to take up weapons and begin the second American Civil War to restore America back to its original founding for all the American people. It would not be long before "the Righteous and Sanctified Armies" would be suppressed, but it was out of this that an army worthy to oppose the Illuminati was born. They called themselves "the Arisen Army." Where The Righteous and Sanctified Armies failed in trying to remain civil and noble citizens, the Arisen Army would see victory with their passionate hate for the Illuminati! The Arisen Army was the only force strong enough to stand against the Elite Occult Orders and against the Antichrist.

The Elite Occult Orders passed through the entry gate of the Black Forest without even the turn of a head to acknowledge these men and women involved with the Arisen. One by one the world's elite drove through the entry gates and were escorted deep into the Bohemian Grove's forest. Every now and then, there was one man in his limo who would shoot a middle finger to the protesters. It was those men who smirked with their middle fingers held high who couldn't wait for the days to come, the days when the average and lower-class citizens of the world would finally be forced to bow in the presence of greatness.

Oh, how they longed to be worshiped like gods among men. How they longed to bring back slavery and the backlash…

Most of the two and a half thousand men involved in the Bohemian Club who filled up this forest were famous celebrities, political figures, CEOs of oil companies, gold mines, and diamond mines, military weapons manufacturers, and families who controlled the world's currency exchange. The list of leaders went on and on, far beyond and dramatically exceeding what was merely listed above; these were just the most commonly mentioned.

Before the ceremony beside the lake, where they would gather to worship their famous god Moloch, they were gathering in their lodges, awaiting the arrival of the High Elder Wizard Lord.

These lodges were nestled deep in the mountains of the Black Forest. The Bohemian Grove was tucked far inside the Black Forest, away from the sight of city lights and humanity.

Driving on the Bohemian Grove highway made one seem suspicious and nosey, considering that the Orders owned most of this highway and the surrounding land. Spies and members were the only ones ever on this road. From the entrance of the Black Forest, it was about a five-mile drive to the parking grounds of the Bohemian Grove. This helped with keeping things secret and quiet to the outside world.

As the afternoon turned into evening, the big names began to arrive. At around five o'clock, the guards who simply carried pistols and looked similar to park rangers now were replaced by Secret Service and military soldiers who carried M16s and M4 carbines. Above the tree line, military helicopters hovered, scanning the woods for intruders. The immense forest looming high overhead had a dark, eerie silence at night, which had a way of pulling the life out of one's soul. All the Black Forests spoken of in movies and books were instantly made real inside the confines of the Bohemian Grove. It was a darkness that one could almost feel cloaking his body.

The silence throughout the forest was no help to the matter. It was like every living thing had died because of its poisonous spells.

The evil practices that had been carried out in this forest seemed to siphon off the very life which kept it full of vim and vigor. All that remained was the smell of the mighty sequoia trees and an empty feeling in one's stomach when he spoke too loudly in the coolness of the night. A man could fear that something evil was looming just over his shoulder, hiding in the darkness of the forest's shadows, waiting to kill him. It was no secret that many Occultists, witches, and warlocks used this ground as their encampment during times of pagan worship.

One of the soldiers began to get hostile with the rioting crowd, just after one of the men in the Arisen Army snuck past the other protesters who stood by making noise and taking no action. He finally took a baseball bat to the side of one of the Bohemian Grove Society members' black limousines.

Firing shots into the air, the soldier radioed to his commanding officer. "Sir. Things are getting extremely out of hand. We need backup at the front gate. The executive limos haven't moved for five minutes. We can't push the rioting crowds back, and now I think we're under attack from the Arisen!" As the rebel refused to step back to make way for the backed-up limos and armored military vehicles, the Secret Service soldiers were given the ok to begin gassing the rioters and sending in the K9s to attack the protesters.

One by one, the men and women who stood as the last source of hope for true journalism were arrested and hauled off to concentration camps to be detained and questioned. There was nothing the Elite Occult Orders wanted more than to discover the location of the Arisen's command station. No matter how much they pushed and pressed, the Arisen soldiers were notorious for keeping a tight lip. "We will never negotiate with the enemy! We will die proudly in the name of Christ before we live shamefully in the name of Lucifer!" This was often screamed at the top of their lungs as they stood in ranks during PT. It was the original creed of the Arisen, even though many in the Arisen Army were not even Christian, but rather men and women who refused to be chipped or take the mark of the beast. That was before their first commander was executed after being captured. After the Arisen soldiers witnessed their Colonel being executed on live broadcast, they turned from just wanting to join with others who wanted to take back the United States of America for its citizens and all joined under the Christian flag as brothers and sisters. They unifyed under one flag to kill the enemy. When the new commander stepped into position, he had a thirst for blood that could not be filled. The Christians had had enough. Illuminati blood began to paint the walls of their torture chambers. The former commander had said, "Thou shall not kill. Do not be like them. They are animals, hateful and incapable of reason. They hunger for death. Do not be like them."

However, the commander's death was a wake-up call. Those involved in the Illuminati were not a joke, and they most definitely were not going to show mercy. It was at this point that the Arisen selected their new commander. On his first day, the Arisen Army Forces broke the lines of an Illuminati fortress and took one hundred

Occult troops captive; they brutally murdered each and every one of the soldiers, until only their gunnery sergeant remained.

They fed him through a feeding tube until he had gotten nice and fat. When he was two hundred pounds overweight, they hung him from a meat hook and cut out his insides. It wasn't a simple slice-and-dice. They sharpened the bones of his men to create the dagger used to disembowel him. Just as they were beginning to dismember his torso, they forced gasoline down his throat and lit a fire under his hanging body.

"No more shall we pretend we are not strong!" exclaimed the commander of the Arisen, watching in glory as the gunnery sergeant of the Illuminati Army was eviscerated and burned.

Once the Arisen became brutal, they had no problem recruiting new members. Thirsty to see justice fulfilled, the lower and middle-class citizens lined up to be recruited to fight for their freedom. The Arisen Army grew from an army of thousands to a global force of millions.

QUESTION: "Why would the Christians who have formed 'The Arisen Army' stoop to acts of murder?" -Reader

ANSWER: "At first, the Arisen Army was a secretive group of wealthy Christ followers who simply were informed of the corruption in the mainstream media and politics. These wealthy Christians built warehouses in secret locations around the world and stored nonperishable food, clothing, infant necessities, medical and pharmaceutical supplies, and light defense armory. The intention was not to stand up and fight against the Illuminati Army; rather, its goal was to be self-sustaining outside of the system the Illuminati had created. Keep in mind that those who came to the Arisen refused to accept the mark of the beast in any of the fashions in which it was presented (ex: RFID, Micro Pill, Digital Ink). In this manner, the Arisen supplied those without food and shelter with the essentials and taught the refugees how to live off of the land. After a few months, the Arisen had grown from the few thousand Christians operating off the grid to hundreds of millions of regular people who were taking a stand for freedom. When the Arisen became an international affair, they decided it was time for new management, a management that could lead an army. Suddenly, believer and non-believer stood side-by-side out on the front lines, defending the right to freedom." -Dexter Rockwell

Silence. What was once a crowded pathway filled with loud rioters, K9s, and Secret Service personnel within ten minutes became a blood bath of dead carcasses scattered about the entranceway of the Bohemian Grove. All that was left standing amongst this massacre was a void of silence. Not one soldier or one society member removed the rioters' bodies from where they had fallen. Many of the limo drivers ran over the dead bodies, not even caring to move them out of the way.

From inside of one of the many black armored SUVs, a government official came over the walkie-talkie to the soldiers guarding the front gate and announced, "The Eagle is on approach. Copy."

All at once, a fleet of almost fifty black armored vehicles zoomed by the entranceway, traveling down the one-lane road, heading deep, deep into the forest until their headlights were no longer seen from the roadway. "The Eagle is on approach" meant only one thing: The President of the United States was under the submission of the Elite Occult Orders. Those who drove in were the inferior-class members who had nowhere near the wealth or respect of the superior-class members. These were the lower-class members who were given orders to carry out. These members were called "puppets."

To identify the upper-class members, one only needs to look up. The military helicopters continued to circle the Grove with their spotlights beaming on the forest. At least ten executive helicopters buzzed in formation, flying just high enough to clear the sequoia forest. These were the elite of the elite. Right on schedule, the Highest Wizard Lord and the Order of the Thirteen had just arrived by way of executive helicopters. They continued to fly deep into the forest, far beyond where most would park and be shuttled to their lodges. These men who flew in on their helicopters ran the show and gave the orders which were to be carried out.

As Mr. Morgan and Isaleer were driving up, the bodies of the Arisen rioters who had been attacked by the K9s were now almost bare bones as the dogs had eaten their victims. The Illuminati attack dogs were trained to eat anything they killed. Eat they did, leaving nothing but unrecognizable remains and puddles of bodily fluid strewn all across the road. When Mr. Morgan caught this scene in his line of sight, he quickly distracted Islaeer by asking if he would look through the carpet of the armored SUV for Mr. Morgan's other cufflink. The last thing Mr. Morgan wanted was for Isleer to see this hideous monstrosity scattered all along the entranceway of the Bohemian Grove. All Mr. Morgan wanted Isaleer to pick up on were the good vibes—at least until the ceremony.

Once Isaleer was standing on stage before the Occult Orders, it didn't matter what happened at that point. The key was to get him through the entranceway and onto the stage.

As Mr. Morgan and Isaleer were driving into the Grove, passing the guard stop, Isaleer's eyes opened wide. He couldn't believe what he was seeing. There were multi-million-dollar lodges everywhere. Nestled under these several hundred-foot-tall sequoia trees was a city designed out of logs and lumber. Beautiful mansion-size log cabins were hidden under the covering of the trees' thick, hanging limbs, which provided shade for the walk ways.

Isaleer looked at Mr. Morgan and said, "Whoa! What is this? I can't believe this. They must have spent a fortune making this landscape look this way. It looks so perfect, like something from a movie."

Mr. Morgan chuckled to himself, looked up from his phone, and said "This is where men can be men, son." He paused. "Oh, yes. Be assured, a fortune has been spent creating this atmosphere. Isaleer, these are the most powerful and wealthiest men in the world. Be prepared to see spectacles which will blow your mind. When we in the secret society get together, we spare no expense on our entertainment."

The security team for Morgan International proceeded to park, and Mr. Morgan and Isaleer exited the vehicle and stretched. It felt so good to get out of the cramped armored military vehicle and move their legs. After they had stood there a minute or two, Mr. Morgan said, "Follow me. It's time for us to retreat to our lodge and get properly dressed for tonight. I will need to introduce you to the warlock over new initiates. Tonight you will be welcomed into our society. You are one of us now. When you meet the warlock, he will give you your very first robe. You will wear it onto the main stage as you perform your first ritual. This is going to be a big night for you, Isaleer."

They walked closer and closer to the transit shuttle which would transport them to different locations all around the Bohemian Grove. Mr. Morgan said to the transit driver, "This is a new initiate. After I am dropped off, he will need to be escorted to the warlock over new initiates."

The transit drivers are trained not to talk much and just simply do as they are told. As such, the transit driver simply said, "Yes, sir."

On their way to Mr. Morgan's lodge, there were men who stopped to high-five and yell out to one another. Joyful to see everyone, these men seemed very similar to testosterone-filled fraternity brothers who acted crazy, caring little about those around them as they raged, rampaged, and acted foolishly. Isaleer couldn't help but notice beers and liquors all over the place. All of a sudden, Isaleer was excited to be here.

In his mind, the only thing ticking down was a little clock that was set to go off when it was time to party.

All of a sudden, the transit stopped, and Mr. Morgan got off and said to young Isaleer, "I'm proud of you, son. I will see you after the initiation. You are going to have the time of your life out here. If you need to go pee, just find a tree."

With that, Isaleer laughed and said, "Haha. Are you serious? That's awesome!" Quickly, the transit pulled away. Unsure of how to act, Isaleer remained quiet until the transit reached a huge cave that had been turned into a lodge, the kind that one might find in his nightmares.

The transit driver said, "Well, here we are. All the new recruits are standing over there awaiting the warlock who will size them for their robes. Please exit the tram to the right. Make sure you grab all your personal belongings."

Isaleer got up from the transit and set off on his way to join the other new recruits. All of the young men began whispering amongst themselves saying to one another, "Hey, guys! Guys! That's Isaleer Horus." Looking at Isaleer in disbelief, the young men kept trying to get the attention of one another. They pointed at him, saying, "Oh my gosh, dude. Dude. Dude. Dude! It's the rockstar Isaleer Horus." One of the young men standing in line awaiting the warlock over new initiates walked over to Isaleer and said, "Can I have your autograph, broseph?"

Sarcastically, Isaleer turned around, distracted by the liquor bar right across the way from where they were standing in line. He said "Five hundred bucks, and plus I don't even have a pen on my person. So… Cool story, bruh."

The young man replied, "Oh, that's no problem, dude. I have more money then you could ever dream of, my friend, and I have a marker. Thank you… Oh, my father is Lord David Rothlefeller. We pretty much own this place. Can we be friends?"

Realizing this young man's bearing the last name Rothlefeller was of some extreme importance, Isaleer began to sign his signature, saying, "Haha… Apparently, I'm famous even in here! Someone needs to get me a VIP section, so at least I have a way to evade my endearing fans before they mob me… Haha. Yeah, man. Got a VIP section around here?"

All of a sudden, the warlock came out to present the robes to the young men. One by one, the young men got their robes and began to put them on proudly. Each robe had an owl symbol sewn into the cover of the left chest area. These black robes were made of a thick cotton-wool mix which helped them remain durable and strong. On the inside of each robe under the left sleeve cuff was a place where the new initiates would sew on a crest which would be given to them by a veteran; each crest and order was different.

Only the children of elite of the elite were chosen to be trained in the dark arts of sorcery and black magic. There were many positions in the dark arts. Some simply trained to put hexes on the music that would be played over the radio. Others learned how to perform rituals for special ceremonies.

These were not the only opportunities available out here in the Black Forest inside the Bohemian Grove. Many famous musicians and actors where discovered on these stages; thus, the the artist would show wondrous gratitude to the secret society through their music's subliminal messages within their music videos.

> "GETTING FAMOUS IN THE WORLD
> WAS EASY ONCE YOU GOT INTO
> THE HIGHEST LEVEL OCCULT ORDERS,
> SO LONG AS YOU WERE WILLING TO OBEY."
>
> −Dexter Rockwell 777

This was a place where young men came and became politicians. Royal families would every now and then take in a uniquely gifted young man and secure him in their bloodline. Accepting the offer of the veterans was how great men now stood amongst the elite.

Again, only hand-selected initiates who were chosen specifically by the Highest Wizard Lord himself got to train under him, learning the dark arts of becoming a warrior wizard. They were taught how to cast spells against anyone who would try to stand against the power of the Occult; they learned to cause death using voodoo and demonic possessions and oppression, along with hexes, evocations, and conjurings. Only thirteen initiates were allowed to learn under the Highest Wizard Lord at a time.

These were not positions given yearly. The only way one could become a member of the Order of the Thirteen was being selected to take the place of one of the previous thirteen members after he died. For the past seventy years, the Order of the Thirteen had remained intact without replacement of its original members—until this year, that is. Two of the original thirteen died after falling to heart attacks during a séance in which they were summoning several principalities which gave orders from Satan.

For the first time in seventy years, two lucky initiates were about to join the ranks of the Order of the Thirteen and control the fate of the world. These lucky initiates were going to be trained to be the highest-ranking sorcerers in the world.

> "The Order of the Thirteen also knew all the secrets hidden from man in the scrolls the religious leaders locked away in vaults…"
>
> —Dexter Rockwell 777

They were referred to as "wizards." Those who got to train under the Highest Wizard Lord also knew him as "the Great Horned Owl."

Those who became wizards were able to carry out animal, human, and herbal sacrifices alone on stage against the Highest Wizard Lord. Many died trying to claim the title of wizard, due to the demonic attacks the Highest Wizard Lord would cast against them on stage during his fight for the title. Those who stood after the séance was complete were deemed worthy to be trained. Only these were given the right to be able to claim their title as wizard.

These tests were necessary because the Highest Wizard Lord summoned the largest demons, and during séances the wizards would need to be able to withstand the demonic presence in the room. If one could not survive, then he was not fit to be amongst the Thirteen.

Every man in the Black Forest Society wanted the chance to even speak to the Highest Wizard Lord for just a moment. It was the honor of those in the Order of the Thirteen to stay with the Highest Wizard Lord in his secluded Castle called the Corridor.

It was located at the farthest end of the forest, only reachable by foot or helicopter. No one was allowed to come near the Highest Wizard Lord's dwelling without being summoned; violation of this rule held a penalty of death.

Everyone secretly wanted to be a warrior wizard. This was a special position that made one instantly among the most powerful and popular of the Illuminati members.

However, in order to be able to train under the Highest Wizard Lord, one needed to be of a certain bloodline, with a heritage established in the Occult. One also needed to have a certain presence about him that greatly stood out among men.

The new initiates were so excited to be holding their very first black ceremonial robes. The only one left was young Isaleer. The warlock over new initiates was not prepared for his arrival, so as all the other young men ran off to go put their new robes on and prepare for tonight's ceremony out by the lake, Isaleer was left standing there in line, robeless.

The warlock looked at young Isaleer and said, "Who are ye? Oh… wait, thou art that Isaleer fellow everyone is talking about? What is your last name? I expect one day you will perform for us. We love entertainment around here, especially good entertainment. Now, what was that last name again, boy?"

Cautiously, Isaleer said to the warlock, "My name is Isaleer Horus. I would love to play some music for you guys sometime! That would be super dope." Isaleer paused and diverted to more important matters. "Hey, so, all these men walking around with beers and drinks in their hands. How do I get a hold of some of these nice, delectable delights?"

The Warlock said, "Oh my gods! Horus… He's alive? Then they were right; it's time. Come with me, boy, right now. I need to get you in a robe, and we need to get you ready for tonight's stage performance.

Normally we don't accept new members under such short notice, but we made exceptions after learning your name was Isaleer. You are quite the popular man around here, Horus. To answer your question, you just simply have to ask for whatever drink you want, and that's it. My dear boy, do you know what size robe ye are?"

Isaleer replied, "I have no idea."

The warlock replied, "That's no problem; follow me." He hastened for Isaleer to accompany him up and into his cave. The warlock's cave was much how one would suspect a witch or warlock's cave to look. It was very primitive and filled with potions, dead animals, spell books, pentagrams, and all kinds of sorcery. As the warlock began shuffling through the robes hung neatly up on a rack, he began holding them up to Isaleer's torso, muttering to himself, "Oh, no, that's not the right size… Uh, fud-woglers… Oh, wait! Ah ha! Marge! You're a marge! My, my, though. Curious that only one marge size was left, too."

Isaleer put it on, and just as the warlock said, it fit perfectly. Of course, Isaleer had to ask the warlock, "What's a marge?"

"It's the size between medium and large. Only in the wizard world are we smart enough to consider the sizes in-between."

The cathedral bell began ringing, signaling that it was time for the ritual to begin. As the Satanic priests began to ring the bell, all at once everyone began migrating to the lakeside for the opening ritual for this year's midsummer encampment. Isaleer still had yet to be informed of what was going on, why he was wearing a black robe, and what all of this was about. Before he reached the main stage, Isaleer had to walk through a passageway, which led out onto the main stage overlooking the lake. As Isaleer awaited his cue backstage, he reached in his back pocket and pulled out that book Haley had given him. Isaleer looked for the book of Psalms just like she said to do. He found Psalms and accidentally stumbled onto Psalms 43.

Psalms 43

(New Living Translation)

"Oh God, take up my cause! Defend me against these ungodly people. Rescue me from these unjust liars. For you are God, my only safe haven. Why have you tossed me aside? Why must I wander around in darkness, oppressed by my enemies? Send your light and your truth; let them guide me. Let them lead me to your holy mountain, to the place where you live. There I will go to the altar of God, to God, the source of all my joy. I will praise you with my harp, oh God, my God! Why am I discouraged? Why so sad? I put my hope in God! I will praise him again, my savior and my God!"

Just then, one of the warlocks came backstage and said to all the young men, "Get ready, initiates. The show is about to begin."

Isaleer quickly put his Bible away, walked out from the shadows, and stood with the other recruits. He could feel that something was not right about this. It was like a monster was being awoken inside of him, and there was nothing he could do to stop it. His eyes began staring off into space and zoning out.

One of the new recruits nudged him and said, "Are you excited? We are about to witness our first real cremation of care."

Isaleer just kept staring off into space. His eyes turned more and more aggressive to the point that they became hostile.

The announcer began to welcome everyone to this year's anniversary in the Bohemian Grove inside the Black Forest. He ended his speech and announced the presentation, which was to follow.

The lights grew dark over the lake. A screen projector turned on, and a mist billowed out onto the water. On one side of the small lake was a huge stage, and on the other side of the lake were carved wooden stands where people would sit and enjoy the speakers as they entertained.

As the fog filled up the lake overlooking the forty-foot idol of Moloch, all of a sudden the crowd began clapping and rejoicing. The laser lights surrounding the forest began to zip around. The lights for the audience's seating went black, and the stage lights went all white. All at once, this was no longer in their control… Unexpectedly, the demons had sensed an unusual presence and, without being summoned, attacked.

"I could hear it in my head just as clear as day. This is why you don't play with magic. Without invitation, that which was uninvited can come forth unexpectedly."

-Dexter Rockwell 777

Instantly, the projector beamed onto the mist. The ritual began with a small movie. The scene showed mankind being transported to a slaughterhouse with cows, chickens, sheep, and pigs. They were going to be killed for not complying with all of the rules the world's elite had created.

3 RULES TO COMPLIANCE

1. Starve the disobedient

2. Torture the resisters into obedience

3. Kill anyone who fights back

One of the wizards in victory sang, making his way out onto the main-stage, beginning the ceremonial séance.

♪ ALL HAIL, SATAN ♪

ALL HAIL, SATAN
A DAY IS COMING
WHEN WE SHALL BE LIKE
MEN AMONG ANTS,
WE SHALL CRUSH THEM ONE BY ONE
OH, ONE DAY SOON
WE SHALL NO LONGER LIVE IN SECRET,

BUT THIS BEAST SHALL AWAKEN
AND THIS MONSTER SHALL THIRST
FOR BLOOD
AND LUCIFER SHALL FEAST
ON THE FLESH
OF OUR ENEMIES.

Written By: Dexter Rockwell
All Rights Reserved
Copyright 2014 ©

The whole crowd went wild, cheering and chanting, "Hail, Satan! Hail, Satan! Hail, Satan!"

All of a sudden, the Order of the Thirteen walked out together, ready to fight off any evil spirits that would try to attack the Highest Wizard Lord. As they walked out onto the main stage, each one had many sacrifices to offer the demons in return for their safety. As the wizards began to speak, the crowd went wild!

Beginning to prepare the burning altar, the wizards pulled from their robes the sacrificial knives. One by one, each of the wizards drove his ceremonial dagger through the hearts of the animals which they brought out on stage to represent their spiritual characteristics. As the animal corpses began to burn, the wizards completely let go and began to freely move around the stage, taking on the powerful traits of the animal they had just killed.

After the animal sacrifice was carried out, it was time for the herbal sacrifice. Each wizard was required to burn his spices and eat his herbs. They all had a special concoction, which they created to help them elevate to the spirit realm through psychedelics. Opiates and psychedelic mushrooms where the two main compounds used to induce the hallucinogens. The wizards used these drugs to see into the spirit realm.

With there being only eleven trained wizards in the Order of the Thirteen this year, they were struggling to get through their séances. The weight of the rituals and the demonic presence began to become overwhelming. The wizards pulled for their wands and began casting spells, but the demons struck back just as hard. As the Highest Wizard Lord made his way out onto the stage, a principality welcomed himself into their presence. The demonic attacks began to inflict actual wounds on the wizards' bodies. This was not going according to plan at all. It was time to do something very dangerous. The Highest Wizard Lord sat down at his throne and said, "Bring forth thine offering of initiates." He knew some of the young men might very well die being exposed to this demonic presence; at least it would give the wizards time to gain strength for their unified attack.

The new initiates were about to be bait in a diversion.

As the young men made their way, terrified out of their minds, onto the stage, many of them began puking up blood. Others began vomiting uncontrollably. Isaleer was the last one to step onstage. When his feet hit the stage platform, instantly the presence in the woods got so heavy the Highest Wizard Lord commanded all the wizards to leave the stage and take the new initiates with them. Isaleer turned to follow the wizards and initiates off the stage, but the Highest Wizard Lord spoke up quickly saying, "One of these recruits is unlike anyone here. One of these recruits has a robe that calls to me. It bears a rare bloodline crest which no longer exists… Horus…Isaleer Horus… Who among these initiates is Isaleer Horus?"

The entire audience was instantly silent. Who was Isaleer Horus? For the first time, the Highest Wizard Lord stood up from his throne and walked down to acquaint himself with each of the new initiates. He walked by each one, unsatisfied, until he got to Isaleer. Then he stared him in the face with an expression of fear and disbelief. His eyes began to glow red, and he said, "This one has a presence about him that is unlike anyone I have ever known. You are not human like us. I am mesmerized by your presence. Can it actually be? He undoubtedly carries the presence like that of our lord Satan...a name I dare not summon into my presence for guarding him are legion armies of principalities which would kill us all. Yet as black as his presence may be, I am spellbound as to how much of your father's blood still lies dormant within you. I see a large light. Odd… This young man is carrying something I fear makes him far too knowledgeable. It is as though Heaven and Earth have parted, and the Jesus Christ Savior walks with him. I venture to even say that you, young Isaleer, have read a passage of Scripture, and now his Spirit has taken form within thee. How can this be? The demons which were attacking the wizards now stand at attention to you. You are not a mere boy. I dare not speak of your origins. I only seek to know how it is that you are here and alive. You died at birth. It was your brothers and sisters who were saved. If you are here, then it truly is time."

It seemed as though everyone in authority within the Bohemian Grove knew exactly who Isaleer was. He had always gotten special treatment everywhere else he went in life. He knew he was different, but he had no idea just how different. Isaleer knew nothing of any brothers and sisters. He was told his whole life that he was an only child. Isaleer thought he was born to a missionary and his wife. The way that the Highest Wizard Lord was talking about his origins brought up so many questions in his mind. Was Isaleer really the son of Satan? More importantly, how did that happen? Confused, Isaleer just continued to stare the Highest Wizard Lord in the face. The Highest Wizard Lord began to speak to the crowd, announcing the return of what he called "the age of the gargoyles." Isaleer was completely unaware of what any of that meant. The speech returned back to him as the Highest Wizard Lord turned his face from the crowd to look at Isaleer again. The Highest Wizard Lord cringed as he tried to reach out for the book that was in Isaleer's back pocket.

As the Highest Wizard Lord went to grab for Isaleer's back pocket, a shockwave shot out from Isaleer's pocket and threw the Highest Wizard Lord back about fifteen feet. The Highest Wizard Lord shouted in anguish, "What is that abomination that you are carrying in your back pocket?" He turned his head sideways, approached Isaleer, and whispered, "Oh. My. God… You're a Christian, and you currently have a Bible on your person?"

The audience of witches and warlocks, along with the world's elite, began to yell, "Kill Him! HE'S A SPY!"

As the Highest Wizard Lord approached Isaleer to stand face to face, he spoke softly, saying, "Do you realize where you are? This is an audience of humanity that would have you sacrificed and burned alive if I gave the word. YOU WILL WEAVE NO WEBS OF FAITH HERE! That infernal thing is not welcome! On this night, you shall burn that Bible and blaspheme the name of your God—or else."

The Highest Wizard Lord smiled, drunk with authority, turned to the audience of men present for the ceremony and said, "My children, rejoice. For tonight, sorrow shall fill the sky as one of God's children spits in his face. This young man has merely brought his Bible to perform an execution ritual upon the Christian faith. Tonight, he shall be like poisonous death that we shall pour into a beautiful, flowing spring of life. He shall return to his world of Christ followers, and he shall infiltrate the churches, interrupt the church services, and perform acts of unspeakable abominations. He shall declare his renunciation of the Lord Jesus Christ, and we shall make him a billionaire for the army of Satan. I believe this young man is the perfect suitor to be head over mainstream media and pop culture."

He then turned back to Isaleer Hord and began to pray in a demonic tongue as the wizards began to séance at the bottom of the altar's staircase. The Highest Wizard began to perform black magic. Isaleer's body then began to convulse and mutate, starting with its color.

As the Highest Wizard Lord continued performing his dark sorcery, Isaleer could no longer recognize his own thoughts. Isaleer began to speak in a tongue with which he was no longer familiar. The magic that the Highest Wizard Lord had conjured over him caused something that had been lying dormant inside of his body to come to life. The struggle between flesh and soul quickly ended when Isaleer quit fighting his desire to hate. Instantly, his voice began to change, though no one in the audience was aware of the change taking place behind the robe. With everything Isaleer had in him, he pushed out these words as his knees buckled, and he was unable to stand up straight. "Jesus! If you're real, give me strength! Help, Jesus, help!"

Just then, one of the Occult masters ushered for the guards to bring forth a human sacrifice. Instantly, it was announced that Isaleer had been chosen with the highest regards ever given by the Highest Wizard Lord. No new initiate had ever been involved in a black magic ritual and ever lived to tell about it. That is, no new initiate had ever delved in black magic without any former guidance. The very fact that Isaleer was still breathing meant he was beyond most veterans. Black magic was deep and dark. If performed wrong, many black magic séances could very well lead one to death. The remarkable nature of this is that, not only did Isaleer live, but now his presence was seemingly being brought to life in its full magnitude. Slowly, he fell from his knees to the ground, paralyzed, and began his transformation.

As the guards dragged the prisoner onto the stage and up the stairs to the guillotine, Isaleer saw the man's face. It was Mr. George, the limo driver. Beating and screaming at the human sacrifice, they threw him under the guillotine. The limo driver began screaming at the top of his lungs, begging the Occult to have mercy and let him live. No amount of pleading was going to change the Occult's mind. For the first time, the secret society was preparing to use a real human sacrifice instead of using a fake wooden dummy as an imitation.

> Normally, if there was to be a human sacrifice, it was done in third-world region.
>
> All the human sacrifices done in North America till this point were imitation sacrifices.

Because of how heavy this demonic presence was, in honor of Isaleer Horus, the son of Satan, the Occult was about to execute a living, breathing human being, openly in the Black Forest. The Occult was operating at their full strength, and those in the audience were going wild.

Tears of hatred began to fall from Isaleer's face. Finally, it was actually happening! His eyes rolled into the back of his head. Instantly, Isaleer blacked out. Something was trying to break through the skin on his back. The mutation was almost complete.

The Highest Wizard Lord approached Isaleer and ordered the Order of the Thirteen to help Isaleer Horus, son of the Dark Lord Satan, to his feet and sit him on the throne.

The Highest Wizard Lord asked Isaleer, "Thou whom dwells within this body, to whom do I address? I seek to lift up an offering which would be pleasing in your sight. I am willing to do whatever thou desires. I ask nothing in return but that you give us orders from our Dark Lord Lucifer on what direction we should move the world."

Something clicked in Isaleer's head. A chemical that had not been present before this moment was now coursing through his veins. His mind and his eyes were colliding in a psychedelic orchestration of reality and phantasm. He could see spirits and demons living among mankind. He could look upon a man and judge him; he could see men's sins reeking off their bodies. When the transformation was complete, he would be able to see one's soul. Just as the Highest Wizard Lord had completed speaking, Isaleer gained his full strength, sat back in the throne, threw one of his legs over the arm of the chair, and replied "Oh ok, so we're gonna speak King James' Version, are we? Ok. My human name is Isaleer Horus. You speak unto me arrogantly, like a king's lord who has gotten much too comfortable in the absence of the king. Thou speaks unto me as a king who is comfortable in his throne room and safely protected behind his knights. Haha. This is not thy throne room. I scare thee, oh great Wizard Lord. I see your knees knocking behind thy fancy robe. Thou enquire about my name as though I am some simple demon which can be evoked and enticed with offerings and gifts. Haha. Who does thou expect? Osirus? Set? Balial? Ahah. Jezebel? Ahah. Incubus? Sucubus? Choas? Rahab? Ahab? Does thou thinke that maybe I am Legion? Or maybe thou thinks me to be the spirit of Sanballat or Tobiah? Ahah. Does thou consider maybe that I might be the spirit of Oreb, Zeeb, Zebah, or Zulmunna? Ahah. I might be the spirit of confusion? What can you offer me that is not already mine? Bow down, and worship me before I call upon thee thy own men to kill you in adoration of me."

No one had ever spoken to the Highest Wizard Lord like this, though no one had ever been sat on the throne either. Even under full demon possession, no one had ever spoken so disrespectfully towards the Highest Wizard Lord. Outraged by Isaleer's performance, the Highest Wizard Lord lashed out. "How dare you make a mockery of me? I bow before you in full reverence before all these men, yet you spit upon my offerings and my loyalty to your father? I was never the king. I simply awaited your father's return. No! I will not argue with a boy, even if he is the son of Satan. I will not be mocked! Curse you and your blasphemy. You are the son of Satan, and yet you seek to delight in the presence of God? You ungrateful… YOU WERE BORN TO THE WRONG FATHER!" The Highest Wizard Lord held up his wand, pointed it at Isaleer, and shouted an execution spell, saying, "Slau tro mus Le Corpus!"

Isaleer began laughing hysterically. "Ahah! Was something supposed to happen? Ok, my turn!"

Isaleer was transforming into a gargoyle. As Isaleer got closer to the completion of this full species transformation, he began putting the puzzle pieces together. Somehow, Isaleer was birthed into the natural realm from other dimensions. Half-man and half-demon, he could only assume he was about to be much stronger than the humans who walked upon the Earth. Isaleer had all the powers of a demon, but his soul was not bound to chaos and destruction. Because of his soul, Isaleer could comprehend reason and weigh out his decisions. Because of his soul, Isaleer still could make a choice. His human body gave him entryway into the lamb's Book of Life. Isaleer was able to choose between Heaven and Hell.

No mortal man could cast spells or take control of him, though. They had to be much, much more powerful. The kind of power needed to affect a gargoyle was a kind of sorcery no man could wield. The Highest Wizard Lord had thought that because he had watched Isaleer fall during the black magic ritual, Isaleer was susceptible to black magic. He had been waiting for Isaleer to fall down dead, but the Highest Wizard Lord was dumbfounded when Isaleer was not even phased. All Isaleer could think was that from the throne of God in Heaven, the Lord Jesus had heard his cry and had actually given him a supernatural strength to stand up and take on his true form.

Just then, the Highest Wizard Lord commanded the executioner to take his position. Isaleer looked the Highest Wizard Lord directly in the eyes. Instantly, his eyes began to glow. The executioner walked over to the guillotine and stood, waiting for the ok to drop the blade. All of a sudden, the transformation was complete. Isaleer had grown fifteen feet tall. Quickly, Isaleer leaped to his feet, crouched down, and let out a roar. As he punched the ground, his wings burst through the skin of his back. Isaleer zoned in on the limo driver. Caught up in the moment, Isaleer ran over to the guillotine and broke the chains which held George captive. He said with boldness and fury, "Puppeteers, wielding your strings of lies and manipulation, meet the puppetmaster.

I am Horus who speaks as the son of Satan. I made it through to this dimension, and now as a demon trapped in the human flesh, I am not bound to the fate of my father. I renounce my birth-father Satan, and I curse his name and all that follow his lies."

Isaleer began to speak in spirit tongues. He then turned to the audience and said with anger, passion, and urgency, "I see deep within most minds a most confounded personality speaking forth in all of my children. I hear words coming forth from the depths of your hearts as you cry out for our own humanities. Will you always run and hide into your hidden worlds and your other dimensions? God looks from Heaven as fire billows from his eyes, glaring in fury, saying, 'When will you look at me? When will you look at me? Have you forgotten me, world? Have you forgotten my capabilities?'"

Isaleer frantically began searching the stage for his Bible. He feared that one of the Occultists had thrown it into the fire "Where is my Bible? With this, I will kill all of you!"

Isaleer ran to his Bible, grabbed it up, squeezed it, and said with assuring power and confidence, "He holds me with integrity as he reminds me who I am. I squeeze him and hold him because he is everything to me, but you here in this audience and on this stage want to call me a coward? Call me a coward one more time, and watch me rip you into shreds."

The wrath and fury of God was about to be poured out on the Black Forest. Isaleer continued to allow God to speak through him saying, "For I, I am God! I am Alpha and Omega, and my patience with you will only tarry momentarily before I subside, allowing every demon in hell to come forth and chase after you, ready to crawl and gnash at your bones as even the fires of Hell come forth burning deep inside your lungs. Do you hear the hounds ready to rip you apart? Submit yourself to me, and I will spare you. I speak not unto the Devil worshipers. I speak not to the women and men who have dived in secret and hidden, inaccessible places to plan evil agendas, abominations, and blasphemous behavior towards God. You, you have made your choices, and the day is coming when you shall beg for death to take you. Death will cry for death, but only the lake of fire shall welcome you. All that you built you shall watch crumble like a sandcastle by a wave. I speak to these new recruits standing up here on this stage right now, preparing to give their souls away for worldly pleasures and manmade power, which can be taken away. As I call forth from the sky, will you choose God? Or will you choose your evil wicked ways?"

God's voice shifted to Isaleer as he yelled in sorrow and urgency. "ISALEER! THIS IS YOUR FATHER GOD SPEAKING. WITH ALL OF YOUR MIGHT, ISALEER, RUN! RUN!"

Without hesitation, Isaleer grabbed George and flew into the sky. Just then, a low rumble filled the Earth, and all of a sudden, booming and crashing, meteorites began smashing against the sequoia forest. God's fury filled the sky with lighting, thunder, and rain that tasted like tears. He knew the day was coming when these men would draw back in fear as God unleashed his full wrath upon the Earth. This was nothing more than a taste of what was to come.

This was day one of the great tribulation...

Chapter 3

CAPTURE THE GARGOYLE

A couple weeks had passed in Isaleer's life since the night he and Mr. George had escaped the Black Forest's Bohemian Grove Society and set off on the run from the Illuminati army.

Before finally being captured and taken prisoner to the island of Eden's science lab within the Illuminati's secret fortress, Isaleer was able to aid George in his escape from the clutches of the bloodthirsty Elite Occult Society. What they didn't know was that the island on which they had just arrived was in fact the Illuminati's largest island fortress located on the island of Eden. Call it being in the wrong place at the right time. Call it luck. Call it irony. Either way, as the Illuminati army began drawing close to Mr. George and Isaleer's trail, Isaleer knew he could not keep up this chase. He was growing weak. Without the ability to control when he would mutate into his gargoyle form, trying to fight back against the Illuminati army alone was far too risky, even if he was a gargoyle—at any point, he could transform back into a man.

Just as Isaleer could hear the Occult army approaching, he also heard a Rebellion helicopter flying overhead, searching the island of Eden for any escaped prisoners they could rescue and bring to safety, far from the clutches of the Illuminati. By the sound of its propeller blades, it seemed to be a rescue unit and not an attack unit. As Isaleer signaled for it to land, the Arisen helicopter quickly descended from the sky and plunged itself into the opening in the brush. Isaleer explained the situation to the helicopter pilot. "Both myself and George have been on the run for months trying to evade being captured by the Illuminati army. They're catching up to our trail, and I think I'm of some extensive value to them. This guy who is with me, Mr. George, was about to be used in an Occult sacrifice ritual." Because Isaleer and Mr. George were so tired and running out of resources, the Elite Occult Orders were catching up quickly to their trail. He needed help, and this Rebellion helicopter pilot was their only hope.

Unfortunately, the helicopter pilot did not have enough room for both of them; however, he could take George if they hurried. That was fair enough. The helicopter pilot and Isaleer quickly devised a plan. Isaleer grabbed George by the hand and said, "Dude, I'm sorry for being such a douche bag to you at the house when you were picking up Haley's dad. I don't know, man… After all that just happened in the forest…I think it's about time I seriously rethink my life. I need your forgiveness, man, if that's ok… Please forgive me, dude?"

George smiled and yelled over the sound of the helicopter blades. "Are you joking? You just saved my life. Those fools were about to lob my head off in the name of your father Satan. I think we both started off on the wrong foot back at the Morgan estate. I will say this, though: Whatever you transformed into… Wow! I have never seen anything like that in my life. I don't even think you transformed into anything in the known animal kingdom. Dude, cut yourself some slack. I mean, if what the Highest Wizard Lord said was true, then I understand why you're such a prick. Hello! You're the son of Satan. Being a selfish and inconsiderate douche bag kinda runs in your bloodline. Seeing you evolve into a fifteen- or twenty-foot monster with wings… It all kinda makes sense now. Actually, you're a super nice dude for having such a hateful family bloodline, I mean, with your dad being Satan and all. I do, want to ask you a question, though. Since you were hardcore standing up for God and Jesus and all, have you ever accepted Christ into your life? We need more Christians like you. Like badly! Really, really badly!"

Just then, the helicopter pilot said, "Guys, I don't mean to break up your new-found bromance and all. Um, just in case y'all have forgotten, I have an Occult army approaching my helicopter! So I have to get off the ground. NOW! Isaleer, hide the best you can. We'll come back and get you as soon as we empty the chopper. Ok?" Immediately, the pilot pressed a button to close the hatch.

As the hatch to the helicopter began closing, Isaleer stood up on his tiptoes, quickly replying to George, "I don't know if I have accepted Christ in my life. I don't even know how to do it."

Before George could answer, the Illuminati soldiers had surrounded the clearing in the brush and began to open fire. There was no time to wait. The Arisen helicopter had to get off the ground. Quickly, George pulled a plan of salvation track out of his pocket and tossed it down to Isaleer in hopes that if he read it, he would learn. Folding the track and placing it in one of his pants pockets, without any awareness, Isaleer felt an extreme headache come on, followed by an absolute black-out. He blacked out, and the gargoyle within him took over.

All Isaleer could see was red as he began running towards the soldiers surrounding the Arisen helicopter. Releasing his hatred towards the Elite Occult Orders and the Illuminati army, Isaleer began his killing spree. Like an uncontrollable monster, he began ripping their heads off and stomping the soldiers' bodies into the ground. Blood began splattering all over the battleground. Consumed with a demonic mentality, Isaleer leaped into the air and slammed down on top of an Illuminati tank. Explosions began to fill the air with black smoke and loud rumbles, which shook the jungle around him.

A couple of military Hummers snuck past and began firing at the already damaged Rebellion helicopter, fighting to stay in flight. When Isaleer turned his head and saw the Hummers trying to shoot the Arisen army helicopter out of the sky, he let out a tremendous roar and then proceeded to run with full force towards the Hummers, grabbing them up and tossing them around the battlefield like an angry child with play toys in a sand box. They detonated, creating large explosions, on impact, and Isaleer realized something: These military transports could be slung towards other enemies and used to take out multiple targets at once. He quickly got clever and began grabbing up Hummers and tanks and throwing them at the Illuminati soldiers. Covered in motor oil and gasoline, they were slowly burning alive. Screams of gut-wrenching terror and agony could be heard for miles around the destructive trail Isaleer was paving. Laughter filled Isaleer's heart as he began to feel the desire to kill and watch the whole world burn.

The Arisen helicopter fled successfully out of sight; at this point, George was safe. The Occult soldiers were beginning to overtake Isaleer just as he began to lose control of his mutation. Yet again, Isaleer was put in harm's way to save George's life. The transformation was wearing off. He sensed he had only minutes before he was outnumbered and brought down. Isaleer had to find a way to escape. If only he could control his transformations from human to gargoyle, he could take this whole army down without a struggle. Every-time the fun was just getting started, something triggered in his body and began the transformation back to his human form.

It was a hopeless victory without having the ability to control his body's rage. Just then, the circumstances went from bad to worse when Isaleer saw six hounds of Hell running through the battle brigade, mindlessly knocking over the Illuminati soldiers with only one thing on their mind, which was to kill Isaleer.

(What are hounds of Hell?)

By the truest definition, these are animals of a demonic type which reside in Hell. These creatures are nothing we as humans have ever fathomed. Furthermore, these hounds of Hell have been given another name: Hellhounds.

For the creation of this book, I wanted to use the hounds of Hell as attack dogs used by the Illuminati soldiers in times of war. I was intrigued by the Thule Occult Society's approach. During the rise of the Nazis all across Europe, Hitler formed a secret Occult society called the Thule Occult Society. Obsessed with blending both science and the occult sorcery, the Thule Occult was my inspiration in bringing the hounds of Hell to life. Below is how I did so.

Illumicorp, Inc.
[Hounds of Hell]

The Illuminati government had been working on creating a genetically-modified creature that could be used out on the battlefield during the great tribulation. Using the highest level of technology and the most up-to-date scientific methods, they were able to use DNA found in ancient fossils to design a mammal that was barely even an animal. Without any hair, these things looked like dinosaurs. They were not dinosaurs, though… They were a perfect mix of the Occult and science. They could slightly speak and could be given commands to carry out. Imagine a hairless pit bull, which stood at the head ten feet tall and weighed nearly three thousand pounds. It was a monster that one could ride into war. It was a beast so ferocious that it could gnaw a car in half in fewer than ten seconds. This was the vision the head of research and weapons manufacturing. He called his creations the hounds of Hell.

They were ready to eat Isaleer alive, so he had to take these hounds down quickly. He was still losing strength and quickly beginning to grow weak. His only advantage over these hounds was that he had wings, and they didn't.

Knowing he wasn't going to have food for a while, Isaleer quickly leaped into the sky and soared over the pack of hounds. He dived down, swooped in, and grabbed one of them with his massive claws. Isaleer ascended into the sky, hoping to kill the hound of Hell when he landed and eat it to regain strength. As Isaleer began trying to make an escape, something went terribly wrong.

Meanwhile, on the Arisen helicopter with Mr. George…

The helicopter pilot came over the radio and said to George, "What in the hell did I just see? What was that thing?"

George quickly spoke up. "That's exactly what you just saw. You just saw the son of Hell. Actually, he's a humongous deal to the Elite Occult Orders. Somehow, he's the son of Satan. I've never seen anyone worshipped by the Illuminati, but I witnessed with my own two eyes them bowed before him. They even sat him on the Highest Wizard Lord's throne in the Black Forest in the Bohemian Grove Society; they were about to worship him by sacrificing me to a guillotine. Then before my very eyes I saw him transform into a gargoyle. The crazy part is that he has brothers and sisters who look like that, too."

The helicopter crew were in silence for a moment. Then the helicopter pilot said, "Well, that thing better never find his way in front of my fifty caliber, or I'll cut him down. Upon my mother's grave, I swear to God I'll cut him down! Anything the Illuminati worships has to die!"

George fired back, enraged by the helicopter pilot's ignorance. "That 'thing' just saved my life and yours! In front of the Occult and the global elite, that 'thing' declared he renounced his father Satan and wished that his father was God Almighty. He begged God to have mercy on his soul and longed to be a Christian so that he may do the Lord's will upon the Earth. That 'thing' has a soul! He could have let me die, but he saved me. If you try to harm him, you will have to 'cut me down' first, you stupid, ignorant buffoon! Did you not just watch him save us? He must have killed over a hundred men and dismantled five tanks before we even cleared his line of sight. In about 2 min, that 'thing' is not going to be a 'thing.' He will turn back to a young man named Isaleer Horus, and that 'thing' will be outnumbered and surrounded, all to save us."

Back on the battlefield on the island of Eden, amidst a private conversation being carried on between Lord Navari and Colonel Fetelli, as Colonel Fetelli is within reach of Isaleer.

"I want him alive," Lord Navari said.

"But, sir, he has killed at least a thousand or more of our men, not including the damage he has done to our tanks and Hummers. He has to be stopped! Your gargoyle is about to destroy my whole army!" Colonel Fetelli replied.

"I DON'T CARE ABOUT YOUR ARMY OF BULLET SPONGES! I WANT HIM ALIVE! THAT'S AN ORDER!"

"Sir, yes, sir!"

In mid-flight, Isaleer fell to the ground and returned to his human self. He lay on the ground, unable to move, while the hounds of Hell surrounded his body, fighting fearlessly over who was going to eat Isaleer.

Dropping his radio communication device, Colonel Fetelli quickly picked up the walkie-talkie for the P.A. and yelled out, "Hey Demon Prince boy-thing! Why don't you quit ^%$#ing $#@! up, and %$#@, and %$#@ing quit killing all my ^$#@ing men, and %$#@. Surrender and make this easy on the both of us. Hell dogs! Stop trying to kill the son of Satan. I mean, I get why you want to do it. Hell, two seconds ago I wanted to kill him, too! BUT QUIT ^%$#ING DOING IT! The Highest Wizard Lord wants him alive."

Hovering in his Banshee helicopter, Colonel Fetelli's commands were instantly obeyed, in perfect timing, too! The hounds of Hell had just surrounded Isaleer's body and were fighting over who was going to feast on it first.

Isaleer was unconscious from the fall and completely drained of his energy. Colonel Fetelli ordered for his troops to handcuff Isaleer and fly him to the island of Eden's secret fortress. Isaleer was on a secret island called the island of Eden. He was to be housed in a science laboratory just as the High Wizard Lord had requested.

Day in and day out, the Order of the Thirteen and the Highest Wizard Lord worked alongside Dr. Killjoy, trying to create a serum that would cause Isaleer to change into a gargoyle again. Isaleer fought back from inside his padded cell, killing many scientists who tried to approach him. The Order tried to convince him that what they were doing was for the betterment of mankind.

They wanted to harness the power of the gargoyle. When they finally concocted a perfect serum, they immediately began experimenting with how much to inject. During the mornings and afternoons, Isaleer was allowed to roam about the island freely. The experiments began when the sun went down.

Without permission, the scientists began injecting him with a chemical which caused young Isaleer to lose control and go insane. In his gargoyle form, Isaleer would be turned loose into an arena and made to fight against animals of the Earth. These top-secret arena fights were tests to evaluate the gargoyle's true strength. After it was approved, the Order summoned demonic animals to come forth and face Isaleer and his brothers and sisters, the other gargoyles.

From all points of the world, Isaleer's gargoyle brothers and sisters were brought to the island of Eden. The gargoyles were an unstoppable force. He and his brothers and sisters were a perfect alliance. Being that Isaleer would black out when he mutated into a gargoyle, he couldn't recollect any memory of his brothers and sisters. He was only told of these things by the doctors.

In a sober mindset the morning after, he would awake remembering nothing from the night before. Isaleer would call gargoyles animals with an unimaginable hatred. Nothing about being the Illuminati's favorite little toy was enjoyable. No matter how much they tried, the Order of the Thirteen could not sway Isaleer's opinion. The gargoyles were monsters with no conscience, and they had no purpose in existing other than turning Earth into a pool of blood.

Realizing that his sobriety was no longer an option, the Occult began forcefully drugging Isaleer. He was never allowed to be sober again.

When Isaleer was sober, he questioned his morals and refused to comply. If Isaleer could ever turn into a gargoyle on his own, he would be a danger to the Illuminati and the plans of the elite.

After a few months of constant drug use and heavy demonic rituals, Isaleer finally cracked. In his new mind, he accepted his position as head over mainstream media and pop culture. He loved the money involved in this position, but he hated the corruption and all the Occult rituals he had to be involved in.

In order to keep dealing with the life he was leading, he had to continue turning to drinking and drug use to find peace. Once Isaleer accepted his position, there was no turning around.

Thanks to plastic surgery and dental cosmetics, Isaleer never once looked like a druggie. At times, when he would begin to sober up, his mind would come back to him. He would see the corruption he was causing and would have to get drunk again to get away from his guilt. As much as the Occult had numbed his spirit, they could not corrupt his soul.

During his sobriety binges, Isaleer would plan his escape from the clutches of the Elite Occult Orders.

Sobriety never lasted too long; soon, Isaleer was forced to go back on the drugs again. When he snapped back to reality after becoming intoxicated, Isaleer knew it was a foolish idea to plan an escape from the Occult. He knew they would only find him and hold him hostage or kill him. So Isaleer had to just keep going along with them and keep doing what they said to do.

Inside of one of the prison cells, they strapped him to a table. They began injecting him with all kinds of psychedelics, hoping to trigger a reaction. They wanted to see that gargoyle again. They wanted to harness the power within him. Try as they might, they couldn't awaken the gargoyle. Because he blacked out when he became a gargoyle, Isaleer had no idea he was able to transform into that creature. He knew only the stories he was told.

Chapter 4

LOCK, AIM, AND PULL

"I felt like unless I was high or drunk, I was not seeing reality clearly. That was the level of witchcraft I had exposed myself to through constant séances and heavy drug usage. It was to the point that sobriety and intoxication had switched places, and I was only connected to life when I was drinking or on drugs."

-Isaleer Horus

Our story continues several months later on that same private island. Little did Isaleer know that a plan was being put in motion to rescue him...

On this day in particular, Isaleer did some drugs and then set off on a jog, running deep into the Jungle. After jogging for some time, Isaleer had gotten lost, and his phone had no signal. He tried his best to recalculate his way back to the fortress. Little did he realize how unprepared he was for what was about to happen.

He spent all day finalizing his decision to escape the clutches of the Occult Elite and take up sides with the Rebellion army against the Illuminati. It only took a couple months of extensive testing and constant picking and poking to finally convince even the psyche of Isaleer's drug-induced, subliminal mind that he had to get free. By now, there was no drug that could numb him enough to convince him that staying was an option anymore.

Getting ready to make his escape, he tried visualizing his location on the island. To the best of Isaleer's knowledge, all he could assess was that he seemed to be some place near a jungle or swamp. Isaleer knew this much: He was running out of time. The sun was going down, which meant all the predators were preparing for their hunt. Before long, this jungle would turn hostile as the nocturnal creatures arose.

Isaleer began running with all of his might through the wet terrain, not stopping once to catch a breath. The sun was beginning to go down, which meant another really bad thing: The natives were preparing to hunt.

The last thing Isaleer wanted was to be mistaken as food for a native. On top of that, all the jungle predators came out at night, and that really wasn't sitting well in Isaleer's gut. Without being able to transform into the gargoyle, he could easily be taken out by a leopard or tiger in the canopy above his head. As Isaleer blindly stumbled across the jungle floor, the animal could pounce on him and easily make him dinner.

The thought of being a Tiger's dinner was not even slightly sitting well in his mind…or stomach, for that matter.

Isaleer began to panic, running faster and faster. Suddenly, Isaleer hit the marshland. What had once been a jungle filled with trees and animals was now a canopy of trees on either side of a muddy river.

"Ahh, freaking great, man. @#$%^&. Got crap all over my shoes now, #$%^." Isaleer slapped himself in the face and scolded himself, "Hey! Quit being negative fool. I know you're scared to swim across this muddy river, but let your last possible words be cleaner than the water you're about to swim through. 'K? Sweet! Now, man up, and let's do this!"

Isaleer stopped to lighten the mood by praying to God. Looking up to the sky, he said, "Scared? Who's scared? Scared? Haha. Psh, challenge accepted, God! Muddy river and all. Ahah. This event is the extreme swim-and-don't-die obstacle. I've got to swim across a crocodile-infested river. The question is, am I gonna swim across a crocodile-infested river? Haha. Hell yeah, I am! YODO! Well, see you on the other side, God."

Y.O.D.O:
You Only Die Once

"Although pop culture has gone mainstream with the term "YOLO," meaning, "you only live once, this term is just not an acceptable slang for us to associate with ourselves as believers in Christ. This is, of course, a completely inaccurate term for Christians, as it is stated in the Bible. We do live more than once. In fact, we will never experience a second death. We will live more than once, and the second time will be forever. To say you only live once means you are denying your right to live forever in the kingdom of Heaven."

-Dexter Rockwell

Isaleer could hear movement on the other side of the river. It was risky trying to blend in with the natives, but after thinking about the wild animals, all of a sudden the natives didn't seem so bad.

Walking in the river on foot, Isaleer kept feeling random things under his feet. Out of the dark, flowing water appeared a human skull, which had a bullet hole in its center.

Isaleer said quietly to himself, "WHAT? Ah. Well, that's not fair at all. How come the crocodiles get to have guns? I mean, what did this man do to even deserve that? He was probably just trying to swim across the lake to get home so he could go night-night, and these hood-@$$, thug-@$$, gangster crocodiles are gonna come rollin' up on a dude and be all like, PEW!-PEW! That is seriously super %$#@ed up. I mean, God, I'm sorry for all the language and all, but no! I'm in the middle of a quarter-mile wide river, and now I found out there are gang-bangin' crocs out killing pedestrians!"

Obviously, the crocodiles weren't toting guns. That is not even slightly logical. Crocodiles can't tote guns; however, assuming that the crocodiles were swimming through the water as unified gang members killing trespassers made the journey across the river much more comical for him.

Isaleer was not an idiot. In fact, Isaleer was a multi-billionaire who controlled the mainstream media, pop culture, and fashion. However, Dr. Killjoy had conducted numerous tests on him, along with his six other gargoyle siblings. This had resulted in Isaleer being a little more out there than a usual person. When Dr. Killjoy was running tests on him, Isaleer never knew what was going on because the scientists kept Isaleer drugged to the point of unconsciousness. During the time Isaleer was a test subject for all Dr. Killjoy's science experiments, he was held captive in a PlexiGlass prison cell, which was monitored by Dr. Killjoy and his team. At any given point, the PlexiGlass could be converted into a padded room, very similar to those in insane asylums. One can only assume this was for moments of Isaleer's uncontrolled out-rage.

Three days before, Isaleer had left Dr. Killjoy's presence in an extreme violent rage. Dr. Killjoy had begun producing a new chemical drug used in combination with the Occult's rituals to force the transformation of Isaleer and his six other siblings into gargoyles. The only problem with the new chemical was that it wasn't fast enough, and the effects only lasted until the test patient went to sleep. Dr. Killjoy wanted Isaleer and the other test patients to permanently be gargoyles. The assumption was that he was preparing an army for a war that was to come.

Dr. Killjoy was obsessed with blending science and the dark arts; he was very much into the Occult. He felt that with these powers combined, it would only be a matter of time until they controlled the world.

WHY DID DEMONS BREED WITH HUMANS?

In the Bible, they were trying to create their own species to overthrow the reign of mankind upon the Earth.

It is thought to some conspirators that these demons were known as "Reptilians." Of course, in the theological circles, these demons were given the pronounced name "Sons of God." They gave birth to "Nephilims," the later spawn of the Philistines who gave birth to Goliath and his brothers. Later, the young shepherd boy David, the seeker of God's own heart, was set forth to slay these mighty giants. He later became the king of Israel.

(This is found in the Bible in Genesis 6)

I further add that this is also backed by both the Church of Satan and the Satanic Temple, given that their translations may vary in terms and titles.

What Dr. Killjoy was trying to do had already been done thousands of years ago, back in the biblical days of the Old Testament. Demons were manifesting and breeding with the women here on Earth. In the book of Genesis, in chapter six specifically, it is noted that that's also where the Philistines came from. David had to go down to the lake and pull out the five smooth stones to take down Goliath, but the other four stones were to take down Goliath's older brothers, considering Goliath was the youngest. Considering that Goliath was the youngest brother, he probably ranged from ten to twenty feet tall. One can only imagine the size of the first generation of Nephilims.

The four other older brothers were probably easily up to fifty, even eighty feet tall. They were all derived from what Genesis chapter six refers to as the "sons of God." In theology, they are understood to be the fallen angels. At this time, the fallen angels were reaching out, grabbing the hottest chicks on Earth, and breeding with them.

The last thing that was said in Dr. Killjoy's laboratory was a coy remark Isaleer made. "What the heck, bro? Why do you always have to be playing God?" He slapped one of the sample vials out of one of the scientists' hands and said with a very angry voice, "Dude, are you freaking kidding me? You have gone too freaking far this time, bro! First it was the chip; now you want to turn our soldiers into test dummies for demons? Dude, I freakin' knew you were working with Navari. You promised me and all of my team under me that you would keep the wizard out of this!"

Dr. Killjoy said to Isaleer, "I have been given orders, sir, by someone much higher up the chain than you to begin human testing as quickly as possible. Your plan to navigate the direction of Illumicorp is no longer needed. You will remain a chairman and a prestigious board member at all of our meetings, but you are too young to operate such a powerful position, so I took it upon myself as head over science and weapons manufacturing for Illumicorp to discuss your reckless spending with the head chairman Lucien Vanderbuilt. He, of course, loves your power of manipulation over the mainstream media; however, he finds your condescending tone of voice lacking in discipline. He agrees with me that you should be stripped of your power over the science and weapons department. You are officially head of media and pop culture. You should consider yourself Mr. Hollywood. Why don't you go tweet about it, Mr. Hollywood?"

Isaleer got up, stomped out of the science lab, and began running through the woods, seeking out the biggest, toughest tree he could find so he could sucker punch that fool's brains out. He could not find a tree big enough to face, though. This was because he was not in California like he was used to, where the redwood trees were big enough to drive cars through the base of them. The fact remained that he was on an island called Eden. The trees were not huge; in fact, where he currently was, all that surrounded him were palm trees filled with coconuts. Angrily, he started towards the nearest palm tree and yelled, "Ah! This is my freakin' Earth!" He ran and tried to tackle the tree to the ground, but as he grabbed for the palm branch in mid-air, he found himself feeling like a monkey swinging from a tree. That only pissed him off more, as he had expected to send the tree soaring into the sea with his power. Instead, a coconut fell on top of his head and knocked him out for a couple minutes.

As Isaleer tried to sleep on the beach shoreline that night, he remained awake, looking at the stars, still furious at Dr. Killjoy. Refusing to return to the Illuminati fortress on the island, he pondered on the beach that night, devising his plan of escape. All of a sudden, an Illuminati space ship came and hovered above the island and landed at the hanger not too far from where Isaleer was currently, not too far from the Illuminati science lab, either.

It was clear to him that what was going on was only going to end up getting him killed. He had to escape and get out of the Illuminati brotherhood. He wanted nothing to do with Illumicorp, Inc. or any plans they had for world domination. He closed his eyes, and before he went to sleep that night, he made a promise to himself that he would find the Rebellion and help them defeat the Illuminati.

Isaleer had now been gone from the fortress for two nights now. He slowly crossed the river, still staring at the human skull. All of a sudden, a young lady his age yelled out to him, "Ew, put that down!" She was bathing near what appeared to be the natives' camp on the other side of the river's shoreline. Isaleer rolled his eyes and yelled back to the girl, "Yes, ma'am. Sassy!"

As he walked onto dry land, he froze, realizing these were not natives; these were the Illuminati soldiers who had captured most of the villagers on this island. The Illuminati soldiers were given orders to eliminate anyone who came against them. Isaleer heard the sound of drums and the gnashing of teeth, just a little ways out of camp, actually.

He quickly followed the sound of the drums. All at once, it hit him. That's what the skull was all about, back in the river. He could smell the vile, rotten smell of human flesh burning. The campsite reeked of it. He began to walk curiously through the campsite; with each step he took, he questioned more and more if this was a campsite at all.

The owl symbols placed everywhere could only mean one thing; the witches and the warlocks were here. Isaleer drew closer to the voice not far from the camp and saw that they were sacrificing the natives in a burning fire to the demon Moloch… They were chanting and dancing around the fire as the bodies burned. Each sacrifice was doused with sweet-smelling oil, burning before their golden god. They could not be stopped. The Illuminati soldiers guarded these rituals with hatred towards anyone who was not welcome.

A few of the soldiers carelessly mistook Isaleer for a fellow soldier. They gave him orders to get properly dressed and to make sure he had his weapons on him at all times. Isaleer, being slick, found a dead soldier just outside of camp and took the clothes off him and placed them on himself. The only problem was that this soldier didn't have any weapons around him. Isaleer walked back to camp and requested new weapons because he had lost his previous weapons in combat.

Without question, the gunnery sergeant handed him a paddle for the canoe, an oversized shotgun that looked big enough to either be used as a sniper rifle or to take down elephants. The barrels of this thing were the size of his head. There were six barrels aligned in a circle like a Gonzo gun, and just like a revolver, the barrels turned counter-clockwise with each shot. Then they handed him a pistol that looked like a nine-shot Desert Eagle. The only difference was that this thing was made to kill and be sure of it. Neither they nor Isaleer gave it a name, but if Isaleer were to give it a name now, it would be "the OHW-18mm," short for "one-hit wonder eighteen-millimeter." The rounds were double the size of a standard nine-millimeter round.

After all was said and done, a man who resembled the most stereotypical military colonel imaginable came out from the bushes. He was tall and strong. He had that old-school military buzz cut and scars all up and down his arms. As he passed, he made a comical remark, saying, "Hey, boy! Do you know how to use them?"

Isaleer assumed he was referring to the guns. Isaleer smiled with all seriousness and said, "Yes, sir! Lock, aim, and pull, sir!"

He laughed and passed Isaleer, slapping him on the back and saying, "Ha, that's what she said." Isaleer knew at that moment that they were on quite a serious mission. The severity of one's thoughts can be discerned by the way they constantly search for humor to keep from becoming overwhelmed.

Just as Isaleer was making his analysis of the soldiers standing around him, out of nowhere they all heard a loud rustle approaching them from the forest. Without the skip of a heartbeat, these men and women turned quickly to mindless robots, ready to flatten the forest and everyone in it without emotion. In a matter of five seconds, there were over a thousand foot soldiers lining up against the tree line. Isaleer found out quickly who the commanding officer was when he yelled, "Soldiers, you will not fire until you are given the orders!" It was Mr. That's-what-she-said. One of the officers radioed the colonel, but the frequency went out over the intercoms. During that time, the sound kept getting louder and closer. Isaleer spun his shotgun from its sling on his back to its ready position against his shoulder. He looked down the sights.

He took a deep breath. This is where Isaleer would find out if he had what it took to kill. He whispered to himself, "I mean, it's just like I said: Lock, aim, and pull. You've got this, dude." Just as Isaleer caught the monster in sight, the engineer had repaired the communication frequency between the officer and Mr. That's-what-she-said.

As Isaleer was about to pull the trigger, he heard a voice come across frantically over the radio. "Do not shoot! I repeat, do not shoot! That's one of ours!!!"

Out from the woods popped a man running at full speed, yelling, "Woo! I've done it! I've done it!" You could hear his man purses slapping against his sides. They sounded completely full. However, while running, Isaleer could see his hand to his head holding a cell phone, so he was obviously on the phone. By the looks of it, both this man running towards them and whomever he was talking to were both extremely pleased with whatever was going on. This man running through the woods was getting closer and becoming very much out of breath, but he continued running till several different cell phones started ringing from his pockets. Isaleer could only assume that what was to happen next was brought on by the fact that this man was running with so many things going on at once, trying to figure out which phone to pick up first. All of a sudden, the man fell right on the ground. Isaleer watched him, with every bit of strength he had, pick up all six bags and place them in such a way that he may carry them accordingly. He brushed off his shoulders, adjusted his safari hat complete with bug net, and began running towards Isaleer and the others again. Then he yelled, "Minion!"

Out of the line of soldiers, one came forth and said, "Yes, Master Killjoy?"

Isaleer dropped his gun on the ground and said with relief in his voice, "Aha, dude, you have got to be kidding me... Nice."

Chapter 5

THE WAVE

Just before Isaleer could say anything, Mr. That's-what-she-said all of a sudden got an official name. Enraged by Dr. Killjoy's ability to make his soldiers break ranks, he barged through the line of soldiers and directly addressed Dr. Killjoy. "Now, you listen here, pretty boy. I run things around here! So before you just come in here declaring your authority, let me make a few things clear. I run the show! Everyone around here calls me Sir, Yes, Sir, but you can call me Colonel Fetelli."

One of the privates nudged Isaleer and remarked sarcastically underneath his breath, "You mean Colonel Fat-belly." Every one of the soldiers standing at attention chuckled but were quickly brought back to attention after seeing Dr. Killjoy present this far in the jungle and this far away from the facility. It was something that puzzled Isaleer's mind as well.

Before anyone could comment on his unusual presence, Dr. Killjoy replied with confidence to Colonel Fetelli, saying as he began walking past all the men standing guard at his approach, "Aha. Whoa, whoa, whoa, what's with the hostility? I am Dr. Killjoy, the head of the science and weapons manufacturing department, remember? Colonel, without me, you would be dead! You will stand down at once, or whatever I have to say to get you to stand down. Psh…shut up! You might run things for your little squadron here, but I run things for this world and for Illumicorp International. I am the science leader.

Sir! Anyway, so are we quite done measuring each other's manhood? Hmm? 'Cause I have some really cool stuff I invented that I want to show you guys."

All at once, an evil black wolf with red glowing eyes that had been deprived of food came from behind Dr. Killjoy and said, "You don't run anything. You have no authority. You make weapons and design technology for the Occult. If Colonel Fetelli has no say, then you have even less say. In fact, you are a puny slave, a mere puppet that shall be discontinued when it becomes outdated. Your creations have apparently given you the illusion that you are God. Ahaha. You are in no position to even think of yourself in such high regards. Without any technology, I can bring you to your knees by casting simple spells, and I am not even the ruler. Remember your place, puppet. Have any of you seen Isaleer? The sun is going down, and it's time to begin testing."

Dr. Killjoy bowed to the ground, stuttering through his words in fear. "I-I-I…I am not a leader, sir. I-I-I…I am a low-life mortal who has no power. S-sorry for my arrogance. I have spent too much time within the confines of my laboratory. In my laboratory, I am the king. I overstepped my boundaries just now. Please forgive me, Lord Navari. That will never happen again."

Lord Navari shunned Dr. Killjoy's presence. "Quit your graveling. We all know how weak and pathetic you are; there is no need to demonstrate the lows to which you will stoop in order to remain in good favor. Your mouth is filled to the brim with the fecal matter of those whom you wish to appease. I doubt you have any more room in there at all actually."

The Illuminati soldiers spoke up amongst themselves. They could not believe a wolf was speaking with a human voice. The colonel said to the wolf, "Navari, huh? What kind of name is Navari for a dog?"

Navari smiled as he shape-shifted into the human version of himself. He said, "The kind of name that will bring forth an army so powerful it will bring down the Heavens."

Turning to his squadron of soldiers, Colonel Fetelli said, "Ha! I hope someone heard that clearly because I think I'm going deaf. He wants to bring down the Heavens, and apparently we aren't a good enough army to do so. Comrades! Last I checked, we're the ones with the missiles and the license to kill. Am I correct? As a matter of fact, I know I'm correct. So let's all stand at attention and get a load of this guy! Listen here, wizard-man-Navari-dog thing. Before you can take on the Heavens, you need to take on your own war down here on planet Earth. As I recall, we soldiers are the ones fighting for you and all these rich boys. They wanted us to patrol the streets of the cities and clear the forests of all the natives. They gave us orders to go into people's homes, grab them up, and put them on trains to FEMA camps. We are doing your dirty work, and apparently that isn't good enough. Now I am fighting for a dog-wizard shape-shifter who wants me to take on the Heavens? Soldiers, get your unicorn killers and change your diet to rainbows. We are about to fight in Heaven with harps and halos. What are the angels gonna do, harp me to death? I have nuclear warheads, Lord Navari. I could blow the Heavens to smithereens."

Dr. Killjoy face-palmed his forehead and said quietly to himself, "Great. Now he's measuring his manhood against a wizard's. Here we go..."

Lord Navari thundered, "Your human army stood powerless to my army of demons. In fact, if I remember correctly, you tried out to be a wizard yourself but didn't have what it takes. One of the demons almost killed you, Colonel. I had to stop one of them from finishing you off. It is thanks to Dr. Killjoy, who sewed you up and brought you back to life, that you are standing here today. If it had not been for Dr. Killjoy, I would have let you die. I do not believe in saving the weak."

The Colonel was brought to silence.

Dr. Killjoy smiled and said, "Now! If there are no more interruptions, Colonel Fetelli, I have created a new weapon! It's called B.I.I.N.D.S. This is short for Binary Illuminant Individual Neuron

Dimensional Seeker. In short, each one of you in the Illuminati military have been inserted with an R.H.F.I.D. chip, which is how you are paid. It's also how your cell phone works, how you store your data, including medical records, how you surf the web, and how you purchase and sell items."

Here is where Dr. Killjoy's weapon comes into play: This chip is also how each person on the planet is tracked. Inside of each of these chips is a radio frequency which is magnified using H.A.A.R.P., a very top-secret mission being conducted in Alaska. Every person on the face of the Earth is tracked using ELF waves and satellites; this is all done from the Beast, which is located in Washington, D.C. It is the world's largest computer storage and tracking device. It takes up six city blocks. This computer is where the information of each and every person with the chip is stored. This is also where a live tracker feed of each and every person's location is sent. Each person receives a certain color on the screen, based on how much they know about what those in the secret society do not want them to know. If one is clueless, he or she is deemed red, and therefore their tracker dot on the screen is red. If someone is researching and wondering about the New World Order, the Illuminati, or any other branches, the dot changes to the color green. However, if one is caught sending these files to other computers or posting secret information on social networks, his color turns to blue, and soldiers are sent to pursue and capture the individual. That person would then be given a choice: life in silence or death for what he knows. …

Dr. Killjoy was just about to announce phase two of the project, in which the soldiers would be made to look like robots. Human skin would no longer be visible, even down to the fingertips. These men and women in the New World Order would now be mindless soldiers who kill innocent people and work side-by-side with demons and principalities.

BEAST FACT #1:

"There is a computer in Washington, D.C. that takes up six city blocks. Did you know it's called the Beast? Something to think about: What if they gave you the chip, and the Beast was used to store your information in a global database and then give a pinpoint location on a government screen of where you were at all times? All of a sudden, the mark of the beast was a controlled device to be inserted and or ingested. We in theology focus greatly on "the mark" as a visual implication displayed on one's body; however, what if the mark, which we think is a tattoo or ink, actually is a dot on a global GPS grid? With the advancement in technology, the idea of a tattoo is just not sufficient for quick individual look-ups. Think about it: a global search engine that is able to track each person on the planet and evaluate our daily lives, while also being able to invade our privacy and implement reprimand for the disobedient, marking those deemed dangerous for apprehension simply by searching a person's R.H.F.I.D. chip. With this kind of technology, no one could ever hide again."

–D. K. Rockwell

"This computer is stored safely in Washington, D.C., not too far from one of our safest locations in America, the White House." Dr. Killjoy turned to Lord Navari and made an inside joke with him, saying, "Now, we just have to keep the Muslim Brotherhood out of there. Oh well, at least it's not the Christians anymore…"

Dr. Killjoy took a moment to breathe and then began again. "Before today, the R.H.F.I.D. chip was just how we controlled the masses, but since the disappearance of millions of people, we suggested that for everyone's safety, they need to have this tracker chip implanted under the skin. So now we can find out just exactly where the hell these people are disappearing to."

HOW COULD THE R.H.F.I.D. CHIP BE USED AGAINST HUMANITY?:

"The truth is, that Illumicorp Int. and all the secret societies just seized an opportunity of weakness during the time of the Marshal Law disappearance to establish the chip, very much in the same way that they passed the assault rifle ban laws. It was a quick, low blow, which played on the hearts of the people.

If you didn't support the gun ban law, you were saying you didn't care about the children who died. The government played on your emotions. As a government, they couldn't have cared less about the children who died. People die every day, in every country. Most of the government officials are lobbyists who want more money and more power. They don't care about us. They don't care about you. If they did, it would be illegal to sell food made with GMOs. The mainstream masses of people are absolute idiots who would believe anything that comes from the White House. Think about it. We didn't ban guns after Columbine or 9/11, but when a random kid runs into an elementary school and goes on a killing spree, the president is moved so deeply that it's not a shooting at a school but a national act of terrorism! The secret societies just sat back and laughed. It was the easiest thing. The plan here was disarming Americans so that when they sent the Illuminati soldiers door to door, they could ensure the Americans' cooperation through intimidation. Meanwhile, moms are crying to their news stations, saying, "Guns are evil!" The mainstream group of Americans fell right into the trap. To win America, all you have to do is play on the heartstrings. In that same manner, when millions of people went missing, the government simply stood up and made it an order to get the chip. During the economic crisis, the government had been devaluing the American dollar simply to set the stage for one world government and the New World Order. When millions of people disappeared from civilization to go into hiding from the military troops who were sending people to FEMA camps for not complying, the masses of people went into a complete panic. The government had to reestablish a new order and control system, so they sent out soldiers into the streets to enforce a complete lockdown. If you were out on the streets, you were taken to a FEMA camp, which was used as a prison camp. At that point, you were held there and given an ultimatum: take the chip and be tracked, or stay in prison and wait to be executed for terrorism. Surprisingly enough, most people stood against the chip...until all of a sudden it was the only way you were getting into any shopping centers to buy food or clothes. People were being starved into submission, and quickly the masses gave in. Even still, there were those resisters who went into complete survival mode, choosing to just steal and pillage. If you tried to sneak into a shopping center with the intention of stealing anything, it was possible but highly unlikely that you could escape safely. There were military personnel who guarded the entranceways of every major convenience store and shopping mall day and night. They had aircraft, satellites, and tanks which could find you even in the dark. You could not grow anything thanks to the chem-trails; the ground and sky were poisoned, and nothing could grow. The R.H.F.I.D. was the new currency because the dollar had no more value. After America had gone into a debt so deep that they could never pay it back, the UN stepped in and had the strongest nation at its weakest point. This was the moment to tell the world, 'WE HAVE AN ANSWER TO FIXING THE ECONOMY: TAKE THE CHIP.'

People said no and began growing their own food. That didn't last long. When the UN caught onto that, it was made illegal to self-sustain. At that point, you needed their food and their water because they took possession of all of the water of the world. Any water that wasn't in a water bottle was unsafe to drink because they purposely began poisoning the water supply. That ended up making the ground sterile and the air unclean to breathe. At this point, they created an air-tight seal around their specific cities, and if you were not in their air-filtered cities, you needed a gas mask. By simply controlling the food, water and air, they had created a silent genocide. I believe this is where you say 'monopoly...'"

-D. K. ROCKWELL

"However, as of today, thanks to the almost-completed Project Blue Beam, and complements of Lord Navari's Elite Occult Society and all of his team of sorcerers, and of course, our High Lord Lucien who is over the secret society's Occult Forces, we are about to make this chip extremely useful to you as soldiers. We are making it possible to transform your robotic body parts into useful things needed on the battlefield."

PROJECT BLUE BEAM:

"Fifty-two million dollars go missing from the United States of America's account. All of a sudden, more than fifty-two satellites start orbiting the Earth, projecting holographic images onto the clouds and the ground from space. CNN announced that the government had projected an image of the Mona Lisa onto the moon. They would most likely use this technology to recreate Revelations, where "Jesus returns in the Clouds." Fooling the world would make them want to follow that savior, therefore giving the masses a God to believe in. Did you know Project Blue Beam is also able to project a voice from the sky?"

-D. K. Rockwell

Colonel Fetelli piped in and said, "Wait, what? So if I need a screwdriver, my robotic suit's right hand will transform into a screwdriver?"

Navari laughed hysterically and said, "No! It's much more than that. In fact, Dr. Killjoy, do you mind allowing the Colonel to be the first to demonstrate what this helmet can do?"

Dr. Killjoy excitedly said, "It would be a pleasure, my lord." Dr. Killjoy reached into one of his bags and pulled out the small head device and said to Colonel Fetelli, "Colonel, here, put this on your over-sized, sausage-meat head."

Isaleer began looking the Colonel up and down, trying to figure out how he could do all of this? Then it hit him all of a sudden: The Colonel was only human from the neck up. Isaleer knew this because as Colonel Fetelli was putting the helmet on, he shuffled some of his hair around, and Isaleer had seen a barcode on the back of his neck—his plastic neck that read, "Illumicorp Inc.," as though his G.I. Joe body was made in China. Hmm…

About ten seconds passed as Dr. Killjoy was turning the helmet on. All of a sudden, the colonel sounded like a little boy who had just woken up on Christmas Day. The colonel with his mouth open wide turned to look at his squadron, immediately zeroing directly in on Isaleer. He said with a loud voice, "This one isn't showing up on my screen as being in my squadron! Hey, kid! Yeah, you! Lock-aim-and-pull, you stay right there, and don't you dare %$#@in' move."

Uh oh. The Colonel shoved his way right through the soldiers, cutting through lines and stopping right in front of Isaleer. He said, "Now, as for this one, I have no giggle-stomping idea who he is."

He looked directly into Isaleer's eyes. Isaleer, without fear, looked the colonel back directly in the face, crossing his arms and waiting for a reply. In the meantime, Isaleer saw a huge scar down the side of the colonel's face that started at mid hairline and went down the side of his head, stopping over the colonel's jugular. Isaleer was entranced at the thought of who or what could have done that. The colonel pulled out his knife, put it to Isaleer's throat, and said with the voice of a true soldier in a time of war, "Tell me who in the Sam Hill you are, now, or I will kill you!"

Dr. Killjoy was about to put a halt to the fight, but Lord Navari grabbed the doctor by the arm and said, "No! This is going to be interesting. I want to see this! You know who that is, right? He's got himself all camouflaged to be one of the soldiers, but look closely. It's Isaleer. Killjoy, we might just see him turn into in a gargoyle today. Maybe if the colonel pushes the right buttons, Isaleer will get angry enough and shift all on his own. Glory be to Satan for giving us his gargoyle children."

Isaleer simply looked at the colonel, completely unmoved and unintimidated, and said, "Psh. Really, dude? Ahaha. I'd like to freakin' see you try!" Colonel Fetelli made no efforts to retaliate; in fact, the colonel seemed distracted inside the helmet.

Isaleer got cocky and said, "Release me, you Illuminati bullet sponge, and I will tell you who I am proudly." Without knowing why, Colonel Fetelli actually released Isaleer. Isaleer clicked his shoulders and cracked his neck and said, "Fear me, for I am your death if you try that psycho @$$ bull $%^& again. Don't ever point a weapon at me again. Are we clear, bullet sponge?"

After a moment of silence, one of the soldiers in line piped in and said, "Umm… I am not ok with all of these creatures around us. We have dogs shape-shifting into wizards, scientists experimenting with humans, and now we have this guy saying he is death. What next, an attack from aliens from outer space?"

Isaleer laughed and, facing the soldier's general direction, said, "My name is Isaleer. I'm here for the sacrifices and ceremonies. How are you doing, Lord Navari? How are you doing, Killjoy? I'm one of the high wizards in the Order of the Thirteen. As your armies keep spreading across the Earth, I keep traveling, hoping someday soon we will have enough blood spilled upon the Earth to summon forth the Dark Lord Lucifer, also known as my father, Satan. I'm just ready for the new world, so I get impatient and come to these ceremonies to track the progress. But uh, no worries, man; we're all on the same team here."

Isaleer hated pretending he was on the same team as the Illuminati; however, right now, as he was surrounded by High Lord Navari, Dr. Killjoy, and Colonel Fetelli, it was not the time to make any slick moves and claim his plan to escape. He had to be wise and keep playing along until the time was right.

Just then, the colonel's satellite tracker began beeping, denoting that the island of Eden was under attack by a foreign enemy. The colonel looked angry and ready for war as he turned to Isaleer and said, "Oh! Well then, Isaleer, I like you again. Sorry for almost killing you. Genocide is what I am doing here, and it's what my platoon is doing here. Anyone who won't comply with our demands dies!"

The colonel looked at Dr. Killjoy, punched the helmet, and said, "Hey! Hey, Killjoy, how do I make this God-dang %$#&^%$ thing transform? We're under attack, and I need to prepare for war!"

Dr. Killjoy said, "Under attack? What do you mean, under attack? This is most technologically advanced Illuminati fortress on the planet. If we were under attack, our radars would have targeted any intruders and notified the command center to fire homing missals that would shoot the intruders out of our no-fly zone within seconds. No one can penetrate our tracking systems. I built them myself!"

Colonel Fetelli replied, "Huh. So then, explain to me why my helmet is notifying me that an entire aircraft fleet is approaching our location and why command center hasn't radioed our platoon that we are being invaded! I repeat, Dr. Killjoy, we have foreign bogies flying in at our seven o'clock, and if this thing can fly or transform into a fighter jet, that would be preferable."

Dr. Killjoy said, "Holy $%&*. The island has been breached! Uh… uh. Press the button on the side of your helmet, and state your name so that the B.I.I.N.D.S. can recognize you… Uh, then, voice what it is you need it to transform into."

The colonel mumbled to himself. All of a sudden, the most epic display of transformation and machinery became a symphony, bursting out of his back and forming two twin turbine engines. The colonel leaped into the sky and flew off as an F-22 fighter jet.

Dr. Killjoy said, "So is there anywhere that we can seek refuge during this attack?"

No sooner did Dr. Killjoy get his words out than Isaleer could hear helicopters and jets flying over the jungle. The island was, indeed, under attack.

Lord Navari quickly turned to Dr. Killjoy and said, "It's the Arisen! They are looking for him! Do not tell him anything. Just protect him from being captured at all costs! His life and our fate is in your hands. Do not fail me!"

Trying to hear his own voice over the helicopters that were beginning to fly lower and lower to the ground, Dr. Killjoy shouted, "I will guard him with my life."

Colonel Fetelli flew over, trying to shoot the helicopters out of the sky, but he was all alone for almost half the fight in the sky. The Illumicorp soldiers began rushing to their aircrafts to help take down these Arisen helicopters.

Lord Navari slammed his staff against the ground and disappeared, leaving the foot soldiers along with Dr. Killjoy and Isaleer running quickly through the woods, trying to seek refuge from the fifty-caliber bullets flattening the forest. Just then, a huge boom was heard, and a low engine rumble filled the sky. It was an Arisen B-52 bomber. He had just taken down three Illumicorp jets by blowing up the side of a mountain. That was a bad idea because that particular mountain range just so happened to be the mountain range that held back the ocean from this part of the island.

The Island had a valley which was about two thousand feet below sea level; in between the mountain range was a huge dam created by Illumicorp. The valley through which they were currently running had a steady river flowing through it, which was what created the energy source for the island in case of a crisis. Well, two bad things happened when that B-52 bomber took out that mountain range. One: There would be no back up power supply for this island for quite a while. Two: that ocean was closing in fast on the forest of the lower valley—and closing in fast on Isaleer.

They watched in disbelief as a monstrous wave came pummeling over the forest, swallowing the scenery in front of them, leaving nothing but a wall of water. It created a shadow that blotted out the sun. The ground shook, and the soldiers who were with them told them that there was no point in running; they would not make it. By the looks of it, all their lives were about to end.

Isaleer began pondering to himself; people think about the most irrelevant things right before they die. He questioned why he picked up that human skull… Ew. His main thoughts were centered on whether anyone was even going to miss him when he was gone. He said quietly to himself, "Dang, man, have I done anything in life worth noticing?" Isaleer calculated about thirty seconds till impact.

He began counting down, accepting his fate. After twenty seconds, Isaleer went back to thinking, "Is anyone going to miss me? What if I'm dead, and my mom and sister come back, and they can't find me? Did I make a positive impact on the Earth, or was I just another rebellious damn black sheep?"

Isaleer apologized quickly for cursing, hoping God had an express pass for forgiveness and would hear him in time. Isaleer began thinking about Heaven and Hell. He realized all this nonsense had helped him count away fifteen seconds. By now, he could feel the mist on his face. Isaleer decided that it was time to face the monstrous wave. He yelled out, "Ahaha. Screw this! I am not going out crying. I'm going out epically!" He fell to his knees and praised this God his mother and sister had talked about. He thanked him for a good life and told him how excited he was to see him. He said, "God, if you would even just chain me to Mt. Zion, I will play music for you all day."

The water pulled back from the river, becoming part of what was about to be the largest wave Isaleer had ever seen in his life. As he counted down from five, he thought of those moments on the shores of Cape Canaveral, counting down till NASA lifted off a space shuttle endeavor.

Isaleer took a deep breath, smiled, and was no longer fearful. He felt like a Chinese monk deep in meditation, as though nothing mattered anymore.

The wave picked him up, and Isaleer was carried to the top of the beast. As he reached the climax of elevation, he managed to get one last glance at reality, at Earth. He concluded he had to have been at least fifteen stories high. Then Isaleer fell with the rip curl, freefalling to his death. Right behind him followed what his heightened senses recognized as about one million pounds of water—at least. He then knew he was not going to die from drowning but from being squashed like a household roach under the weight of someone's shoe.

His last thought as he hit the ground and blacked out was whether he was a roach in God's eyes. Was Isaleer a petty being minding his own business, disgusting to his viewer's eyes? Must he be squashed and killed simply for being like the roach, which was created to do as they do? Like the roach, must he be destroyed for simply being alive? A tear fell from his eye when he wondered... Had his sin made him unsanitary? Just like the roach, without question, must he, too, die?

They say before a person dies, there is an eight-second transition period from life to the afterlife. In Isaleer's last eight seconds in his body, he wondered why he was so cruel to God's animals, never minding everything else he had done to humanity. His last concern as his eyes glossed over was coming up with an explanation for being an ant bully his whole life.

Chapter 6

YOU ARE A GARGOYLE TOO

"You minuscule delinquent, trailing your echoes through this monastery, be silent at once! Who are you? I don't believe we have met. I also fear that your ignorance has led you to this place. Do you know where you are?"

Isaleer shook his head, the way one shakes his head after waking up to jog his memory, except no amount of rubbing or shaking his head could prepare him for answering where he was. Isaleer looked up at the man dressed in his red and black cloak and then closed his eyes, hoping things would start making sense when he reopened them.

Violent lightning struck all around him. The sound of ravens and evil creatures filled the forest floor below him. As he began to look around, he remembered falling from a wave, but that was it.

Isaleer about to ask the cloaked man where he was, but all of a sudden the black wolf came up next to Isaleer and shape-shifted into Navari, the wizard lord. Looking at Isaleer with his eyes glowing red, one single strand of drool falling from his mouth, he said, "You are not dead because I saved you. You are too important to the Illuminati, and the Eye has given specific commands that I am not allowed to let you die. Dr. Killjoy had the responsibility to keep you safe. I told him to get you to safety. He failed to save you because he only cares about himself. One day, you shall be fully unleashed and you shall never know your human body again… I know it must pain you to live inside of mortal flesh. Your father would hate to see you trapped in human skin, but we cannot figure out to how to contain your outbursts. Your power is too great to risk you turning against us. If you were to be unleashed before you have been tested, you could jeopardize all of the plans your father has set in motion. If only we had gotten to you before your earthly stepparents had manipulated your mind with the knowledge of God and Christ. It makes no sense for a demon to be brought into this world and then be given a soul, only to think poorly of the origins of his ascension. Oh, how I wish to see you side with us and truly take form. It saddens me to see such potential gone to waste as we wait for your soul to darken. I await the day I can call you Master Isaleer. the son of Satan."

As the lightening continued to strike all around them, Isaleer could hear sorcerers singing like monks. They were chanting an eerie kind of music that had haunted his dreams for years. The trees around the castle stood hundreds of feet tall. Isaleer then knew where they were.

He said to himself, after taking a large whiff of the air around him, "Never mind. I know where I am. Home sweet home. There is only one smell like that. I'm in the Black Forest; I'm in the Bohemian Grove."

As he stood up, he could see the cremation of care miles off, just over the lake. Isaleer immediately succumbed to his worst nightmare. Isaleer questioned Lord Narvari, "Dude, do you realize how crazy you sound right now? All I want is to be free of this curse. If I could be a human and never have this power, I would give it away in a moment. I hate being bound to a spirit that is damned to Hell. Do you realize what is waiting in Hell? Have you ever stopped to consider the horrors that stand even at its gates? King Asailatine himself… I can feel the walls of its dungeons cloaking my body like a robe tampered in abominations and fire not known to this Earth. Being that I am the son of Satan, you presume I am damned to his same doom? That I should share in the torture of the lake of fire? How can such a horrifying fantasy be what drives you? It's like you get off on the thought of your doom. I choose not to be like my father because I don't want to share in his fate. How can you look at a field of flowers blooming ever so true and not find comfort in the eyes of a bumblebee that buzzes from flower to flower collecting pollen? His only care is to pollenate and drink of the sweet nectar. How can you see such a gorgeous expanse of land and not want to venture its valleys? All you men wish to do is watch the whole world burn. How can such chaos and destruction be appeasing to your tastes? You drink bile and vomit and try to find joy in your upheavals. Why do you force yourself to enjoy such bitter, disgusting things. This world could be paradise, yet you and all these men hide in secret, conspiring of ways to bring down the sky. Do you not realize you are bringing it down on yourself as well? If I am a gargoyle as you say that I am, then you are right. If I ever was given control of this mutation, I would undoubtedly stop you. I am not my father's son, and I do not partake in his blasphemy. I am held hostage under your witchcraft; I am spellbound and told what to do. I am an unwilling puppet who is bound to its strings. Let me go!"

Wizard Lord Nevari replied, "No! We will never let you go. You will never be free. Your words shall never prevail against me." Wizard Lord Navari's eyes began to illuminate with a deep anger. "Yes! I see fields of flowers. I gaze far and wide over the landscape. Do you know what I see? I see the works of God's hands. I see an unstoppable king who has created a dream world unlivable by man. He has given us free will and forced his children to give their free will, give up our power, and be his slaves. How can you taste such power as you have known and not once question why God mocks humanity? He sits on a throne in Heaven guarded by legions upon legions of angels seeing beauty and perfection, yet has cast us down to gaze into the sky to question if there is more to life then this...

"So we build. We could wait on this God, or we could fashion for ourselves a Heaven here on Earth, simply by putting our hands to the plow. Though we cannot attain the ability to live forever, at least we can say we have known the best man can build, and I do say I think

Babylon would be proud. We most definitely have the capability to bring a whole new meaning to the Tower of Babylon. If we lived in the ways of the Christian, we would strive to never once please our flesh but rather reject our desires, as we are supposed to. We would live our lives casting away from ourselves our true nature, our animalistic tendencies, what makes us man. 'Sin not,' right? Yet what is sin? Hmm? What is sin?

"Sin is doing what we were designed to do. Isaleer, you are too quick to go on these spirit hunts through the different dimensions. You forget, we are human. Nothing that happens there is real…

"Let's talk about what is real. Do you know what happens when you take all that spirit energy, move it to reality energy, stay away from downers, and get your energy up? When you see a beautiful girl, is it not primitive nature that, if you two click, you want to acquaint yourself with her and then have her bend over a glass table so you can have your way with her body?

"God gave us this Earth and all the things in it. Is it not our job to enjoy them all? It's like God looks down upon man and says, 'I created you to be lions with large teeth, to kill zebras and gazelle,' but if you drink the blood as you were created to do, God rains down his judgement, saying, 'I shall cast you away from my sight for being an abomination in our existence.' What kind of God is this that which would create us with a flesh that longs to be pleased but expect us to not obey the voice of our inner desires? What kind of God says he loves his people with a jealous love and then watches them suffer as they take a stand for him, while he does nothing to save them? Say whatever you want, but it seems all you are doing to yourself by trying to be a believer is making yourself and everyone around you miserable. We were created with lusts and desires, just as the lion that is dissatisfied with the taste of green herbs. His hunger shall only be truly fulfilled when he releases his inner beast. It is foolish for him to deny who he is. He is not a gazelle, lapping up the river water and delighting in herbs and berries. He is a bloodthirsty, stone-cold killer. By accepting this, he takes his rightful place on the food chain and in the animal kingdom. At least by aiding Lucifer in his lust to rule the Earth, maybe we shall all live together in Hell without hostility. No! It's not a pretty place. I am not a fool! I know it is a place of damnation, a place without life and without beauty. I ask you, demon prince, how can you look at a God and his Christ who speaks so hatefully against you and say that you love him? Remember something: God cast your father out of Heaven and never gave him a chance at redemption. When he looks upon your face on judgment day, do you not think he shall see your father when he looks in your eyes? Do you not think he will smell the hate in your sweat or notice that your blood reeks with the fragrance of thousands of rotting corpses? You are not one of them! You are not a child of God. You are a demon in a human body because we can't let you be who you really are until you quit trying to side with God. Do you realize how crazy you sound? A demon cast out of Heaven, a prince of darkness, the son of Lucifer no less, saying that God is his true father, and he will never comply with Satan. How does this make any sense?"

Isaleer said, "I say that I love him because I am not only a demon but also a man. I have a soul. I am not bound to the fate of those without a soul. God created us to live with him. Yes! He gave us the ability to make choices and decisions because once upon a time, evil was not among us. Once, choices and decisions were not wicked but simple and beautiful. Evil seductively approached Eve as a serpent. He slithered up a tree, and while Adam was gone, he took advantage of Eve. Oh, what a serpent to wrap his coils around the legs of a beautiful woman and slide his scaly skin over her body. How it must have felt as he was whispering in her ear the things she was capable of, touching her and making her feel sexy and powerful with his half-truths. I'm sure as she lay with the serpent, in her climax she yelled, 'Yes! 'Yes! Serpent, yes! Yes! I will eat of this fruit which you say will make me a

God." I'm sure when Adam returned and Eve was limping towards him, eyes filled with witchcraft and adultery, Adam was easily spellbound by the thought of power and control. For that evil serpent who was my father to offer a man and a woman that which was already theirs only to create a separation between Creator and creation, tells me that serpent was jealous of the union that Adam and Eve had with God. That Serpent had lost his position because his position and status had begun to make him feel like second only to God in Heaven. His position and status had begun to make him feel like he actually had the ability to replace God by overthrowing him. As if to say, Pinocchio had the ability to murder Geppetto. Satan was never created as a God or God like. He worshipped God as Lucifer and God adorned him with every precious stone and ever precious metal, as a display to all of Heaven that this angel named Lucifer was special and unlike all the rest— but the gifts and adoration began to fill Lucifer's heart with lust for power and greed. It was Lucifer who became perverse with all the attention. God gave gifts out of love and appreciation, but Lucifer confused the gifts of All Mighty God; with weakness and lost sight of the gift giver. Lucifer began to ponder on a dangerous thought. He began to fill his own mind with evil illusions that there was only one other who got more attention then him and that was All Mighty God himself. In Lucifers jealousy he sought to take out his competition. What part of any of this labels God the criminal? If anything it labels Lucifer as ungrateful and filled with dangerous doses of greed and lust for domination. God does not enjoy watching anything suffer. This is life, and this is the price we pay for the separation made by Adam and Eve. This life is us paying for the sins of our forefathers, and you want to make it worse? I agree that at times it seems as though God has abandoned us. It is in those moments that I have to remember not to look at reality in my situation but look with my spirit mind, my third eye, and see the process."

Navari quickly replied, "Gagulesisus-Du-Cranium-En-Twangle-Mi-Vanacular. Silence! Your words fall upon foul soil. $@#$ God! %@$# Heaven and %$#$ all of your words. One way or another, you will do as you were created to do. We will make you obey!"

Isaleer replied, "Uh, was something supposed to happen? Ah-ha. The Highest Wizard Lord tried casting a spell on me, too. He tried to stop me from glorifying God's name. All it did was put a fire in my eyes and make me want to glorify God even more. That you want me silent means there is truth in my words. Your sorcerous tricks don't work on me, bruh. You will have to make me a prisoner before I will ever do anything you ask willingly! What have you done to the Black Forest surrounding the Bohemian Grove?"

"An awkward silence fell over the balcony. Isaleer began looking around from atop the tower's balcony. He could see for hundreds of miles, though all he could see was what looked like a valley of death. Since the Night Isaleer was 1st brought on the stage in The Bohemian Grove and confronted by The Highest Wizard Lord, The Bohemian Grove had been scorched and burned in the fire storm God sent pummeling over-top of The Grove. Since that night these great and mighty woodlands have been reduced to ash and wasteland— with Volcanic activity becoming a concern from the mountain range surrounding The Bohemian Grove."

"All I see are patches of dry and barren wasteland. The rest of it looks like the outer courts of Hell."

Navari quickly said to Isaleer, "Oh, I'm sorry, Mr. Horus, head over mainstream media, pop culture, and Hollywood fashion. Don't like how the new decorator is decorating?"

Navari opened his mouth to speak, and just as he did the cloaked sorcerer spoke up. "The closer the master gets, the more nature is going to die, young Isaleer. Life doeth not follow that which is death. What thou seest is the world being strangled of its right to flourish. We seek chaos and destruction, for to have order there must come a rebuttal against the current. That which is current must be done away with. The masses have been trained to look to the sky to seek a high power. We must squeeze that hope. We are training them through misery to accept that there is only man. We are the hope. Soon, they will learn to look to us; we shall be like gods among men. They shall look no longer to the sky but to us for hope. We will never have to force our beliefs on them. We will just take them low enough that they turn from their faith in the unknown and reach for someone to fix their reality. It is said that the more that is stripped away from a man, the less he thinks ahead to the future. Eventually, when he has nothing left, his only instinct is to survive. It is in this state of mind that we can showcase our previsions and offer elevation by persuasion by means of food and water. When we are the only ones who have the necessities to live, the masses will choose to do as we say or die. This is the New World Order. It is a world where leaders supply as long as you obey."

Isaleer upchucked and shouted, "Obey. Obey. Obey. Obey. That seems to be all I keep hearing, this stupid freaking word: obey. I have never met men and women who were thirstier to be God in my life. You all are sick and disgusting. You would watch innocent children die just to get off on watching their parents kneel before you and call you "king." I hope Revelation is right, and God does cast every one of you into the pits of Hell. How can you hold the keys to humanity's existence and dangle them above their heads? You are billionaires and trillionaires, living the life of kings and queens, and you watch the world work their hands to the bone just to put food on the table. &%$# all of you, you sick bunch of ^%$#ing &^%#s. You are not getting away with murder. God is up there, and he is watching with fire billowing from his nostrils! He will avenge our blood."

As Isaleer opened his eyes, he saw hundreds of miles of dry wasteland. If nature dies the closer Satan gets, he must be close. Isaleer's heart sank, but his face remained frozen. This was not a wasteland in some desert. This was something that had never seen sunlight. The ground was a blue-gray clay which had cracked from draught. What rain that did fall was toxic and filled with pollution and poison that was killing the ground. Isaleer squinted and looked deep into the sky, but all he saw was smog and clouds which blanketed the atmosphere and refused to let sunlight or moonlight in.

Navari looked at Isaleer and said, "Whether you believe it or not, in your unconscious mind you have done many great and wonderful things for the Order. What you have done is merely clear the way. There is still much work to be done. It is time for you to meet the minds behind all of this. Come, follow me!"

Isaleer turned away from the balcony and followed Navari down the winding stairs, staggering with each step he took. They walked for some time down a long hallway. Thoughts began racing through Isaleer's mind. This must have been a side entrance to the throne room because it's never this easy to access the king's quarters. When they reached their destination, Navari looked at Isaleer and said, "Shhh. Do not speak unless spoken to. Do not answer with long replies. Be direct in your responses."

Inside Isaleer's head, he was questioning what or who could be behind this door. As lightning continued to toss itself mercilessly across the sky, rain began pouring down, almost drowning out the sound of the tremendous claps of thunder which followed each bolt.

Death was praised and worshipped through the decor of the outside castle walls. On either side of the moat were two large pillars which acted as the entryway onto the bridge. These columns where decorated with a statue atop their mighty structures. The sculptures were that of the serpenscilla. He who rode on the back of this beast must kill the serpenscilla's mate, though no one had ever killed the Asailetine. Whosoever killed the mighty King Asailetine was cursed with an illness which could only be cured by drinking the blood of a dragon each lunar eclipse.

The serpensillas were the only full-blooded serpents. The king of all dragons was named King Asailetine. The serpent king had many queens. If any of the serpenscillas became with child, King Asailetine would attack the serpenscilla and kill her, eating both her body and that of her offspring. He feared a child being born that would overthrow him as the king serpent guardian of Hell's gates. These statues on the pillars represented monsters that were to make their way to Earth during the time of the apocalypse. These serpents were under the authority of Heaven and were assigned to Hell's gates to assure that no demons could get free of its grasps.

The Illuminati were hypnotized by the desire to ride these beasts into war. Thinking that they could harness the power of a serpensilla and make it work to their advantage, they sat up night and day thinking of ways to form an army of serpensillas that could be raised and trained to be used on the battlefield. The Eye passionately dreamed of the day he would ride on the back of King Asailetine and terrorize the Earth from the sky. They did not know that only a holy and pure rider could ever tame the Asailetine.

Awaiting permission to cross the castle bridge, Isaleer began to look around. The moat below was filled with crocodiles and piranhas. It had a pungent smell, probably from all the dead bodies that had never been reclaimed from the murky water. Because the castle was created in the middle of a meadow, a forest surrounded the castle grounds on all sides. About a mile away in every direction was a dry lakebed. Ravens swarmed over the forest, screeching and clamoring their anger at all the owls who controlled the hunting grounds just outside the castle. As the storm began to pick up, the lightning began to strike the ground with an unimaginable force, leaving burn spots in the dry lakebed large enough to fit a suburban home. The thunder from these strikes rumbled the ground and could very well make one go deaf if he were standing close enough.

As Navari spoke to the guards protecting the castle's entryway, Isaleer stood patiently, waiting for entry into whatever could be behind this drawbridge. After a minute or two, the guards signaled to the tower that it was ok to open the doors and lower the bridge. As the bridge began to lower and the door began to open, loud music poured out. At first, it seemed as though Isaleer was walking into a wealthy coven. However, as they approached the castle walls, all Isaleer saw were extremely bright lights gleaming through the entranceway. They made their way through the castle hallway and walked through the door, which was shaped like a large tunnel. Fog machines and laser lights began to make their presence known. Fog billowed through the cracks in the doorway. The bass from the music being played rumbled the floor, making it hard to hear Lord Navari as he spoke.

Witchcraft Terminology:

coven |'kəvən|

noun

a group or gathering of witches who meet regularly.

◇ figurative, often derogatory: a secret or close-knit group of associates: covens of militants within the party.

ORIGIN mid-seventeenth cent.: variant of covin -D. K. Rockwell

After walking about one hundred feet, Navari grabbed Isaleer's shoulder and shouted over the music to Isaleer. "This is where the rulers of the Illuminati reside. These men are the richest among the richest. You are about to walk into what we call the Corridor. This was where you were to train under the Highest Wizard Lord before you escaped. The throne inside was supposed to be yours to fill one day. At the moment, mere mortals sit upon that throne, basking in the power of its magnitude. Are you ready to see what could have been your home?"

As the Secret Service guards opened the doors to the Corridor, Isaleer smiled and said, "Huh. Well, that escalated quickly. I thought this was gonna be a huge demonic séance ground. Dude, this looks like a huge party! There's nothing threatening about a lavish party, right? All of a sudden, this looks just like home.

It was a one hundred thousand square-foot corridor filled with everything that the wealthiest man could ever want. All across the Corridor were the most beautiful naked women. Aligned at the bar was the largest selection of alcohol in the world. Any liquor, beer, wine, rum, tequila, champagne, or mixer that could be imagined was made present for their enjoyment. The world's best live DJs and the wealthiest rap, pop, and R&B artists were playing live on a stage made for an arena. Of course, wealth like this required drugs and a flying trapeze performance happening overhead. This corridor bankrupted California when it was build. The price tag was over fifty billion dollars, and no one was allowed in unless someone from the inside requested someone from the outside. Not even Isaleer had been in this castle. In comparison to any magical castle that one could think of, this one scaled over it by about a thousand times the size. However, though everything was expensive and lavish, it also was extremely twisted.

There before Isaleer's eyes was a throne, and a man sat upon it. Fake blood dripped from his golden throne, and naked female slaves played blood-wrestling on the floor in front of him. With fury in his eyes, Isaleer set off towards the throne. There was every evil nature there before him. He saw a rich whore trotting around on the back of a pig and holding a beer mug. The walls were crawling with bats. As he reached the stairs, the man seated on the throne looked at him and said, "I will open your eyes."

Navari began laughing hysterically, sending chills down Isaleer's spine. His audience of misfits all rejoiced over his name. Navari said, "Master, I must go. Our savior is close, but I have brought this one to you as you requested. This is Isaleer Horus."

Just then, the man on the throne looked down at Navari and said, "Yes, I know you are quite the busy wizard, Navari. Very well. Leave him with me. When I am finished, he will be returned safely to the island of Eden. I assure you, Navari, his mind will be changed when I am through with him."

Just like that, Navari brought his hands together, and with a pop and a crash, he disappeared.

"My name is irrelevant as I will only be with you shortly, and you will never see me in person again—or, at least, you as your human self will never see me again. I dwell with the kings and queens of the world. However, you, as you have been told numerous times, I'm sure, possess a very unusual capability. You share the same blood as our Lord Lucifer. I have been told he is your father. I will need you for the war against the Heavens when God returns. Now, am I to understand that you side with God?"

Isaleer boldly responded, "Yes! Yes, I do. I do plan to side with God against my father, Lucifer."

The man sitting on the throne said, "Ah, I see. Why is this? May I ask what exactly your father has done against you to make you hate him with such passion?"

Isaleer replied, "Uh, look at this. Look at all of this. You guys are so bent on making people your slaves and forcing them to conform to your agendas that you are willing to starve them till they bow. All in the name of Satan… Oh, my bad, I mean Lucifer. What is the difference? Look at the evil one as the angel of light, or look at him and the lord of darkness; what difference does it make? Either way, with a smile or with a frown upon his face, he wants to dominate, to be worshipped as God. I would never allow humanity to suffer such a horrible demise as to become soulless robots. They would only worship him to be given provisions to live another day. That is not true worship. I hate this thing you call my father because he wants to destroy mankind."

The man on the throne replied, "Of course, of course. You want to be the hero. How noble of you. Blindly, you seek to stop the New World Order your father is bringing to life, yet you can't accept that his plans are already set in motion. God? God has abandoned his people to die. If he wishes to stop the killing, then I beckon for him to stop it! Hmm, nothing. Nothing at all, not even a sign that he is up there.

I beckoned for him to stop his people's suffering, and nothing… Where is this God, Isaleer? Now, I urge you to accept your rightful position. You are a prince, and we need you to do what a prince does and begin planning the war. I will have none of this nonsense anymore. You are the prince of the Dark Lord. I want you to see the new world we have created. I think after you see the power of the Occult, you will obey. If it is the winning side you wish to be on, I urge you walk with me. Our teams of scientists have developed a small-scale transporter. We were unsuccessful at bringing the powers of darkness to Earth. Instead, we want to bring the people of Earth to a whole new dimension. We have found a portal to the Garden of Eden. It is a paradise where things only spoken of in fairytales and myths exist. It is a place where we can live and grow. Granted, it is not yet complete, though what we do have completed is very much livable. At first, we were going to bring everyone to a virtual reality world, but that is so outdated and far too overplayed. Instead, let's give people the tools to unlock the spirit realm within reality for themselves. Let's show them what is going on around them. Let's show them the mystical animals they think are phantasmal. Let them stand in awe of the colors that their normal eyes would never be able to see. All these thousands of years, we have minimized mankind's perception of the spirit realm. Now, it is time to open them up to it and show them it exists. When they see dragons and trolls and goblins and aliens for the first time, they will cry out for God and believe in him. Then we will give them a God through Project Blue Beam. We will provide a face in the sky and a soundtrack to life. It will be a marvelous display of technology, the Occult, and science. Come! Let me show you the new world."

Isaleer was lost, but he just played along, nodding his head, hoping something in here would make all of this make sense.

The man descended from the throne and quickly proceeded to the lower levels of the king's stairs to escort Isaleer down the hallway. He continued to speak to Isaleer, saying, "Through that door over there, you will find a drone waiting to escort you through the castle grounds and display the capabilities of Project Blue Beam. Go now, and enjoy! It was an honor meeting you, Isaleer Horus, prince and son of Satan!" The man extended his right hand, pointing to the door, and Isaleer saw "666" inked there on the back of his palm.

Without a thought, Isaleer walked over to the door, turned the handle, and walked through the doorway. He closed the door and found himself standing in an empty twenty square-foot room. He went to open the door to go back out into the corridor, but the door was locked.

A simple speaker system was set up on the corner of the wall. A voice came over and said, "Hold on. Let me activate the portal system." The man began pressing buttons and proceeded to start the sequence initiation of the portal system. All of a sudden, the man on the speaker said, "Ok! Go ahead and walk through the portal."

Isaleer stared with his eyes wide open and said, "No way, dude! H-e-double-hockey-stick, no. I am not walking through a freakin' portal, bro! Uh-uh. You picked the wrong brotha for this mission, homeboy. You need to check the color of my skin and go get yourself a crazy white boy for that mess." No one could hear him. He was alone. Without a second thought, he came close to the portal system and said, "Uh, well ok. So here I am about to do everything stupid known to man. I am about to walk through a portal to another dimension with my human body being awake and present. I don't even have a camera phone to record me doing so. Wow, the number of 'likes' I would get for this one. Well, here's to all the times my friends said I don't take enough risks. I hope this shocks the %$#@ out of all of you."

He walked through the portal and found himself in a room similar to the one he had just left. Isaleer whispered to himself, "Hmm, was something supposed to happen?"

The speaker system was replaced by a drone that walked through the door and replied, "Oh! Hello, Isaleer! Are you ready to tour the new world?"

As the drone gave the tour, it would stop periodically and explain certain features this new world had to offer. They began to make their way out to the outer courts of the back of the castle, where the drone was delighted to explain how this was a dimension where demons and principalities were living amongst humans. This was a place where animals and creatures could speak.

All Isaleer could say as he stood dumbfounded by all of this was, "Wow! %$#$ %$#$ what the $%$#. Dude, animals can talk to us here?"

Just as the man on the throne had said, there was music playing all around them constantly. The music was coming from the sky. For the first time, reality had a soundtrack. He couldn't continue lying to himself; this was quite delightful. The drone turned to ask Isaleer, "Do you like it? The music in the sky, that is? Now, keep in mind that this is only a preview of the world that will actually come to Earth. What you are seeing is only a technological breakthrough in science. This world is not reality. It is the possibility that awaits us in the new world. What do you think?"

Isaleer replied, "I mean, I can't keep pretending that this isn't probably the coolest thing I have ever seen. No doubt about it, I am having a complete mind change right now."

The drone replied, "It gets better, though. Because you are over pop culture and mainstream media, it will be your job to pick and choose what music comes out of the sky. Wouldn't that be fun?"

"I get to pick the music? I get to pick the music?" Isaleer replied.

The drone replied with joy, "Yes! Not only do you get to pick the music, but Project Blue Beam controls the color of the sky, and with it you can display a light show and even music videos. All of it will be yours. You are the prince, and you will help your father bring in a whole new era, an era where anything is possible!"

Skeptical, Isaleer questioned this. "Yeah, but what is the catch?"

As Isaleer gazed off into the night sky, lost in the thought that this would be his to control, a large beast snuck up behind the drone, snapped its neck, and threw its robotic head deep into the forest. The rustle alarmed the witches in the woods. As they went to investigate the loud thump, the beast quickly tossed his robe over his body and sat down, waiting for an unsuspecting Isaleer to turn around.

Isaleer repeated himself. "Drone! Hello! What is the catch?"

Still gazing into the night sky, listening to the music, and enjoying the simple light show taking place in the sky, he was almost completely sold on the idea that he would control this satellite system. He was almost ready to side with the Illuminati and bring humanity to their knees, but he was still desperately curious to know what the catch was.

He turned his attention from the light show in the sky as he heard a tremendous roar. For the first time, he could see dragons flying overhead. The dragons were flying in formation, and a serpenscilla was chasing them. It was much larger than the dragons. Watching the frightened dragons flee from the presence of the serpenscilla was humbling. The monster picked off one of the dragons in the back of the formation. It cried out in agony, screaming for the others to turn around and save it, but they showed no signs of helping the dragon. Never once landing, the serpenscilla began chewing through the dragon's neck. The dragon curled up in the serpenscilla's claws and let out a terrifying gasp that sent chills down Isaleer's back. The serpenscilla flew off far into the distance, and Isaleer's attention was brought to the lights coming from the forest. Those lights came from the tips of the witches' wands as they were casting spells. In this new world, witches, warlocks, and wizards no longer relied on voodoo and translucent magic, which could not be seen as it was being casted. In this new world, magic was real. It was tangible and extremely powerful, so powerful it gave off light and looked like fireworks when it shot from the tips of the wielders' wands. This world quickly turned from a paradise to a real-life nightmare about to enter the reality of Earth. To think that this power was being just handed out so freely made one wonder how many villains would rise from such an overload of unlimited power? Mass murders could come from the tip of a wand on every street corner.

Isaleer had an epiphany. His mind began conjuring up visuals and scenarios, and, astonishingly, it all came together.

The Epiphany:

My God, this is a full-out anarchy world, an anarchy ruled by a leader who in the midst of chaos demanded for full control. Let them kill each other, they said to one another. The genocide we shall unleash will be worse, but let them do most of the work. Let the masses kill each other.

—Isaleer

Isaleer glared in horror at the nightmare the Occult had created in this new world. He was puzzled as to why any man would want this to be a reality. He noticed a large silhouette behind him, and he turned quickly to face it. The gigantic beast that had taken down the drone was now sitting on a dead tree stump. This beast had to have been twenty or thirty feet tall. It was dressed in a cloak to hide his appearance. Isaleer had never seen anything like this beast before.

The beast said, "That's the catch."

Startled to learn that this was not a statue but a real, breathing creature, Isaleer cautiously approached the beast. "Who are you?" he asked.

The beast said, "Shhh. Dude, hold on. We don't have much time before they realize the drone is down. When they figure out the drone is down, the whole castle will be alerted. No one is watching, so I must be quick. Follow me! Hurry! Stay to the shadows!"

They ran quickly to get into the shadows created by the castle walls.

"They wanted you to come through the portal because they wanted to show you the power you will harness. According to Luciferian law, they have to present the concept of their plans before they can bring them to life. They are not allowed to create action without presentation. This is what they want to bring to Earth, man! A New World Order! The Occult and all the Illuminati Orders want to manifest demons and dragons and magic. They need these creatures and this magic for when God declares war on all the Earth. Anyone who lets the government or any world power put a tracking chip or currency chip or whatever you want to call it, man… If you take this thing, there is no turning around. You belong to Satan, and when he goes to Hell, so will you! First, before God can establish a new Jerusalem on Earth for all those who were willing to die before taking that chip, there must come the war of the apocalypse. The Illuminati holds you in such high regard because they expect you to fight alongside your birth father Satan against the Kingdom of Heaven. Satan wants to take the throne of God. Satan needs his children. The Occult have been working night and day on a large machine that they have hidden in the tower of Babylon in the Middle East. When the time is right, they will try to open a portal to another dimension."

Isaleer replied, "What? This plan is so much worse than I ever could have imagined. I will never fight for evil. I am confused though. Satan's children? So it's true?"

The beast replied, "Yes, it is true. You have six other siblings, two sisters and four brothers. Everything you have been told is true, all of it, every last word, every last psychotic word."

Isaleer replied, "Where are they? I want to see them."

"They want to see you, too! I promise they want to see you. They think about you night and day."

"They do? Wait, how do you know this?"

The beast replied, "Shh. Look! The witches are running towards the castle with the head of the drone. Quick! We need to get you back into the castle and through the portal before they send out the search party."

Isaleer stopped the beast. "Wait! Since you're all-knowing, answer me this. When I walked into the castle, I saw hundreds of beautiful naked women all present to entertain the men. What is the deal with women? Why is the core of entertainment always nudity? The critics who are under me are always demanding for more nudity. Then I walk up to a sketch @$$ castle, and I'm thinking this is a demonic haven. I walk inside, and it's a billionaires party, and there's nothing in the Corridor that you wouldn't see in a club. I saw liquor, money, women, and people acting crazy. I don't get it…"

The beast replied, "What don't you get?"

"The critics never demand drugs and money. They always demand more nudity. Real talk, what is the big deal with a woman's body?" Isaleer asked.

The beast looked at Isaleer with an unusual happiness, as though he was catching on and learning quickly. It said, "Dude, the biggest downfall of men is that they base their whole life on what they can see logically. Bro, do you know how powerfully gnarly the woman's body is? Your worldly leaders teach the masses to accept perversion because it's a woman's body that can hypnotize and entrance the human mind. A woman's body is just as dangerous as a serpent. In fact, it took both of them to get Adam to eat of the Tree of Life. All they have to do is dangle a little meat in front of these selfish humans using mainstream media, and they crawl to the television and computer screen begging for more. The mainstream media use sexuality and nudity as a distraction from much larger and more pressing topics, such as correcting the corruption within the governments. They do not want their citizens involved with their political choices, so they pass out porn as a way of keeping the masses focused."

The cloaked creature motioned for Isaleer to follow him. Isaleer was trying to keep up, but the creature was much too fast. He grabbed Isaleer up, ran with him on his back, and said, "Hold on tight, bro!"

Isaleer could feel wings on this creature's back, concealed underneath the beast's cloak. Before he was able to ask him about that, Isaleer saw something much more important coming quickly into sight. At first it appeared to be a barricaded field for the soldiers to call home when they were not guarding the castle.

Isaleer asked, "What the %$#@ is that?"

The beast replied, "Do you want to see it for yourself? We will have to be quiet and quick, but here, let me show you. Prepare yourself; this isn't going to be easy to see."

Isaleer replied, "Wait… No! Dude, no, no, no, no, no. There's no way!"

Isaleer and the beast found a way to get close and observe without being seen. Isaleer vomited as he saw men and women lined up in formation in prison jumpsuits. Inside of one of the cell blocks, the prisoners were reaching out of the windows overlooking the prison yard, screaming and shouting from their holding cells, begging to be the next one to be executed. Isaleer asked, "Uh, please tell me these are terrorists?"

The beast replied, "Yes! They are as you say. These are men and women who are deemed a danger to society. They have refused the mark of the beast and were caught trying to meet in secret to worship God. These are terrorists who have exposed the plans of the Illuminati on television stations and radio. These are men and women who know too much and wouldn't keep quiet and obey. So if you consider non-conformists and followers of Christ to be terrorists, then yes, these are terrorists. These are members of the Arisen who have fought back against the corrupted government. These are the tribulation Christians! They represent all of those who will experience great torture and starvation before being killed in the name of Jesus Christ. Here stands a concentration death camp, and there arrives a military train bringing in brand new prisoners who will not go along with the New World Order. You wanted to know what the catch to all of this was. The cool position as head over mainstream media would offer you… Well, here it is. This is the catch. As you're running the pretty little soundtrack for the Earth and displaying your cute %$#@ing holographic shows in the sky, millions upon millions of people are being dragged out of their homes, brought to these camps, and killed. All in the name of progress! All in the name of progress…"

All of a sudden, fear gripped young Isaleer, and in fear he said, "Killed? What do you mean, killed?"

The beast said, "Yes, killed! Where did you think all of this perversion and corruption was going to lead? All of this is all about a choice, Isaleer! A choice that has been made since the beginning of time: God or Satan, good or evil. Whose side are you on?"

Just then, Isaleer had a flashback to something his mother had said… "Son, you can't ride the fence and not make a choice. You must choose because if you don't make a choice, you have made your choice. When you refuse to accept that Heaven and Hell are real, your worldly leaders will choose everything for you. They will choose who you worship, what you wear, who you marry, and how much money you make, and they will make you take the mark of the beast. You may be Mr. Hollywood Horus to everyone else, but you are my son, and you will always be Isaleer to me. There will come a day when even the wealthiest man will have to choose, and no amount of power or money will make you exempt. What good is it to gain the whole world and lose your soul? Control starts with knowing where you are at all times with that chip, and all these ingestible microchips are only phase one. I don't understand why are you supporting this."

There were many things that Isaleer's mother had talked about from the Bible, but when she brought up the mark of the beast and the unholy number, a chill came through the room. It was made clear when she spoke that there was no turning around after one had renounced God. One could only make that choice one time. There was no going back. Removing that chip or cutting off skin could not make it right in God's eyes. At that point, one was Satan's property.

Isaleer begged for the beast to explain. Just then, two hounds of Hell came and tried to cuff Isaleer, thinking he was a prisoner who had gotten loose. The beast let out a huge roar. He was a gargoyle. He grabbed both hyenas and slammed them on the ground, bashing their heads into the concrete. When he was done, he said, "I didn't mean for you to know who I was, but since you've seen me, I am a gargoyle. I am one of your brothers. All your siblings can transform into gargoyles. When they let us roam free on the island one night as gargoyles, we all conspired together to escape and seek out the Arisen. My name is Number Six. Isaleer, you are Number Seven. You are able to transform into a gargoyle, but you need a certain chemical that the Arisen has created. With it, you will be able to transform at will, and you won't black out anymore. Unfortunately, I don't have it on me, so next time we meet I will bring you the chemical." Number Six was unlike any other gargoyle in that he wore a black knight's helmet with a red cross over the forehead.

Isaleer asked him, "How is it possible that the animals can speak to us?"

Number Six said, "Everything talks to us, but humans never listen because they are selfish." Urgently, he reached out for Isaleer's hand and said, "Quick, we must go. Jump on my back."

The castle was now aware of Isaleer and Number Six; all of a sudden, war sirens began sounding. Number Six said, "If you can get through the portal, you will be safe. What goes on in this dimension is not kept track of in reality."

They flew into the air and over the castle. Number Six pointed to the guillotine and shouted, "They will be using these to kill the resisters. First, they will put them in concentration camps, but if they will not conform, then they will kill them… Isaleer, you must find the maker of guillotines and stop him. Killing him will buy us some time."

With Isaleer on his back, Number Six raced down the hallway and back to the portal system. He said, "Go! You don't have time to waste. They will not know I am sending a team to save you. The team is on the island looking for you right now. Do not act like anything is different, or the Illuminati will suspect something. Don't do anything to push the hand of the Occult any faster, but when it is time, do exactly what the Arisen says, and follow them to safety. They know where your stepparents are. You must kill the maker of guillotines. Now, go!"

Chapter 7

TREES AND MONKEYS

…Isaleer was quickly thrust through the portal, but this time he wasn't sent to the room at the castle. This time, he was sent directly to the island of Eden…

He appeared on the shoreline just as his dot appeared on the screen inside the war room of the island's castle. Dr. Killjoy was notified of Isaleer's arrival by the head of the island security. After notifying Dr. Killjoy's laboratory of Isaleer's arrival, the island security sent forth the military war drones to greet what the security guard could not decipher. It was either a man or a monster standing on the shoreline. The war drones notified Dr. Killjoy that they had Isaleer in their sights. The drone was little help to alarm, though. Dr. Killjoy knew when Isaleer had arrived back on the island far before the drones had realized.

This was no surprise, of course; in fact, most of the world's population by this time had a tracking chip in their body somewhere. The corrupted government knew where most everyone was at all times. Dr. Killjoy secretly used this same technology on Isaleer to track his every move.

WHY IS THE CHIP SO VITAL TO THE ELITE?

"The R.F.I.D. chip has so many purposes. It can be used for the new global currency. In the same manner you swipe a credit card, you would swipe your body, and the amount would be added or deducted from your electronic account. It can be used to store medical records; with a quick scan, the doctor can get a read-out of medical history. It can be used as part of an advanced internet experience. Though, truly the biggest reason of all that the global elite would want you to have any chip, electronic pill, smart blood, smart ink or any type of foreign object in your body would be to have a global position on you. When everything hits the fan, they will want no one to be able to hide."

-Dexter Rockwell

During the science experiments, Isaleer had been unwillingly 'chipped.' In case Isaleer escaped again, the elite societies wanted to be able to easily find him. Isaleer had no idea he had a tracking chip implanted in his body.

Luckily, it was not the third-generation chip. Regarding the third-generation chip, Dr. Killjoy said, "It's how you are paid. It's how your cell phone works, how you store your data, including medical records, also how you surf the web and purchase and sell items." The first-generation chip was not the chip they used for buying and selling. Unlike the third-generation chip, the first-generation of these human 'chip-ins' only stored important information…or so the government said, but the government lied. Secretly, it was a tracking chip used to maintain global positioning on the masses. Although Isaleer did not have the mark of the beast in his body, there was nowhere he could hide. By now, the first-generation chip was merely a thing of the past, being that the mainstream society had advanced to the third-generation of human 'chip-ins.'

Isaleer was far beyond his due date for an upgrade; the only problem was, if the society told him they had implanted a chip in his hand, he would demand for it to be taken out, and then he would forcefully escape. The societies were in a bind. Isaleer had not given them permission to place that chip in his hand. Because of this, Isaleer had not taken the mark of the beast. (The rules where clear, not only in God's law but in Luciferian Law as well. Anyone given the mark of the beast had to willingly accept it knowing full-well what it was.) Although the societies of the government and the Occult Orders were not going to risk losing the ability to secretly track Isaleer, their patience with Isaleer was dwindling quickly. Soon he would have to be confronted and given the choice of taking the mark of the beast or being executed.

HOW DID THE GLOBAL ELITE INTRODUCE THE R.F.I.D. CHIP?

Phase 1: At first it wasn't a chip. Before they could go shoving needles into people's bodies, they needed to warm people up to the name "R.F.I.D." Welcome to the age of smart phones. The R.F.I.D. chip was in your phone. It made it so you could surf the internet at blazing speeds and gave you the ability to use GPS if you ever got lost. To the simple-minded, the smart phone having an R.F.I.D. chip was an extremely good idea.

Phase 2: They needed a way to transfer the R.F.I.D. chip from your gadgets to you. How? You can thank the major theme parks for that one. They made simple rubber bracelets that fit like a watch around your wrist. To access the theme park, you simply swiped the wristband. To pay for food, you simply loaded up the wristband's account with a money deposit. Then all you had to do was swipe your wristband, and you just paid for lunch. To access your hotel room, all you did was swipe your wrist, and the door opened. Smart wristbands were the wave of the future. No more money. No more credit cards. No more carrying around your driver's license. All your information was on the wristband.

Phase 3: The first-generation chips they passed out came at a perfect time. When they declared martial law everyone was kindly required to take the chip. It was so that they could cypher out the resisters. The world's elite in the Illuminati knew there would be an uprising against them. They just needed to know how many. The first-generation chip seemed harmless because the chip wasn't even active unless it was within two feet of a scanner and was being scanned at the doctor's office. The first-generation chip 'only held your medical records,' so any resister seemed like a radical paranoid obsessed with conspiracy theories. Social networking, of course, started helping with getting everyone used to having their every single move tracked and posted publicly. Wall posts gave everything away. When people tagged you in a photo and posted it on the internet, your name came up, along with a pinpoint location. Fake names while operating on the internet were always a good idea. However, they used the chip along with your cell phone to activate your chip and gain entry to your personal information, along with a pinpoint radius of where you were…but they never told you that part.

Phase 4: People who had taken the chip started questioning why the government needed to track them. Well, until they established **martial law,** they didn't. In fact, the chip lay dormant inside of their bodies for a good minute before they actually became useful to the government. By the time the world's elite had established martial law, it was mandatory to have the chip. Your rights were taken completely away by a corrupted Occultist government you never knew existed. This is how it was after the disappearance. Hundreds of millions of people went missing, and the government wanted to blame the aliens for the abduction. Martial law gave them full control by putting the military out on the public streets. Then it got ugly. They began rounding up the resisters and sending them to FEMA camps, but the revolutionaries, mostly made up of tribulation christians, never called these camps that. To the revolutionaries, these camps were concentration camps. That's what they were. They had gas chambers, guillotines, fiery furnaces, and firing walls, though these were only the popular forms of execution. There were plenty of camps that practiced unique and foreign motives of slaughter. Until the Illuminati decided to make a sport out of it. This is when they got creative, sending the resisters off in trains to concentration camps and, in random instances, sending them on planes to the Coliseum to fight and die for their right to live as entertainment. It became the most popular sporting event on Earth. Men and women who wouldn't take the chip were now forced to fight to live, all in the name of good sport.

We return to the story...

On the beach's shoreline, Isaleer was approached by Dr. Killjoy and his team of escort drones. He found one of the B.I.I.N.D.S. helmet systems washed up on the beach. Considerably interested in how this helmet is able to function, Isaleer picked up the B.I.I.N.D.S. helmet and began trying it on. Peering his head into the helmet, he expected to see a wondrous light show of sorts, but when he looked inside the helmet, nothing amazing happened at all, not even a light display on the main screen. "Eh, the water must have gotten to it," Isaleer said to himself.

Just then, Dr. Killjoy ran over to Isaleer and said, "Ah, you are not properly designed to be able to use the B.I.I.N.D.S. system, though I must say, I am not entirely against you wearing it as a helmet to cover up your stupid baby face." Out of breath from jogging down the beach, Dr. Killjoy took a moment to catch his breath. He collected himself and then said with a smile, "I'm kidding, Isaleer. Quit getting so butt-hurt over me making fun of you." Isaleer remained unresponsive to Dr. Killjoy's words. Isaleer saw a barcode on the inside of the helmet: 616161. Isaleer paused in his tracks and was unable to catch himself. The guards at the death camp just outside the Corridor had these helmets on, too! He could remember it clearly. Being thrust through the portal to the other dimension had brought so many nightmares to life.

All Isaleer could hear in his head was his brother's voice saying, "Do not act like anything is different, or the Illuminati will suspect something. Do not do anything to push the hand of the Occult any faster. When it is time, do exactly what the Arisen says, and follow them to safety. They know where your stepmother and stepfather are." On the double, Isaleer needed to regain his equanimity before Dr. Killjoy noticed something was wrong.

Dr. Killjoy flailed his hands around, waving them in Isaleer's face, saying, "Hello! Earth to Isaleer! You act as if you died and saw a ghost. Can I request for a moment of your attention, or is that too much to ask of you?"

Quickly, Isaleer shook his head and snapped out of it. Remembering what his brother Oxford, Number Six, said about not being conspicuous and just going with the flow until the revolutionaries instructed him on what to do further, he replied to Dr. Killjoy, "Haha. Dude, Doctor, you have no idea. That wave was a doozie, man. I have to thank Lord Navari for saving me. Of course, no thanks to you and your $#@! @$$… P^$$#. Good to know when $#@% hits the fan that you are your only concern. %$#@ you, you selfish #@!$! Oh, dude, guess what? I went to the Corridor. That castle is so ratchet on the outside. I was so sketched out. The crazy part is that once you get inside, it looks like a gigantic rave. By the way, how did you make it out of the wave alive, Killjoy?"

Dr. Killjoy replied to Isaleer, "Hey! %$#@ you, too, man! I saw a huge wave coming towards me, and the only thing on my mind was to run! I was hoping you would follow me, but you just sat there like a stupid @$$. Who the $%#@ just sits in a river when a giant wave is coming towards them? You saw the Corridor? Is it nice? You know, one day we will be able to live there, too, right? I'm surprised Lord Navari took you there. As I saw the explosion, I was able to escape the wave by just climbing the nearby mountain."

That night, after the whole day of interrogation, the soldiers who had survived along with Colonel Fetelli were beginning to get cranky and weary. After being asked every question that the Highest Wizard, the Council of the Warlock Brethren, and the One World Government Overseer could come up with, the soldiers were released from questioning for the night. The Arisen army was successfully becoming an eminent threat to the plans of the Illuminati. This attack actually momentarily crippled communications for much of the Illuminati army forces. The Arisen was beginning to get smart with their attacks. If the Occult and the Order could not get this under control lickety-split, the Revolutionaries would be able to decide the outcome of this war.

For the first time, Isaleer was favoring being around the Illuminati troops. When he saw that the Highest Wizard had dismissed them from interrogation, he dismissed himself from the luxuries of the fortress to go join the soldiers around the campsite. They sat around a huge bonfire in the center of the camp, awaiting the hunters to return with something to eat. This was not normal. In fact, most days they all met in the mess hall and ate food the fortress had prepared, but tonight was a time of celebration. They thought they had defeated the revolutionaries' army, so they were feasting and partying. The soldiers were allowed to mingle with the fortress women. This was never ok unless it was a time of celebration. On nights like this, everyone got sloppy drunk and partied.

It was just before sundown when they set off in two military Hummers, locked and loaded with their machine guns. By now, the moon was high overhead, and a good portion of the wood in the fireplace had turned to white ash. Isaleer and the soldiers who were too tired to hunt had collected before sundown had completed. They collected twenty-four palm trees, thanks to the gracious tank commander who chained up the palm trees and uprooted them like they were toys in a sandbox.

To Isaleer's recollection, he was only aware of four families of palm trees; there was the queen palm, the sago palm, the tropical coconut palm, and the ones that grew all around swamplands and Ocala. They had a name, but Isaleer had forgotten it… He ventured to say it started with a "W," something like washington palm or swamp palm. Either way, these exotic palms were nothing like anything Isaleer had ever seen before. They grew close to the camp; of course, this placed them right by the ocean. It was weird for Isaleer. For a moment, he felt like Dorothy… They weren't in Kansas anymore. This thought came along in Isaleer's head at one moment when he couldn't believe his eyes. It was almost like the tree had feelings, and when they uprooted it, it cried tears of sorrow. Every tree they pulled out of the ground secreted a sappy liquid from its palm fronds. It got worse after they realized these palm fronds went from a vibrant green to a pure black as the bark turned a pure white, ghostly and pale in color. It was as though they had taken the very life out of it. The fruit began shriveling up, but before they died, they grew little crab-like legs, fell off the tree, and began trying to dig itself into the ground to begin trying to grow a new tree. Before they could succeed, they lost all life, killed over, and died.

The rest of the boys caught on and made a pact that they would never tell Dr. Killjoy about the fruit that walked. The tearjerker came when a monkey came out from the bushes and started trying to help the fruit dig holes that they could reside in. When the monkey realized the fruit was dead, he looked at us and uttered little monkey mumbles. He picked the fruit up and handed it to Isaleer, as though he could fix this.

Isaleer told the monkey, "Listen, Monkey, I can't help him." That situation ended with Isaleer adopting a new pet. That little monkey saw right into their hearts and knew that they had no clue what was to come on this island. He jumped onto Sergeant Grinder's shoulder and then leaped over to Commander Bolen's lap. Considering a military outfit found this monkey, he had to be named appropriately. All those who were gathering wood for the bonfire gathered around the tank and Isaleer's new pet and began thinking of names. "Beretta!" Private Jackson yelled out. That was a great name, and they almost called him it, but even though it was witty, it sounded like a girl's name. They had two Black-Ops teams who begged for the name "Lo-Key." They were asked why, and they said, "Because a Black-Ops soldier has to be able to get in and get out, always staying low key." Everyone smiled and knew they were getting close. A bunch of Marines put in the names of their M1s back in boot camp at Parris Island. Of course, that was an obvious no, considering this monkey was a boy, and soldiers are supposed to name their guns after their girlfriends back home. The last thing they wanted was for the monkey to be thought of as some girlfriend back home. Then they might start spreading AIDS through bestiality.

Just then, the sniper team came up. It consisted of ten men. They told a story about a mission they had to execute called "Silent Mission." They were guarding in two-man teams over five mountain ranges. Their job wasn't to kill but to study and observe an operation. They were to relay that information to Homeland Security for discussion in the Pentagon. After a full week of little movement, the sun was shining really brightly that last day. They all were watching the last bit of the transaction between two foreign parties as they were exchanging a lethal biochemical. The sniper team watched through their scopes and binoculars as their targets completed the swap. A briefcase of money was exchanged for a vial of the purple bubbly; the trade was extremely simple. As they began walking back to their own cars, one of the men holding the vial stopped and noticed a glare coming from the mountain. All of a sudden, the sniper team realized they had been spotted. The only thing that saved them was reaching for some moss and crawling into a bush. They looked at each other and said, "Long story short, that moss saved our lives. We were wondering if we could name the monkey Moss."

All the soldiers clapped and cheered as Isaleer yelled, "Moss it is!"

Of course this never explained to Isaleer, who was still wondering, how and why these trees changed colors when they were chopped down. More importantly, Isaleer wanted an explanation for the fruit growing legs…because to say, "Plants have feelings," just wasn't cutting it for Isaleer.

The soldiers packed up and brought the trees they had uprooted back to the campsite. Seeing that the trees were about fifty feet in length, they cut them into fours and dug out a hole about twenty feet wide in diameter. Isaleer gladly shared Moss with all the soldiers and let them teach monkey, Moss, about how humans live. It was amazing to see how quickly Moss caught on to the soldiers; he impressed everyone when he could open a beer for Captain Brutus.

Chapter 8

EVERYONE HAS A PAST

eanwhile, Colonel Fetelli had not been heard from since he set off with his troops to go hunting. The men around the campsites' stomachs were rumbling like something fierce.

Isaleer's stomach was growling with attacks that felt like a hyena eating a screwdriver through his eye socket.

No sooner had the band quit playing their covers than all of a sudden, Colonel Fetelli got ahold of the microphone in the Hummer and yelled out in belligerence.

> **belligerence** |bəˈlijərəns| (also **belligerency** |-ənsē|)
>
> noun
>
> aggressive or warlike behavior : *the reaction ranged from wild enthusiasm to outright belligerence.*

"Good afternoon, ladies! Anyone in the mood for all-you-can-eat ribs?"

Jumping up with the happiest faces, the soldiers all came running to help carry the dead carcasses of the wild hogs over to the fire pit. They began dismantling, seasoning, and cooking them. Colonel Fetelli came over to Isaleer with a smile and said, "Welcome to the pit!"

Isaleer in return smiled, pointed at the fire and all of the surrounding area, and said, "Oh, I kept hearing everyone say "the pit."

Ok, now this all makes sense!" For the first time, Colonel Fetelli was showing interest in Isaleer.

After all the hustle was said and done...

Staring deep into the stars, Isaleer was reminiscing on the girl who kept him strong. When he finally got the chance to sit back and relax, he realized he had almost forgotten how. His past kept coming to mind...

Looking deep into the fire, he zoned out. He imagined he was pulling up to an arena, ready for his tour with the other famous musicians touring with him. When he arrived, the crowds had to be held back by the police. People were going wild; just seeing him pull up made people faint. At this show, he decided to pull up in a concept car that no one else had. He was tired of the typical exotic-car hype; it was time to blow them out of the water. He did just that when he pulled up in a concept car which had a mind of its own and conversed with Isaleer.

Before he could even think about entering this building, he had to contact security to surround his driver's side of the car and get him from his car to the VIP door. Isaleer was treated like royalty because he was a member of the Illuminati. He was put in charge of overseeing and controlling mainstream media.

He was Mr. Hollywood. He attended all the exclusive parties, from the rock, porn, and rap star parties to everything in-between. He attended all the famous charity fundraisers, all the celebrity dinner banquets, and every A-list private wedding. He was the face of mainstream media, and when he walked in, the party had arrived. Behind the scenes, he set the standard for the men and women's fashion. He knew his job was to demoralize women by making it fashionable for them to dress like sluts in public. He also knew his job was to make men consider women pieces of meat. What he didn't know was that this was more than just making the masses perverted and lustful. This was about keeping the masses focused.

To assure Isaleer's loyalty to the brotherhood, he had to perform acts of unspeakable evil in the initiation process, most of which he was unconscious for. After he was initiated, music videos went from containing sexual and explicit content to containing Occultist subliminal messages. Thanks to Isaleer, hand gestures forming the shape of a pyramid, hand signs over one eye, messianic pillars, Freemason checkerboard floors, Baphomet, the goats of men, and Molach, the all-wise owl, were mandatory in all the music videos. Isaleer brought on the doom of man when he exposed the mainstream to one of the most deadly hand gestures: 666. It looked very similar to an O.K. sign. As your index finger and thumb formed the circle your middle finger, ring finger and pinky were layered over each other as you held the circle over your eye. This told everyone this artist stood for the New World Order. If any artist used this symbol, they had renounced Jesus Christ as Lord and they were sold out to the devil.

After he made his way through the celebrity entrance, he rendezvoused with five of the top rap artists at the time. They were then all escorted into the arena by military personnel with assault rifles. After the concert, Isaleer went over to the bar to grab some drinks, and there, standing before his very eyes, was one of the most visually appealing young women he had ever seen in his life. This girl had curves in all the right places. Her very eyebrows were shaped to be thin and say, "I am a vixen." She had tattoos from the neck down. She was wearing the all too familiar red dress he had written songs about all his life. It was just long enough to barely cover her body properly. The highlight that showed her attitude was that she had one black heel and one white heel. They were the same style of six-inch stiletto heels, but they were just different colors. Isaleer was standing at the bar, and as he was throwing back shots, for the first time he heard her speak. She seductively asked for a shot of sex on the beach.

Her voice sounded like Barbie's. It was a higher pitch, but with the way she pronounced her words, all the "S" words were so crisp. Isaleer put away ten shots of vodka and then called for a bottle of spiced rum. The bartender said, "Anything for you, Isaleer!"

She walked over to Isaleer all hot and bothered. She grabbed him by his tie, pulled him by his shirt into a nearby private room, and said, "You're mine. Right now, baby! I want you."

Isaleer lit up a blunt and hit it for about one minute, back to back, just to get faded. When he felt the high, he picked her up. She wrapped her legs around him, and he slammed her against the wall with all of his might. He said, "Designer all the way down to the panties. God, I love expensive taste!"

As they were making love, she had yet to take her clothes off. She stood up to strip for him. Little did Isaleer know that she was a porn star. He asked her what her name was. She licked her top lip and said, "Evette Moore." Before she started her tease, she said, "Do you %$#@ ing love me baby?"

He lightly smirked and said, "I do right now."

She began dancing to the music playing in the room. Her seduction was entrancing to Isaleer. She finally got naked, tiger-crawled over to him, and said, "Anything you want, it's yours."

Isaleer's last words before he was hooked were, "Ight! Prepare to not to be able to walk straight for the next two weeks!"

That night sparked a long and passionate relationship. All of a sudden, Mr. Hollywood had found Mrs. Hollywood. The rumors flew about long vacations to private islands. The magazines and tabloids were writing, "Isaleer and Evette were spotted in Fiji getting sleazy on the beachy." That was just one of so many headlining ads. The thing that made this so beautiful was that they really were in love; Isaleer had never met any girl like her. Isaleer wanted more to come of this; he wanted her as a wife! She knew how to quench his lustful side, and for a moment things seemed to be going perfect.

One night, Isaleer met up with one major record label. They bought a pound, broke it down, and put it in a stogie. They talked collaborations. After that night, they became the faces of utter darkness. Of course, to the masses they were gods! These were men and a woman who could have the hottest chicks, the nicest cars, and the biggest homes on the planet. Of course, that was perfectly fine for young Isaleer. He went from being a millionaire to a multi-millionaire. One of the leaders of the record label said, "Money left in irresponsible hands has many nay-sayers. Whether the careless playboy wishes to splurge all of his liquid assets on the simple pleasures of weekly raunchy brothels amongst the world's elite, or whether he wishes to feed and clothe the low-life peasants, the power of those who hold the most money is non-negotiable. The one with the most money is playing God, and he is winning." This let Isaleer know that no matter how much the poor people hated the rich people, they only hated because they wished they were able to be rich, too. Isaleer realized that in this world, money was power. In the same aspect that faith was the currency of Heaven, money was the currency of Earth. In young Isaleer's mind, it seemed that with enough money, one could most definitely move a mountain. Why could money not bring happiness as well?

Night after night, Isaleer drugged himself to oblivion. Having sex with Evette and all her girlfriends helped momentarily, yet nothing seemed to satisfy his heart. He would lie awake at night after the drugs and alcohol had worn off thinking about his family. He hadn't seen them since he had gotten in the limo with Mr. Morgan.

That night kept playing over and over in his head. If he tried to rise up against the Illuminati, they would only kill him. He was forced to cut ties with his family to keep them safe. Night after night, he tossed and turned. It was not uncommon for Isaleer to wake up at three in the morning in cold sweats, hearing evil voices telling him he needed to make a new song or travel to Mr. Morgan's secret mansion and devise a particular bill that needed to pass in congress. Isaleer had to break it off with Haley after the night he was forced into the Illuminati. He knew her safety was at hand, but at times he dreamed about her, dreaming of how they could just run away together. Isaleer wasn't truly married to Evette; it was only a Hollywood marriage. He still thought about Haley. It seemed that heavy drugs and drinking along with excessive amounts of sex were the only things that kept him numb enough to deal with the life he was living. Though, as rough as things were, nothing prepared him for what was to happen next…

As Isaleer was coming home one night, he came in through the doors of his mansion and saw Evette shooting porn with a guy she had met at a club that night. The man Evette was stripping for was shooting a POV when Isaleer walked in. He was sitting on the couch and holding a camera in his hands. Evette climbed on top of him, begging for him in a moaning voice. As she sat down on him, she screamed as she began talking dirty to the viewers who would be watching this in the privacy of their own homes. Isaleer's fury became uncontrollable. Without even thinking, Isaleer ripped Evette off of this random man and shot him in the face with a desert eagle. He then slapped Evette, knocking her on the ground, and dragged both of them out of his house. That was all he needed to make him go heartless. He looked at the camera crew. When the police arrived, Isaleer bribed the officers with twenty million dollars. They gladly accepted and covered up the crime, and on with life Isaleer went.

He dumped Evette and began a suicidal downward spin. Night after night, he would sit by his bedside crying and reading his Bible, trying to muster up the courage to put the pistol in his mouth and blow his brains out. If this was what being a rock star was about, Isaleer was over it. Even though he wasn't married to Evette, he had trusted her, and she broke his trust.

Now, it was either end his life, or end the life of those he influenced. Then an evil light bulb went off in his head. He ran to his music studio on the other side of his mansion and began to devise a dastardly plan to pull the masses so far into the dark that he could feel the numbness in their eyes. He made a call to several of the top rappers and said, "Listen, if you're in, I have an idea that is going to revolutionize every single rapper's approach. We are going to flaunt our lifestyles in front of the masses and make them go broke trying to keep up with us. When they have no more money to spend, we will rule the world. When we can control the masses like this, we will no longer be musicians, but we will be right-minded politicians. If this works, we will be able to work hand-in-hand with the government, controlling the world. Are you in?"

Without a moment's notice, the conference call unanimously voted. All those on the line agreed and said, "Absolutely! We are in. It's time we do our thing and quit being so generous to an ungrateful audience!"

That was when they made a whole new breed of rapper. They introduced a female rapper with a Barbie body and a Barbie voice. Many people called her talented, and she was, but her job wasn't to be talented. Her job was to toy with men's heads. Isaleer called his plastic surgeon, and all of a sudden, only perfect women were allowed to appear in his music videos. Every morning, the female rapper was to wake up, look at herself in the mirror, and repeat to herself, "I must be seductive at all times and, when the camera is on me, do everything I can to make men want me." From there, the Illuminati used video vixens as a way to control the masses and keep them focused. Really, it was just a fun power game for them until one night on a rap television station, for the first time they unknowingly let a Christian rapper hit the microphone live on television. He exposed the Illuminati and the Devil for the entire world to see the true agenda of Isaleer's evil plan, while shutting the worldly rappers down.

That night, the arch warlock called a ceremony at his aristocratic mansion deep in the Black Forest. Christians were making their attack on the kingdom of darkness, and all of a sudden, secular rap stood powerless to the lyrics these Christian rappers were putting out there. These Christian rappers were talking about hope, love, and Heaven and were stirring up faith in the masses' hearts in a revival that was about to break out across the world. The Illuminati freaked out and called for the Wizard Lord Navari to prepare for spiritual warfare.

A mandatory meeting was called in the Black Forest. Every major musician in the secular world was to meet and séance. Devising battle plans, the Occult were in the West Wing beginning the Satanic rituals. A ram was brought in and sacrificed to Satan. The blood was used to draw the pentagram on the ground. Out of the center of the pentagram came forth smoke, and a demon spoke and said, "It is time! Beat the nations down into an economic crisis. If they won't obey, then begin taking away their rights; force them into submission at whatever cost. I will not tolerate this talk of God and Jesus Christ anymore. Cut the subliminal messages out of the music videos. They have been presented with the plan. Follow through, and bring it to life."

All of a sudden, they went too deep and what was supposed to just be them sitting down and discussing how to come back at an attack from the church became a séance summoning demons to possess all the headlining musicians. There were over two hundred musicians present in the room. Mistresses of darkness came out and began to orgy with Isaleer and the musicians and began to speak hexes over their enemies. Through sexual intercourse, the possession was complete, and as they consummated, they spoke in a demonic tongue.

As they began to speak in their demonic tongue, Isaleer could understand it as clear as day. Not even the Wizard Lord could translate what the demons were saying through these mistresses. Isaleer not only understood, but he could not be possessed because he already was half-demon. Isaleer walked to the center of the pentagram and spoke in the demonic tongue to the demon standing there, saying, "From where thou comest, thou also must return. Thy presence overflows with baffling fear. I sense terror in this room of a mighty power which is much greater than that of Lucifer. Art thou afraid, oh demon?"

The demon lashed out, saying, "Comest much closer unto me, boy they call Isaleer." Isaleer stepped closer and awaited the demon's reply. The demon drew back and said, "Truly, the tales of this day were foretold many years before today. I was not told of your existence yet, son of Satan. Surely I do fear that which is to come, just as you should. The armies of Heaven are beyond our power. We are outnumbered. We are doomed, and our fate is sealed. All that we can do is make the masses to be as livestock that we can lead to the never-ending slaughterhouse. Why does thou not fear our fate?"

Isaleer looked the demon directly in the face and said, "Because I am not like you, oh demon. Thou comest unto me as a demon who is assigned to bring forth chaos with not one single inkling of knowledge, speaking to me as though you are superior unto me. However, I command you to bow down unto the prince of darkness."

All at once, a silence filled the room. All those in the room watched in disbelief as the demon fell to the ground and silenced himself before Isaleer. The demon spoke with his face pinned to the ground, saying, "What fate has thou that differs from the rest? Thou has not yet to seal your soul to your father?"

Isaleer said quickly, "Why doth a man who is also the son of Satan have need to be bought and sold like mere peasants? I am not like the greedy aristocrats in this room. These are those who have come desperately. I come neither desperately nor willingly. I have been brought into this world unwillingly. I am sitting in this room, too, as these among us know that I always carry a Bible on my person. Perhaps thou should depart from me and summon forth my father that I may speak to him. Or, is he too busy fearing his fate that is soon to come to speak to one of his sons?"

All at once the demon said, "You will regret those words, or I will one day have the honor of peeling those words off your foolish speaking tongue, son of Satan! I will request for Satan to come and speak to you. If I were you, I would back up a little bit, for he is much bigger than I."

Isaleer stepped back and said, "Good. I await his arrival." Hours passed, and nothing happened. The men and women of the Illuminati remained, awaiting the arrival of Lucifer. One of the musicians got up and left the room, saying, "He's obviously not coming."

One by one, the musicians left the room, returning back to their lives. Lord Navari spoke to Isaleer, saying, "Your authority to summon and send forth demons is stronger than anyone I have ever known, even more powerful than I. Are you truly the son of Satan?"

Isaleer replied to Lord Navari, "I am."

Lord Navari quickly bowed before Isaleer and began to worship him. Isaleer said in anger, "Get up! I am not the maker of the universe! I am not Christ that takes away the sins of the world! Nor am I a man who is even worthy to speak his name. I am a sinful man who was brought into this world by hexes and spells. My brothers and sister are shameful accounts of unspeakable abomination. I wish I was never born."

Lord Navari rose from his bowed position, wrapped his arms around Isaleer, and said, "You are more valuable than we ever had imagined you to be. You are much more than a shepherd unto the masses. You are a beacon of hope to the darkness. You have restored hope unto my heart that we may stand a chance on the day of apocalypse. If you were to die, all hope would be lost. Never again wish for your death to come before it is time. We look to you to speak to the other dimensions on our behalf."

Isaleer said to Lord Navari, "This is such a burden to bear. Every day the weight gets heavier and heavier. Every day I care less and less for humanity. I wish to know love and joy. I do not wish to destroy or bring chaos. I want to see the world come together in peace and love. I want to see strangers holding hands, saying we are one!" Just then, Evette came into the room where Isaleer and Lord Navari were standing.

As she walked over the pentagram drawn in ram's blood, she spoke to Isaleer, saying, "I love you, Isaleer. I was foolish to ever allow anything to separate us. I was stupid. I got a call from my former producer, and they wanted to try a revolutionary idea. Because of all my awards in the porn industry, they chose me to shoot 3-D porn. I never meant to hurt you. If I could take it back, I would. I was glad when you shot him. I hated him. I still hate him. Tonight, as I watched you command that demon, I realized there is something about you that is much greater than anyone upon this Earth. I stand humbled by you, baby. You're enormous among men. It's like you're not human. Everytime I see you in these séances, I can't help but question if reptilians are real. Because of you, I joined the Illuminati. I'm nowhere near the level you are, but I did it for you. I wish that you could forgive me."

Isaleer said to Evette, "As you asked for my forgiveness, I have already forgiven you. The Bible says to forgive 'even as I, Jesus, have forgiven you.'"

Evette looked at Isaleer and smiled. She said, "The son of Satan still clings to the Bible. How are you able to quote the Goetia in Latin? Isaleer, how can you bring such a heavy dark presence into a room and yet bring such a light as well? You're so hot. You're literally perfect. You're the best of both worlds."

Isaleer opened his arms to Evette and said, "Come, embrace me and know me. Feel my heart beating against your ears. See that I am a man who bares a soul. I am not my father's son. I seek for what is written in this book." As he held up the Bible, Evette continued to hug him. He prayed, saying, "Father God, teach us how to be pleasing unto your sight."

Evette followed his words, quickly saying, "Amen."

Lord Navari smiled and said, "Amen. Never have more blasphemous words been spoken in a room filled with sacrifices and pentagrams. Allow me to say a prayer as well."

Lord Navari lifted his staff above his head and said, "Lord God of Heaven, as we drink the blood of damnation, pour out upon all men the judgment we seek. Fill our hearts with hatred. Join these two in seductive matrimony. May they both come to see that they need each other. Jesus, as you hung on the cross spilling your fizzy juices all over the ground, may each of the soldiers who tore your skin be blessed one thousand-fold for having the strength to pierce those hands of abomination. As you are seated at the right hand of God, may God favor his left hand and look not upon your corpse. May God see fit to spoil the wishes of Lucifer and grant us the strength to do your will and kill anyone who does not bring forth the last days. I wish never to see Heaven, for I wish not to dance and sing with a harp. For, God, you loved the world so much that you allowed separation between you and that which you love. Your love is as soft as a razor and as holy as a whore giving her body to anyone who asks. May the evils of man be strong enough that when the blood of the innocent is shed, it will be enough to resurrect Satan and bring Heaven to its knees."

Evette laughed and said, "Amen! Amen! Amen! Death to all resisters and anyone who stands in our way. Amen!"

Lord Navari said, "One day, Isaleer, you will give up that foolish Bible and all its childish hopes. One day, the Bible's light will be stomped out, and nothing shall be left but utter darkness. You shall see…"

Evette said, "Yes, baby, when it is stomped out, you and I shall reign, and we will spit in the face of God. Once and for all, you and I shall be one again. We shall set fire to the rain and watch it burn the Earth."

Isaleer said in defiance, "No, Evette, you and I shall never be again." Then he turned to Lord Navari and said, "I see the enemies of God bowing down in front of his feet and saying, 'God, have mercy on me.' It is on that day I shall weep and mourn for your soul as it is dragged off into the pits of Hell. The demons you think you control will one day control you. They shall peel back your skin from its bones. They shall wear your corpse as they trod through the lake of fire. A day is coming, and one day will be when the plans that you have devised will only leave you running for the mountains, seeking refuge from the wrath of God. God may be quiet now, and he might not retaliate at this moment and strike you down with lightening as I would. However, it is always calmest right before the storm."

Lord Navari laughed and said, "Isaleer, you always have such a way with words. We shall see soon enough, but until then, let's celebrate the glory of our prince, Isaleer."

Evette said, "Yes! Let's party!"

Isaleer quickly came back from his memories saying, "Dude! What's going on?"

Just as things started falling apart in Isaleer's mind, Colonel Fetelli came and sat next to him by the large campfire. Isaleer could smell straight liquor on his breath.

Colonel Fetelli said, "Horus, I haven't talked to you much, so it's about time I stop to get to know you."

For a drunk, he put his words together quite well. Considering Isaleer had just been thinking about life before the disappearance, he replied, "Well, Colonel, there's not much to get to know about me."

The colonel smiled and replied, "Well dang, kid, I'm not asking for a sob story."

Isaleer laughed along with the colonel and said, "Girls, bro!"

Fetelli nodded and said, "Was her rack nice?"

Isaleer smiled and said, "They were perfect, sir."

The colonel began talking about how, when they made him do the surgery to be able to operate with the B.I.I.N.D.S., he woke up realizing all they did was take his body organs and place them in a plastic and steel shell. He was having a hard time accepting that he was partially a robot.

That night, Isaleer tossed and turned. He had a tattoo of the all-seeing eye on his right hand, and until today he had never thought anything of it, really. It was like something he had gotten when he was drunk. It was time to get answers, and Dr. Killjoy was the only one on the island of Eden who could give them.

Chapter 9

WHAT IS THE NEW WORLD ORDER, AND WHAT IS MY PLACE?

It was three in the morning, and as Isaleer lay tossing and turning in his cold sweats, all he could hear were the tribulation Christians crying out from their prisons cells, begging for execution. How could someone be that bad off?

The part that was making Isaleer sick to his stomach was that he had had a hand in making all of this possible. The question came back to his mind: Where was his family? When he found whoever took them, he was going to kill them. In his mind, he feared that because his family were Christians, they might have been taken as prisoners to one of the prison camps. The next question rolling around in Isaleer's head was what this pyramid on his right hand was all about. It was the same as the one on the American one dollar bill.

Queasy from his nightmares, Isaleer awoke from his nightmare gasping for air. As he was punching the ground, he rolled off of his cot. On the ground, he at once turned to vomit. With each upheaval, he could feel the weight of his playboy lifestyle being brought to its knees. After the BBQ and alcohol from the night before projected out of his mouth, soon all that was left was bile. He choked and dry-heaved on the blood from the acid tearing away the lining of his throat. Then Isaleer hocked up his final loogie and wiped his face with water from one of the canteens. The splash of water helped him come to. He needed to accept that his nightmares were true; he had to accept the reality of the damage he had caused. Standing up inside his tent next to the campfire, he quietly made his way outside.

More questions began flooding his mind. What was he really involved in? What was martial law? Why was it that only the Christians went missing off the Earth? Wait, and yet Christians were also locked up in prisons or in hiding? What role did Isaleer really have in all of this by being over the media and entertainment? Who was the maker of guillotines? What was the Antichrist? What was the mark of the beast? What was the New World Order?

"Who has to take The Mark?" Isaleer wondered to himself.

He searched the Illuminati soldiers' backpacks one by one looking for a flash light. He then set off with a pistol and a flashlight, heading out of the barracks to the facility's underground science lab, which was located inside the Illuminati fortress. When he reached the fortress, he stormed into the underground science lab's testing facility in search of Dr. Killjoy. Isaleer was hostile and had the mind to kill anyone who got in his way. As he reached Dr. Killjoy's office, Isaleer could see him hard at work putting together some sort of equation, no doubt for an experiment.

Isaleer grabbed Dr. Killjoy and threw him off his chair and onto his desk, landing him on his back. He yelled with extreme anger, "Where is my family?"

Dr. Killjoy could not reply. Utterly terrified, all he could do was gasp and wheeze. "Uh… We… I…"

Isaleer lashed back unmercifully. "Answer me! Where are my mother and father?"

Dr. Killjoy strangely collected himself enough to smile and say to Isaleer, "I have been waiting for this moment for almost twenty years. I knew this day would come one day. Your questions most definitely have answers. Just please don't kill me when the story I tell you doesn't end happily ever after."

Isaleer was tired of the games. Again, he asked, "WHERE IS MY FAMILY?"

Dr. Killjoy calmly pushed the gun barrel out of his face. "Very well. You're digging rather aggressively in a hole that has never had a floor. By the time you reach the bottom, darkness will have long since cloaked you as a garment. Before you even come close to the bottom-dwelling creatures which live in the depths of utter darkness, they will have acquainted themselves with the touch of your skin. They hop to and fro as they can see in the dark, and you cannot. They are the kindest of these, those who only torment the mind in utter darkness but await the prison guards as they tie you in your chains. But yea! For your story's origin is the darkest story of Earth's history. Your origins were foretold from the beginning of time through the fate of your father and the conspiring of Hell, from whence a desire for separation was first conceived, where beautiful creations are re-birthed as foul predecessors of an abominable beast which has, since his falling, never seen the light of day. The darkest and most blasphemous of man's comprehension: This is only the beginning of your story. I cautiously advise that you remember what curiosity did to the cat..."

With the snap of Dr. Killjoy's fingers, the lights in the room went off, and Dr. Killjoy began his presentation. "Twenty years ago, the Order of the Thirteen came to my aristocratic mansion. Together, we successfully carried out one of the most powerful rituals I had ever experienced. A principality came forth and made an offer on behalf of Lucifer himself. Wielding black mag..."

Interrupting Dr. Killjoy, Isaleer redirected the argument back to the initial question. "I DON'T CARE ABOUT MY PAST. WHERE ARE MY PARENTS?"

Dr. Killjoy, having little time to think, had run out of diversions and needed to think quickly. "Isaleer, they're safe."

Furious, Isaleer replied, "No! Shut up. I didn't ask if they were safe. I asked where they were. Tell me where they are before I lose my patience with you, you foul, gloating minion, unprepared for the death-stroke which chases your shadow each passing day."

Dr. Killjoy said, "I don't know where they are. I don't know. Ok? I don't know."

"What do you mean you don't know?"

Dr. Killjoy replied, "When the Occult found you, they viewed you as an invaluable asset. They viewed your family as a distraction, and therefore you needed to be peeled away from each other immediately. We had never officially used the prison camps. Your family was sent to a prison camp to be evaluated and monitored. What happened once they got behind the razor wire fences, I have no clue. It's best that you just forget your adopted family."

"What!?" Isaleer, blown away by this response, looked up to the ceiling and then to the floor and then from the floor back to the ceiling, each time finding a new way to hold his head with both hands in complete and utter shock. "Have you all lost your f***ing minds? Do you know how many times I passed those prison camps wondering if maybe my family could be in there? Do you know how many times I had to remind myself that these people would never do this to my personal family?"

> "In this moment, Isaleer now realizes this has affected even his immediate family. He never considered that this would even slightly affect his family. It was in this moment he knew that no one was exempt from the prison camps."
>
> –Dexter Rockwell

By this time, Dr. Killjoy was cowering behind his desk, terrified of the horror he could unleash if he pushed Isaleer's anger too far. "I… Isa….Isaleer. C-calm down. They have food; they're taken care of. If you're worried about them, they're not in there by themselves. In fact, soon they will have lots of people in there with them. When we bring on the New World Order, anyone who resists will be put there. Your family will be surrounded by guards and all the Bible-thumpers who, like them, will be persuaded to adjust to the changes. Isaleer, you have to remember that you're the head advisor of the media for the world. Stay focused! You have a lot on your plate. I know. Just let us take care of your family. You have a world awaiting its superstar. Put the gun down. You're stressed; it's ok. Let's see if we can get you back to your happy place."

"Why are there prison camps in the first place?"

"The prison camps are here for the radicals, terrorists, extremists, disobedient, heretics, and non-conformists. I'm sure your family aren't considered a part of any of those groups, but are merely mixed up in a… The Illuminati soldiers are just being thorough. Anyone who isn't taking the mark will be rounded up and brought to a prison camp to be questioned and rehabilitated—that is, except for the heretics and extremists. They get executed immediately, but I'm sure your family aren't extremists."

Dr. Killjoy knew full-well that Isaleer's family had been taken to a prison camp. Because they were Christian missionaries who refused the mark of the beast, they had been executed under the New World Order law. Dr. Killjoy had deceived Isaleer into a lie. Dr. Killjoy cut his eyes, hoping that Isaleer wouldn't pursue the discussion any further.

Chapter 10

THE COMPUTER LACKS DISCREPANCY

Isaleer was speechless. He replied, "I joined because I wanted to be famous. I knew the Occult was serious, and I was aware of the sacrifices. I just never took it that serious. Dr. Killjoy!" Isaleer raised his voice. "Did you know this was all a Satanic bloodline?"

Dr. Killjoy replied, "Duh… I descended from the thirteenth bloodline of David. Do you have any more questions, Isaleer? I am really busy right now."

Isaleer, mind-blown that the doctor was shrugging him off as some inconvenience, quickly corrected Killjoy by saying, "SIT DOWN! YOU AREN'T GOING ANYWHERE! You haven't answered all my questions! Turn on your computer, Killjoy. I don't trust you anymore, so we're gonna play a game. I need facts, and you're not giving them to me. Each time you piss me off, you're getting a strike. You get three before I kill you. And guess what? You just earned strike one. LET'S GO, KILLJOY! TURN ON THE COMPUTER, BRUH!"

Dr. Killjoy said, "Hold on." He cleared his throat and continued, "Computer, begin start-up sequence."

The computer replied, "At once, Dr. Killjoy."

Dr. Killjoy looked at Isaleer and said, "I will give you voice-command over my computer. You can ask it anything. Will that help?" Dr. Killjoy thought this would excuse him from the room. He weaseled his way to the door of his office, preparing to exit.

Isaleer rushed quickly over to the door Dr. Killjoy was opening and slammed it shut. Grabbing Dr. Killjoy by the throat and dangling him by his neck, Isaleer slowly walked the doctor back to his computer desk. He said, "Tell me something. When your parents gave birth to you, who was the coward, and who was the weasel? Seeing you wiggle your way to the door was most entertaining. You can learn so much about a coward by the way he stays on-tempo with a conversation while struggling to find his exit. Don't want to answer my questions? Inch by inch, your death is closing in on you… Strike two, weasel. I've got an idea. Let's ask the computer.

"Computer! What does the owl shrine in the Black Forest represent?"

The computer replied, "The owl shrine in the Black Forest is also referred to as Moloch."

Isaleer said, "Computer! Define Moloch." The computer began retrieving the files and then said…

Moloch: It is pronounced (Mo-lay).

-, a Semitic root meaning "king") – also rendered as Molech, Molekh, Molok, Molek, Molock, Moloc, Melech, Milcom or Molcom – is the name of an ancient Ammonite god. Moloch worship was practiced by the Canaanites, Phoenicians, and related cultures in North Africa and the Levant.

As a god worshipped by the Phoenicians and Canaanites, Moloch had associations with a particular kind of guiltless child sacrifice by parents. Moloch figures in the Book of Deuteronomy and in the Book of Leviticus as a form of idolatry.

Leviticus 18:21

"And thou shalt not let any of thy seed pass through the fire to Moloch."

In the Old Testament Hebrew Bible, it says that Gehenna was a valley by Jerusalem, where apostate Israelites and followers of various Baal and Canaanite gods, including Moloch, sacrificed their children by fire.

(2 Chronicles 28:3, 33:6; Jeremiah 7:31, 19:2–6).

Isaleer replied, "Yeah! Ok, so if the Bible was a lie, then how come is it able to foretell and even give a history of this Moloch the Owl shrine? And how about the men in the Black Forest sacrificing in the same manner as those in Deuteronomy? Killjoy, you know something I don't. I'm going to find out the secret. Computer! What does Horus mean?"

A silence took over the room…

"Computer, what does Horus mean?"

Isaleer waited nearly ten seconds for a reply, but none came. He looked at Dr. Killjoy, who was laughing under his breath. Isaleer asked, "Why won't it answer my question about Horus?"

Dr. Killjoy said, "Because it's none of your damn business what it means. Yes! Your name has a reason, and it was given to you specifically, but if you knew, you would know too much. By tampering in the Egyptian history, you are learning way too much about stuff you aren't prepared to understand. Again, Isaleer, you are diverting the minds of the masses and distracting them so we higher-level members of the brotherhood can establish and set in place the necessary puzzle pieces. It's none of your business what goes on above you."

Just then, the computer screen started to glitch, forcefully loading and replying…

Horus: also known as "The eye of Horus."
In one myth, when Set and Horus were fighting for the throne after Osiris's death, Set gouged out Horus's left eye. The majority of the eye was restored by either Hathor or Thoth (with the last portion possibly being supplied magically). When Horus's eye was recovered, he offered it to his father, Osiris, in hopes of restoring his life. Hence, the eye of Horus was often used to symbolize sacrifice, healing, restoration, and protection.

Isaleer said, "Wait, dude, so my name Isaleer Horus means "the eye of Horus?" So this all was a plan? You gave me a last name?"

Dr. Killjoy replied, "Kid, obviously! What do you think the pyramid which has been on your right hand your entire life has meant? It's your sacrifice to the Dark Lord Lucifer! You will belong to him. He will come calling for you to fulfill your oath. The beast will expect you to take his mark."

Isaleer quickly said, "Take his mark? Whoa, whoa, whoa… Take his mark? Who said anything about taking a mark, as in the mark of the beast? I didn't ask for any of this. I was going on a vacation with Mr. Morgan. I never once said I wanted VIP seating for the drinking of the chalice which will bring forth the full wrath of God."

Dr. Killjoy said, "No. It's not the wrath of God. Finally, we have our master here on earth with us. To take the mark means to join in the marriage supper of master and man. When Lucifer comes, we shall be free! You don't seem happy even in the slightest bit, Isaleer…"

Chapter 11

666THE666MARK666OF666 THE666BEAST666

Isaleer turned to look at the computer. He then turned back to look at Dr. Killjoy. With his right hand, he gripped his temples on either side of his brain and said, "Computer! Give me a Biblical run-down of the mark of the beast."

Isaleer, mumbling in confidence, said, "I want solid truths. I will no longer entertain this foolish philosophy of riddles. You are leading me to and fro. I have not yet once seen anything that stands alone as truth coming forth from your mouth. All your words are held together by support beams, which hold together other support beams, which hold together other support beams. Your words are rigged together as a web being weaved together only to trap your victims and exhaust your prey. Holy Spirit of the one true God, harken unto me. Give unto me keen discernment, for I see no rock on which this corrupted man's foundation is laid."

Isaleer fearlessly looked the doctor in the eyes and said, "Perhaps your foundation is laid, but your hiding it's unveiling. If you are unwilling to share these plans with your known allies, then perhaps your plans are in fact maniacal."

Just then, the computer retrieved the information. As the files loaded, the computer replied, "The mark of the beast: This is known in two forms, one of which is the most popular. In its first and most well-known form, it is identified as "666." However, in other cultures, it can be identified as "616."

Just as the computer began to explain the relative facts about the the mark of the beast, without request a video began uploading. Dr. Killjoy's computer had retrieved a signal being forcefully transmitted to the computer's media window.

Dr. Killjoy simply said, "Computer, what are you about to play?!"

The computer replied, "ATTENTION! System compromise. Recommend immediate shutdown. ALERT! System compromise. Outside source breaching through video feed. DANGER! System is breached. BEGIN RUNNING ARCHANGEL"

What is Archangel?

The acronym A.R.C.H.A.N.G.E.L. means:

{Anti
{Religious
{Communication
{Hindering
{And
{New
{Global
{Electronic
{Law

It's an anti-virus system with a spiffy acronym.

Isaleer made this up off the top of his head. Its primary focus is to control the exchange of information and limit the audience from talking amongst themselves, though this is not its only function. Archangel has the authority not only to monitor but also to remove, enforce, administer and dispatch. This means this system can remove and enforce information, laws, and guidelines. This software has the ability not only to administer punishment via restriction but also to dispatch authorities to one's location using the technological device as a satellite tracking system. This anti-virus software dispatches authorities and army personnel when suspicious behavior is discovered. Dispatch is notified by software and given the location to go in search of the dangerous, rebellious terrorist.

Dr. Killjoy told the computer to track the source.

Isaleer demanded the computer to stream the feed, so he could see what it was. All of a sudden, a live webcam transmission began streaming, and a man who called himself Awa replied, "Isaleer Horus! This is an urgent message from the Arisen. We tapped into the fortress and overheard your conversation with one Dr. Killjoy. You asked what the mark of the beast is. This is what it is…"

An unexpected video began playing and said, "Isaleer, I am so sorry we couldn't come sooner. After the rescue team returned from its mission over the island of Eden, one of our helicopter pilots reported meeting a man and then witnessing him transform into what one Mr. George called 'a gargoyle,' who was an alleged 'child of Satan.' We have returned to the island of Eden and have breached the main gate. We are searching for you. Make your presence known! We are here to rescue you. You must trust us. We will meet you in the center courtyard of the fortress. Be prepared to fight; we may need your help getting out of here!"

Just then, the whole fortress went into complete lockdown. Ten heavily armed guards made their way into Dr. Killjoy's laboratory to find the doctor sitting hostage behind his desk as Isaleer was frantically trying to discover what the mark of the beast was. The guards barged through the doorway and yelled, "GET ON THE GROUND! ISALEER HORUS, GET ON THE GROUND, OR WE WILL FIRE!"

Isaleer rolled his eyes in frustration and lifted his hands above his head. Was Isaleer about to give up? No way! Isaleer just needed time to come up with a plan. In the meantime, the guards checked Dr. Killjoy and then helped him to his feet. He ordered for the guards to arrest Isaleer.

Isaleer was put in handcuffs, unable to escape.

Dr. Killjoy began walking in circles around Isaleer, saying, "You think the Arisen can save you from the inside of this fortress? They will be dead in minutes. Once they reach the hallways of the inner-court, they will be greeted by five hundred heavily armed Illuminati soldiers who hate the Arisen! Oh, but let's assume they make it past the inner-court, and they pass through the cell block. They will be greeted yet again but this time by twenty-five of the finest Illumicorp humanoid drones. These humanoid drones are fitted with concept weapons which were designed for immobilizing tanks. What are men on foot against tank destroyers? Still… they press on. Getting through the security center will be their hardest task yet, not because of the armed forces but because the whole island is on lockdown, and those blast doors won't open for anyone. Let's say they find a way to forcefully push past the blast doors; they will have no other choice but to pass through our ceremony building. There they will meet the impossible task of bringing down Lord Navari, who we both know is not just a mighty sorcerer but also an animal shape-shifter. Five men against Lord Navari? They're dead, Isaleer. Dead! Just like you, if you won't take the mark of the beast…

"Guards! Escort this prisoner, Isaleer Horus, to the center courtyard. The Arisen are expecting to meet him there; let's make sure he's on time. They won't be able to get to him. We all know this, but I can't help but want front-row tickets to see this all play out. Let's go!"

They escorted Isaleer through the laboratory. He was brought through a side door right out into the center courtyard.

It was fitting for Dr. Killjoy's lab to be right next to the center courtyard, as this courtyard also had another name: the execution court. When they would dispose of bodies, Dr. Killjoy would have his minions come and pick up the remains and bring them into his office for experiments.

The alarms from the interior of the building could barely be heard once the large steel hatch to Dr. Killjoy's lab was closed.

There before Isaleer was a guillotine. Until this moment, he had not realized this machine was actually present here at this fortress on the island of Eden. A gut-wrenching feeling grabbed his stomach.

This was actually about to happen.

Isaleer was about to be a martyr for the Christian faith. As the Illuminati soldiers dragged him to the guillotine, Isaleer was trying not to reveal the horror in his eyes. He began focusing his attention on all the details of this carefully handcrafted work of art.

The guillotine was complete with a forward head basket, a throne for the Dark Lord to sit upon if he so pleased. It was almost as though the creator of this execution device envisioned Satan asking the condemned personally if they really planned to die over a microchip.

Dr. Kiljoy said, "Now, you have refused to complete your last task in sealing your oath to the secret Order. Don't make me do this, Isaleer. You are a valuable asset to the Illuminati. This is such a waste. I'm not asking you to bow down and worship. You're the son of Satan; you'll be the one being worshipped. I'm just asking you to take this chip so that you will be registered in our network. Don't you want to make money? Look down at your right hand right now. Guards! Uncuff him."

In seconds, Isaleer was released from his handcuffs. Isaleer refused to look at his right hand. In fact, Isaleer glared into Dr. Kiljoy's eyes instead. Dr. Kiljoy said, "Isaleer, look at your hand, not me. Why are you still looking at me? Ok. You won't look at your hand? I'll tell you what's on your hand. That is a full gold pyramid with an all-seeing eye at the top. Correct me if I'm wrong, but doesn't that symbol represent the immense wealth of the pharaohs? In essence, Isaleer, you are already marked. That's just not binding enough."

An awkward silence took over the center courtyard….

Dr. Kiljoy looked at Isaleer and said, "Ok, enough of the foolishness. You're Isaleer Horus, son of Satan, gargoyle prince, head over mainstream media, pop culture, and fashion. You are an A-list celebrity. The world needs you. So are you ready to secure your future?"

Isaleer said to himself, "You mean seal my fate."

Dr. Kiljoy said, "So what is it going to be, my dear prince?"

Isaleer replied, "What are you talking about? I will never take that mark. I'm a Christian who believes in his holy blood. I was at the ceremonies, rituals, and any important séance. We all openly discussed what this chip was about. It's about slaves and pharaohs. If you are really gonna kill me because I won't play this game, because I won't take this micro-chip, then I accept that my game is over."

Dr. Kiljoy was on the execution throne. Sitting on this throne without authorization and approval would warrant instant death, no matter who did it. Killjoy had no business sitting on the throne. If Lord Navari could have seen Dr. Kiljoy at that moment, they'd have probably killed him for treason or heresy. It was neither his throne to sit on nor his choice to make. That chair was reserved only for the Dark Lord. Not only was he about to execute someone without permission, but he was about to execute the Satanic prince, Isaleer!

However, Dr. Killjoy cared nonetheless for his fate. He jumped up and down on the throne as though he owned it and said, "You made a deal, Isaleer!"

Isaleer laughed and said, "And you're really short. Not only are you short, but let me remind you that you are not a Dark Lord. I bet that throne felt really good to sit on. Oh, science boy, always seeking to be a sorcerer, but your facts and knowledge have locked you out of the spirit realm because you allow no room for unimaginable possibilities. I'm sure you would love to cast a spell to levitate me off the ground, but the facts just simply say that you can't. You don't know how to wrap your mind around a concept that cannot be explained with tangible facts and solutions. I see you in your laboratory at night when no one is watching, secretly pulling sorcery books and black magic Occult chapters out of your desk, glancing around your office and making sure no one is watching. I see you as you pull out your laser pointer and call it your wand. You know all the technological languages known to man, and yet you can't even pronounce your ancient Latin properly for the Goetia. I think you try to overcompensate for your inability. Now it all makes sense. These concept weapons, your humanoid drones, your need to fashion a man's body to be plastic—these are all your attempts to call yourself equal to mighty sorcerers who need nothing more than a wooden spoon to play God."

Isaleer barely completed his insult before the guards threw him on the ground and removed his valuables from his pockets.

Dr. Killjoy said, "As I recall, I was the leading scientist in the development of the DNA strands for the son of Satan. Creating the Devil's son and being able to wave a wand and make a wish—are they really too different when it comes to playing God? Of course not. Playing God is playing God, whether you're the scientist who creates Isaleer Horus, or you're the powerful wizard who twists his arm. Now, if you will not accept the mark, then you will die."

The guards picked Isaleer up and dragged him through the execution courtyard. This yard had once been used for terrorist and treasonous traitors. So many Al-Qaida members had died in this courtyard. Isaleer, being over mainstream media, was unaware of it all. They used to announce executions, broadcasting them all throughout the facility for everyone to witness, but when the apocalypse hit, this courtyard got used much more frivolously. Here, they captured, experimented, and executed men, women, and children who were not involved in any acts of terrorism or treason. These were simply martyrs who were being killed for refusing the micro-chip.

As Isaleer lay under the guillotine, they raised the headstock, allowing his head to get through, and then proceeded to lower the headstock down on his neck. After locking the headstock, the other guards proceeded to shackle Isaleer's hands and feet to the body table.

Dr. Killjoy proceeded to sit on the throne created for the Dark Lord. He sat with his left hand hovering over the kill-switch, which was formed into an image of a snake's head offering Eve an apple. In this regard, the whole throne was a handcrafted reminder of the Tree of Knowledge of Good and Evil. This, of course, was the reason for the separation between God and man because Adam and Eve followed Satan, instead of obeying God.

A portrait of a man representing Adam was crafted on the throne's right leg. Adam's two feet supported the weight of the right side of the throne. On the throne's left leg was Eve, extending her hand up to the left armrest and embracing the apple.

Meanwhile, the serpent's body was etched around the backrest, trailing to the left armrest. His mouth was holding the apple, which was designed to be cupped and pushed to drop the guillotine blade. The spectacle of this twenty-four-karat gold throne was located at the top, far above the human head, where the Eye of Horus peered down in the form of the world's largest diamond. The right armrest was a cup holder for the Dark Lord's chalice and bread saucer. The idea was when that the Dark Lord executed a Christian, he would drink a chalice of their blood and eat a portion of their flesh as mockery of communion. The blood was a poison to the beast which burned his insides, reminding him of the lake of fire which was to be his eternal damnation.

He drank the blood and ate the flesh of man with a never-ending hunger. The blood made him strong for a time, until he needed to drink and eat again. He knew his time was near, but he longed for innocent blood, for death and for control. It's all he wanted. He was consumed.

Isaleer knew the beast all too well. That same blood flowed through his own veins.

The Tree of Knowledge of Good and Evil was Lucifer's trophy and seal of doom, but right now, Isaleer's doom was this guillotine.

Taking a deep breath and exhaling, closing his eyes and resting his head on his fingertips, Dr. Killjoy asked him one more time, "One… more…time… Will you take the mark and complete your destiny?"

Isaleer shouted, "NEVER!"

"Then you shall die like the pigs in a slaughterhouse, and I shall laugh as your body convulses in its last moments." Killjoy then ordered the Illuminati soldiers to place goggles over Isaleer's eyes and fill the head basket with water. The goggles were there so that when Isaleer's head fell into the water basket, his vision would not be distorted; there would be no running from reality.

They placed a strap around his skull and knotted a rock to the back of his head.

Dr. Kiljoy said, "As you're sinking in the head basket, think of the moment when I could have saved you from the wave but instead left you to die. Let the last thing you hear be the screech of the blade bringing the might of 666 down upon you. I hope you stand before God, and he spews you out, you man who lived for Satan and died for God. I hereby sentence you, Isaleer Horus, to death by execution under the guillotine. for the refusal to comply with what is to come. At 3:33 A.M., you refused the mark of the beast. So now you are a threat to the plans of the Illumanti. Isaleer Horus, do you have any last words?"

Isaleer replied, "Hello, Jesus, my father sucks. Can you share yours?"

The blade fell, and in a matter of three seconds of fall time, Isaleer thought to himself, "I hope that's all it takes to be a Christian."

Isaleer thought about the innocent he had led astray, but those thoughts were quickly made irrelevant when he needed to prepare himself for a blade going through his throat and spine. No doubt, this was about to hurt. Isaleer could feel the wind from the blade. Isaleer flinched. There was no way to prepare for the excruciating pain that was about to hit him…

All of a sudden, the blade stopped. Out of nowhere, there was a breach. A sword had stopped the blade from hitting Isaleer's throat. It was five of the Arisen soldiers. They had come to save him, and they had made it!

The Arisen soldiers opened fire on the Illuminati soldiers standing guard of Isaleer's execution. Unprepared, the Illuminati soldiers were instantly killed.

Dr. Killjoy fled for his life. One of the Arisen soldiers pointed his submachine gun at the back of Dr. Killjoy's head, but the Arisen commander yelled, "Leave him be. We have to get Isaleer out of here before we are outnumbered."

They unlatched Isaleer and broke him free of the shackles that held him to the guillotine.

Quickly, they ran to the wall of the fortress. The Arisen soldiers threw ropes and anchors over the side of the fortress wall.

Climbing up and over the wall, they, along with Isaleer, began their escape through the jungle. As they were striding through the forest, Isaleer could hear a helicopter in the distance. In no time, Isaleer could see the helicopter. Soon, they were on the helicopter, fleeing the island of Eden.

Isaleer was so overwhelmed, and the flight was long, so Isaleer lay back. He awaited the landing and longed to learn more of the evil plan that was to unfold.

At this point, Isaleer just wondered to himself how he had gotten that close to evil and allowed all of that mess to be a part of his life without ever questioning why.

More importantly, how far along was the Illuminati's plan, and how could Isaleer stop it?

Grateful to be with the Arisen soldiers in their military transport helicopter, Isaleer collapsed from exhaustion, fearing the thought of these visions beginning again…

Chapter 12

DRESSED FOR THE THRONE ROOM

wa began poking Isaleer, trying to awake him from his slumber. "Is… Is… Hey Isaleer, wake up. We are here."

As Isaleer began to wake up, he noticed that the propeller blades on the helicopter were no longer moving.

As Isaleer came to from one of the greatest naps he had had in ages, he just barely heard something he hadn't heard in a long, long time: praise and worship Music. Far off in the distance, he could hear worship music being played on a soundtrack. Being that he was still half asleep, he wondered if he had died and gone to Heaven. Of course, he was very much alive, and what he was hearing was music coming from a home just down the street from where they landed. By this time, the soldiers had long dispersed from the chopper.

Isaleer asked the man dressed in all white, "Why did no one wake me?"

The kind gentleman told Isaleer, "I was told to let you sleep, but it's been two hours. By now, we really need to get this chopper as well as ourselves quickly underground and out of the sight of the Illuminati satellites."

Isaleer laughed and said, "What?"

He couldn't believe he had been knocked out like that. He quickly jumped up, folded his blanket, and jumped out of the chopper. One glance was almost too much at one time. For the first time that Isaleer could remember, he was safe. Isaleer was taken out of his daydreaming when the man in all white coughed, cleared his throat, and said, "Hello, Isaleer. My name is Awa-baka Norniquo, but it's easier to just call me Awa. Welcome to Fort RS-7. This is our recovery station and one of the main entrances to the underground. The priest is expecting you. Come; it's time to get changed into your new outfit. Come. Follow me."

Isaleer was quick to follow. As they walked through the empty suburban neighborhood, Isaleer was lost as to how this was the Arisen's station when there was no one here. Stopping to take a deep breath of the autumn air, Isaleer got caught up in a feeling he thought he had lost. As he held his breath, he felt the cool air rejuvenate his lungs. It felt like an autumn evening, one of those evenings cool enough for a hoodie. It was a feeling that reminded him of having the most amazing time rolling around in the leaves without fear of a random bug crawling into his clothes because the cold had killed all the bugs off. It was the cool sensation of the holidays and family coming together.

Just as Isaleer exhaled, the moment passed, and he snapped back to reality. Awa walked up the driveway and to the front of one of the homes, looked around, and said, "Come on!"

They walked in the home. Before Isaleer shut the door, he saw the helicopter descend into the ground on a platform, leaving the road completely barren. A whole helicopter had just been swallowed by a secret helipad-lowering dock. Isaleer quickly peered out the house door and looked for the helicopter he had just exited. It, too, was gone. Clearly, the helicopters where on elevator docking pads which just went into the ground surrounding this ghost town which Awa kept calling Fort RS-7.

Isaleer shook his head and said, "Huh. You don't see that every day." He shut the door and followed Awa.

Awa asked Isaleer if he was thirsty; Isaleer asked for a selection.

Awa said, "We have all sorts of pure fruit juices, all kinds of teas, and the purest water on the planet."

Isaleer said, "Let me knock back a few of those fruit juices, and then I need to pile on the water!"

Awa tossed him some fruit juices and then threw him four water bottles out of the refrigerator. After Isaleer drank the juices, Awa said, "Let's go upstairs and get your outfit."

He led Isaleer to the second floor, where they proceeded down the hall to the master bedroom. As Isaleer began looking around at the bedroom, he noticed that there was no dust; this room seemed to have been walked through a lot. Just as Isaleer's brain juices were flowing, Awa yelled, "Here, catch!"

Isaleer caught the clothes and whispered to himself, "Huh…how did he know my sizes?"

Either way, Isaleer changed from his black suit to this white get-up: white skinny jeans, white V-neck T-shirt, white glowing bottom slip-ons, and a white faux leather jacket. Isaleer sarcastically yelled from the bathroom, "What? No hat? And what's up with these shoes?"

Awa yelled back, "White glowing shoes because everything is artificial lighting where we're going, so we get really creative with its placement. Call it a cliché—'Light unto my path.' I mean, we can get you a hat, but no one really wears hats."

Isaleer came out of the bathroom and looked in the mirror. Awa asked, "What do you think?"

Isaleer replied, "Is everyone wearing this?"

Awa chuckled and said, "No, everyone gets a completely custom outfit made to fit their use and personality."

Isaleer laughed and said "Ok…so then you got this wrong. My primary color should be black."

Awa looked at Isaleer's shoes and said, "The mischief of the color black is what got you in this mess in the first place. Perhaps you should retire that color for a while until you've learned its proper use."

Isaleer would later learn that black was reserved for the special forces team; it was a very powerful color, which required a very powerful person to control its need to want to rebel and do evil.

Awa said, "Many become consumed by its false sense of security because many use black as a color to hide in, very much like the shadows. For us in the Arisen, it's only used in times of war so that we can get close enough to strike." Then he said something that stuck with Isaleer. "Black is not a color worn by conquerors; it's a color to be hidden behind."

With that statement, Awa had just pressed the kill switch and set off a bomb in Isaleer's head; that literally blew his mind.

A silence took over for a second. When Isaleer came to, he said, "Wow, dude! I have never heard it put like that, but you're definitely right on, bro. Well, I mean, you're definitely passionate about your perception that black is bad or whatever. Yeah, bro. Anyway, so like, I look like an LED snowball, bro. Everyone better look just as gnarly as me, man. I feel like I'm about to perform a concert at an arena or something."

"But wait, there's more!" Awa said, smiling as he walked over to the door to one of the closets. Awa opened the door for Isaleer and said, "Come here, Snowball. Pick out a few weapons for your person. Oh! You're getting a modified motorcycle for scout missions, just so you know."

Like a baby with an unlimited supply of grade-A breast milk, straight from the factory, Isaleer began cooing like he was in breast milk Heaven. His eyes were so full, they almost needed to be rolled around in shopping carts. Everything from wallet guns with two shots, to 9mm handguns, to hunting rifles like the 7mm, to the AK-47, the M4 carbine with laser point and grenade launcher attachment, to RPGs and anti-aircraft missiles, to sniper rifles like the Barrett 50-cal., to concept weapons. Inside this huge walk-in closet were knives, lethal blow-dart guns, crossbows, bow and arrows, axes, machetes, and katanas. The room even had chemical weapons, gas masks, Hazmat suits, and weapons Isaleer had never even seen before.

Isaleer asked Awa, "How many do I get?"

Awa replied, "As many as you can carry, I suppose. The war against the Illuminati is not over now that you're with us. In fact, now that you're no longer with the Illuminati, they are going to seek for you. They will scour the globe day and night looking for you. They will not sleep. You're their secret weapon, and you just got away. They're gonna want you back. In the meantime, I assure you that many innocent people will die—just because of their frustration with you now in the possession of the Arisen. You're gonna need to be ready to fight and fight hard. So honestly, I would say to take as many as you can comfortably carry. Straight up."

That was all Isaleer needed to hear. After that, it was simple. "The crossbow goes over the shoulder, M4 carbine is in hand, Desert Eagle is my left side arm, Glock .38mag is my right side arm, two K-bars for each thigh, two string-loaded blade launchers for my inner thighs, a folded-up night stick for my outside right calf, a flashlight for my left calf, and a ball and chain pulled through my belt. Now, as for the motorcycle, do we have a shop I can take it to and get weapons installed?" Isaleer said in complete joy.

Awa replied, "Yes, we do. The mechanic's name is Levi. If you can think it, he can build it."

Isaleer said, "Boom! Round two. Ding! Let's talk heavy weapons."

Isaleer grabbed two Uzies, a box of twelve grenades ready to be welded to the motorcycle's swing arm, a small turret to be welded up front, and a couple boxes of fogger bombs for a solid escape.

Awa said, "Wow, bro, you aren't playing at all!"

Isaleer began laughing so hard and said, "Yeah, I know! I packed super heavy, but all of this can be left behind or used for different missions. But just in case..." He grabbed two large leather belts and grabbed two 50-cal. turrets, threw them on his back, and said "For those days when I need to just sweep a street."

Isaleer finally looked at Awa and said, "Ok, I think I'm set."

Barely able to carry his weapons, Isaleer couldn't help but laugh when Awa looked at him like he was crazy. Nevertheless, Awa led Isaleer to a walk-in closet and said, "After you."

They walked in. Awa closed the closet door and pressed a button on his vest, and then down they went.

All of a sudden, something dawned on Isaleer. He said aloud, "Whoa, so when you said underground, you really meant underground."

Down, down, down they went, fifty-five floors underground until they reached the bottom. The elevator opened up, and both Isaleer and Awa walked out and onto the underground's main balcony, which acted both as the main entrance and as the overlook of the entire fortress. The only better view was from the general's quarters. Just then, Awa went ahead of Isaleer and said to a couple soldiers, "Help Isaleer carry his weapons! Guy ended up having tastes larger than his capacity, and watching him carry all of these is really getting tiring for me to watch." They ran over, took Isaleer's weapons, and carried them to his quarters. Awa said to Isaleer, "Come see our city!"

Isaleer walked out of the cave tunnel, and it opened up to a humongous city below him. Looking down from a rock balcony, Isaleer realized that it was a whole new world down there. He saw people, horses, villages, all sorts of life, and festivities going on all around him.

Awa said with so much pride, "And this is just the recovery station. All of this leads all over the USA. We have found a place to hide from the Illuminati, inside the underground."

No matter how close Isaleer thought he was to understanding everything, he was miles from understanding anything. All of this just wasn't logical. Where did the Arisen get the funding to be able to build such a mighty structure?

This was much greater than anything Isaleer had ever seen the Illuminati build. This was a city of lights and life, all located underground.

Isaleer looked at Awa and said, "I thought America was wiped out?"

Awa looked at Isaleer and said, "That's what we wanted everyone on the ground level to think, but we started finding survivors and bringing them here. Until Jesus Christ comes back riding on the White Horse, we have to stay strong and fight back against the beast!"

Wandering through the vast city that night, Isaleer was grateful to have found such a wonderful group of people. Though they didn't dress the best or drive the best cars, these people were extremely loving and accepting of newcomers…as long as they didn't have the chip or the mark.

No one with either of those ever got close to finding or entering the underground fort RS-7 because this city was far out in the country, and no one from the city dared leave the city for fear of being captured and questioned.

After all the hype was over, Isaleer made his way to his sleeping quarters. Being yet again overwhelmed by his surroundings, he passed out in his room, awaiting his next move, which would come all too soon.

The next morning, Awa came to wake Isaleer up and said, "We have packed everything for your journey to see the elders. First though, you have to go see the throne room."

Isaleer, got up out of bed and whisked his way over to the sink. He looked into the mirror and saw a man he hadn't seen in quite some time: a man of valor and courage. He splashed water on his face, threw on his new outfit, and walked out of his room and into the hallway of the sleeping quarters.

Awa said, "Look at you, all dressed for the throne room."

Awa led Isaleer down, up, over, through, and to the throne room door way. He said, "When you go in there, take off your shoes at the door. Then lie down on the altar and begin praying and talking to Father God. His Holy Spirit will come and reveal to you what you need to see for the journey that is ahead of you."

Chapter 13

Δ THE ALMIGHTY APPROACHES Ω

Isaleer shouted through the silence, "Hello? Hello? Am I alone in here? Is there anyone in here?"

As he lay on the altar, apparently talking to himself, Isaleer began to notice peculiar things about the room. First, Isaleer noticed the old-fashioned lights being used. The room was candlelit; it looked very much like a gigantic cathedral at night. The ceiling was so high that it faded into the blackness. These little candles were scattered all throughout the temple. They lit the surrounding area where they were burning, but they were no match against the size of this room. Mild exaggeration was necessary to explain the immense size of this structure. When Isaleer spoke, he heard his voice carry for quite some time. Truly, Isaleer couldn't see anything to make a true evaluation. All the incense that had filled up the higher part of the atmosphere in the throne room was beginning to fall, filling up the temple itself.

The ceiling was at least one hundred feet tall at absolute minimum. At least that's what Isaleer could see before the mystery of the ceiling's height was concealed behind a blanket of incense.

Isaleer waited about twenty minutes on that altar, crying, praying, confessing his sins, and asking for forgiveness. This room had a way of making one want to confess his every wrong and completely open his heart. Not once was any of this required; it all just seemed to flow out of Isaleer. His eyes filled with tears that eventually began to spill out onto the altar.

The atmosphere began to come to life while Isaleer wasn't paying attention. Some of the smoke began tunneling downward in a small vortex, subsiding around him.

Isaleer got up and began walking around, pacing back and forth at the front of the throne room near the altars. He had not even noticed the vortex following him around. His eyes were full of tears, and it was hard to notice anything other than the deep pain and anguish he felt inside of his heart.

Isaleer's emotions began to be more then he could handle. He needed a way to release his bottled up feelings. Knowing this was a church temple, Isaleer searched around through the dark and found a grand piano sitting to the left of the throne room's stage. He hardly even got the chance to sit down at the piano and play his first chord—instantly, the tears began falling uncontrollably.

Barely understandable, Isaleer cried out in a song to Father God. "God! I'm a #*&% up. Straight up. I led all these nations to the ledge and then pushed them into this utter darkness. I am unworthy of your presence. I was hungry for the money. I wanted to leave my family with a legacy and a fortune. I wasn't trying to turn my back on you, but I did. If there is anything I can do to make it up to you, anything I can do to one day live in Heaven with you, tell me, and I will do it. I love you, Lord Jesus! You are the Savior of the world. You died for people like me, people who are selfish and greedy and in need of a Savior. You arose from the grave and ascended to Heaven, and one day you are coming back for us…for me. Until you return, what would you have of me?"

As Isaleer began to sing, he was still unaware that the vortex of smoke was following him. Slowly, as Isaleer played the piano, the vortex began to grow. The vortex grew until it was large enough to be a spectacle. Turning faster and faster as Isaleer continued singing, the atmosphere began to grow powerful and quickly becoming much more than Isaleer could handle.

All of a sudden, Isaleer was taken away from his song and brought back to reality. He could feel the gusts of wind from the vortex as though a Hollywood fan were blowing on both him and the piano he was playing. Isaleer gazed in awe at the vortex behind him, and he was interrupted by angelic voices saying, "Blessings and honor, glory and power forever unto God!"

The voices got louder and louder; mercilessly, the whole temple began to tremble and echo mighty roars. Singing and music… Was it? Was it?

A light penetrated the room. It was so bright. Isaleer could feel the light on and around him moving clockwise. As the light grew strong and bright, Isaleer fell to his knees, bawling with all his heart.

Angels descended from the clouds, one by one filling up the room and carrying the train of God Almighty. It was so long that it did not all fit in the temple.

Isaleer looked above him. Heaven was literally manifesting above his head; he could see angels and a great city forming in the clouds. Out of that city in the clouds, a mighty king came to the forefront riding on a great white horse. It was nothing like any earthly horse. This horse had wings and predator teeth; it was much more like a mighty lion and eagle mix than a horse. Either way, this horse had the ability to fight back against dragons, something earthly horses could not do.

Isaleer muttered to himself, "Damn, Jesus—looking like a mother*&^%ing bad*$@ and $&*#. I'm not gonna lie; you look freakin' dope, Jesus."

---

train |trān|

noun

a long piece of material attached to the back of a formal dress or robe that trails along the ground.

[So what is a train?]

The cape a king wears around his neck.

Did you know? The longer it is, the bigger his kingdom is.

Just then, the cloudy vortex following Isaleer in the temple began forming a silhouette.

As the angels were lost in their praise and worship to God Almighty, a voice came from the vortex, soothing like water and comforting like a deep, passionate embrace. The silhouette formed in the vortex began to speak to Isaleer. His voice alone captured Isaleer's full attention. With an indescribable authority which no one could explain, the voice from the vortex urgently shouted, "Before you die from the glory of God, with all of your might, Isaleer, run! Run!"

All of a sudden, string instruments, drums, and guitars began playing. It was a choir of angels with a resounding voice singing, "Star of the morning, light of salvation! Majesty!"

The anointing fell so heavily in the room that Isaleer fell flat on his face, unable to move. No amount of alcohol, drugs, sex, money, cars, or clothes could ever make him feel this happy. The voice in the vortex continued to urge Isaleer to leave quickly. No matter how much he wanted to move, he couldn't. Isaleer was too happy to move. The Holy Spirit ordered two angels to carry him out through a doorway and onto the balcony.

Isaleer could not stop crying tears of joy, much less muster the strength to stand up. The anointing in the room continued to become more and more concentrated. He had become completely disoriented and had no idea where he was—nor did he honestly care.

Above the temple building, the sky opened wide. A voice that silenced every demonic force and paralyzed every Illuminati member to a prostrate position all across the world began to speak. The whole Earth bowed in reverence to the King of all kings. Interrupting reality to come speak to Isaleer, the Lord Jesus Christ needed to give Isaleer guidance for the journey ahead of him. It was the Alpha and Omega standing before him, holding a veil over his face so that he wouldn't kill Isaleer with the sight of his full glory. The only thing Isaleer could say with tears streaming from his face was, "JESUS! WORTHY! HOLY! JESUS!"

Just then, Isaleer felt a touch on his shoulder. This man had a hole in the center of his hand. Isaleer grabbed this hand, lowered his head to the floor, and said, "Jesus! I love you! I'm not worthy."

Jesus Christ said, "I love you, too, my son. Why do you cry? You have called out for forgiveness. God has heard you, and you are forgiven. The God of the universe sees you as spotless and blameless in his sight."

The whirling vortex spoke forth with an omnipotent voice as the Holy Spirit took human form. He came and threw his arms around Isaleer and said, "My baby boy! I love you! I love you!"

God spoke with an omnipresent voice that shook the ground of the temple. God said, "Isaleer…"

Isaleer said, afraid, "Yes, God of all gods?"

God said, "Isaleer, you are to lead the Arisen army to victory against the Illuminati army. You are also to learn about Heaven and my son Jesus and prepare yourself to give your life for me at any moment. The world is going to be much different now that you're not the head of mainstream media and pop culture. High Lord Navari is going to try to assemble your brothers and two sisters. He will try to turn them against you. Now that you are defending my people, I will place my blessing upon your life. You will need to unite the gargoyles and begin seeking out the prison camps. I want my people freed from this persecution. Do you understand me? Can you do this for the one you call Father?"

Isaleer, humbled, said, "As you command, so I will do, Father God."

Isaleer was then able to look around from atop the temple's second-floor balcony. From here, Isaleer saw the most beautiful landscape spread out before him. Predators and prey were standing next to each other.

Isaleer saw every kind of tree, full of life to their absolute brims. Kingdom and nature had come together in this moment, this moment Jesus Christ had with Isaleer. That which should never be was. Common enemies made amends and stood side-by-side just to be close to the presence of God Almighty.

Even the sky was celebrating the Lord's coming by creating a light show of auroras, shooting stars, asteroids, and comets. Clouds formed hearts and spelled beautiful words of endearment to the King of all kings. All creation was drawn unto him. The entire Universe was drawn unto him. The planets drew closer to the Earth for even the chance to be near the God from whose hands they were created. For the first time, the sky filled up with hundreds of planets and galaxies. From Earth's surface, one could see Saturn along with millions of planets never before seen by man's eyes. All thanks to God Almighty making an appearance in Isaleer's life, the Earth was seeing a phenomenal spectacle.

As the Lord Jesus was talking to Isaleer, he smiled and said, "You want nice things? You should try standing next to me sometime. You should see all the things that just come to me because they want to be near me. I promise you, Isaleer, I make your politicians look like beggars on the street."

Without self-control, everything having a mouth resounded praise after Jesus Christ had spoken.

Jesus spoke again and said, "Isaleer, decimate every slaughterhouse and every guillotine factory you find. Win as many to the kingdom of Heaven as you can. Save those who are held captive in the prison camps. Use the gargoyle inside you to protect my people! Make the blood in your veins cry many war cries. Make your curse be your blessing. You, too, are a mighty, young son of God."

Isaleer asked if Jesus Christ hated him.

Jesus replied, "No! Finish the assignment Father God has given you, and you will join us in Heaven, in eternity forever."

Before Isaleer could ask anything else, Jesus Christ and the Holy Spirit began to ascend back into the city in the clouds. Before the Holy Spirit left Isaleer, he declared all manners of confusion and darkness to leave Isaleer's mind! The Holy Spirit commanded one million angels to guard and protect Isaleer. The Holy Spirit spoke and said, "Anoint his wings to fly like an eagle. Take away the scales and replace that which was evil with feathers of victory."

After the Holy Spirit had finished, he joined his spirit with Jesus and God in the sky. They joined all of Heaven in rejoicing that Isaleer had given his life to Christ.

As the clouds began to fade, off in the distance one of the trees expressed its sorrow for the departure of Jesus Christ by releasing one leaf to fall to the ground. As the leaf hit the ground, all the leaves of every tree Isaleer could see fell in unison. What was, for a moment, one of the most beautiful scenes of paradise was now a valley of death.

Suddenly, Isaleer had a vision flash before his eyes as the Illuminati members rose quickly to their feet after being paralyzed all across the globe. During the time that Isaleer was speaking with the Holy Trinity, all throughout the world, all those involved in the Occult were simultaneously brought to their knees without question or control.

After Jesus Christ left the galaxy to return to Heaven, the Illuminati members slowly came to, and the demons roared out to the sky in hatred.

For a moment, while Jesus was there, things were perfect. After he left, though, it was back to reality.

All of a sudden, the final leaf hit the ground…

All at once, the animals of prey which had stood next to their predators were instantly demolished and torn to shreds without mercy. Below Isaleer was now a blood bath that reminded him he was living in a dark and evil world in the age of the great tribulation.

Right as the clouds closed from Isaleer's encounter with God, Isaleer was brought back to the apocalyptic world he now called home. The vision Isaleer was experiencing on the balcony of the Arisen's throne room became extremely intense.

As if things weren't bad enough with the corruption of men turning to black magic, now things were about to get really interesting. Somehow Isaleer could feel the age of the apocalypse was about to begin, just as the age of the great tribulation had started.

The vision took hold of him, and he could see clearly some of the things that were to come…

Isaleer watched, horrified, as the beast was released from the inner core of the Earth. Out of the bottomless pit, he came forth.

Suddenly, the skies turned to blood. A black hole in the sky began to open, looking like a portal from another dimension. From this opening from outer space, a conglomerate of sky creatures began falling to the ground, making their way to a middle-Earth filled with mystical creatures that sought to serve the Dark Lord. They soared high in the sky, awaiting the order from the Antichrist to kill all of mankind.

And there…after these sky creatures fell a monster so large in size, it appeared as a meteorite slamming into the waters of Earth. Taking up the canvas of most of the sky above, this monstrous beast plunged deep into the ocean, blaspheming the fires of Hell in a tongue not spoken by man.

His impact on the waters caused a tidal wave to set forth in all directions. This beast, after making his plunge to the bottom of the ocean, quickly swam for a coastline. He made his way to the shoreline. Standing on land, he posed, looking in all directions. He sought his only rival, the serpenscilla. This beast called for his opponent fiercely, though he was met with no answer. After several days of awaiting a proper challenger, he took to the ocean, never to be seen again. Before he left, though, during those few days that the beast called out for the serpenscilla, man marveled upon this beast's magnificent size. Within minutes, the world news crews began flying around the beast, airing live on television graphs that showed this beast to stand thousands of feet tall. They compared this beast to the Empire State building. He was so large that he didn't even bother attacking humans. They were ants compared to him and the serpenscilla.

In that moment, all of the powers of darkness came alive, and the imaginary was now made real. The demons roamed the Earth, searching out the trail of the Arisen, but now they had mystical creatures to embody. They began seeking and killing everything they pleased. The principalities loomed high over the cities as large dragons, waiting for orders from the beast. Water spirits filled the clouds and poured down on the masses in the cities, burning their skin like acid. A few of the highest ranking in the demonic hierarchy were big enough that they did not live upon the face of the Earth during this time; rather, they looked over it like monsters looking at a snow globe…

Snapping abruptly from his revelation, Isaleer turned around to walk back into the throne room. When he did, he said to himself, "Every demon in Hell must have been set loose. The sulfur smell is strong in the air. Psh, welcome to New World Order. I feel like I'm gonna need a gas mask really soon."

Darkness filled the temple as a thick, black smoke clouded view inside the throne room the view in the throne room. What had just been one of the most magnificent places was now filled with such a heavy Satanic presence. Isaleer began to push his fingers into his eyes, trying to pull out his very eyeballs. He clawed at his skin and began trying to rip his clothes off, so he could run around the throne room naked. Isaleer could not; instead, he picked up one of the knives used for cutting the communion bread and began cutting himself, trying to commit suicide. Isaleer could not control himself. The demonic presence was so strong that he became self-destructive in that atmosphere. No matter how much harm Isaleer inflicted upon himself, he could not die. All of a sudden, a new vortex was being formed from the haze in the temple and out of it. A demonic beast took a form, a form which could fit in the throne room. It felt as though Satan was making his way into the temple. The room began to fill with an evil stench. Isaleer could smell the aristocratic mansion again. The smells of sweat, body odor, blood, death, maggots, and rotting flesh filled the room. He began to dry heave. Soon, the dry heaving turned to vomiting. In a panic, he reached into his bag, pulled out a gas mask, and quickly put it on.

It took three breaths to clear the mask. Then Isaleer tightened the gas mask's mouth-out-port so that all he was breathing in was pure, filtered air. It felt so good to get rid of that rotten smell. Something was terribly wrong. Isaleer ran over to a large fifty-square-foot mirror placed in the temple to check and make sure his self-inflicted cuts on his face didn't look too severe. Of course, this required Isaleer to remove the gas mask he had just put on.

Isaleer quietly said to himself, "What was the point of the gas mask if I'm just gonna take off?"

As Isaleer was examining himself, his biological father Satan's left-hand ambassador, the fallen Persian archangel, appeared behind him. He was unlike anything Isaleer could explain. He brought fear to one's eyes, the kind that leaves a man standing breathless as a statue. His eyes overflowed with the darkest knowledge only learned by sitting amongst the counsel of death and death alone.

He said to Isaleer in a demonic tongue, "Come away from thou's fixation in the mirror. Gaze into the depths of darkness, and behold your master." Taking in a deep breath, Isaleer began searching the darkness with his eyes. He could see nothing—until the demonic ambassador's eyes began to glow.

"I can smell blood covering you. Doth thou think me to be a mere demon or principality to be fooled into thinking thou art free of your father's grasp? Just because thou ran away from the Illuminati, dost thou think that I am one from whom thou may at will walketh away, Isaleer? For I tell you, I am not the one. Your father has commanded me to seek you out. 'Search far and wide until you find all my children,' he said. 'When you have found them, bring them to me. For it is time.'"

Isaleer spoke up and said, "I do not belong unto him. In fact, #*$@ est you. By blood I am his seed, though I entertain not the thought that Satan art truly my father. You and the rest of his demons are soon to be extinct. I have called for his demons to send word to Satan that I do not belong to him, and he does not own me. Yea, I was formed against my will when Lucifer raped a thirteen-year-old girl who was my birth mother. That's what High Lord Navari told me. Harken unto me; I did not choose to be here by this path. Unto my mother, boldly I say I am grateful, for at least from her I have been given a soul—a soul which now is granted a choice, a soul, which calls out to the one that you call Jesus Christ. His blood is that which courses through my veins now."

Satan's Ambassador smacked Isaleer unmercifully onto the ground. He stood over him and said, "Lucifer hath given unto thee everything that thou seeks! Crawling through the halls of your mansions, possessed and enlightened, you have sought and summoned for more, more, more! You may not have willingly chosen this path knowing its full outcome; nevertheless, you stayed, and on this path you began to build. Doth thou think to try to walk away from a debt thinking there is no price to pay? Your savior is gone. For seven years Satan shall reign. How he chooses to rule will be entirely up to him. In the day, he shall be the bright and morning star. Soon, night shall fall upon the face of the Earth, and the sun and moon shall no longer shine. By night, Lucifer shall rid himself of the masks, and he shall forever be known as Satan. All shall kneel before his feet, either in death or in obedience. Thou art no acceptation. Thou art unmatched in the world of man. None have the power to stand against thee, oh great Isaleer. I shall have mercy on thee this once, for perhaps if we are clear with one another, things shall be as they should be. No man can bring harm to you, but I am no man. My sorcery is a demonic black magic no man has ever witnessed. I am the fallen Persian archangel. My only enemy is the archangel Michael. None can stop me. Your fate shall be decided in this room today. Perhaps in your gargoyle form you could stop me, but I see no gargoyle standing before me. I see pliable flesh which I could contort in all sorts of directions. Isaleer, I can turn thy own limbs against thee, for my power is demonic just as yours and is not watered down by man. Care to see?" He lifted his hand and began conjuring a spell.

"mi–du–i–Control–le–Corpus.

ye–Hov–Air–tu–di–Luk–ing–Glass.

De–Appende–mi–sae–Serade–de–Palm–tu–de–Altar.

Re–vil–tu–mi–de–Opposition–de–mi–mae–Curect'e–des–one.

Admin–de–Trans–Tru–Form."

For the first time, sorcery took over Isaleer; he was being completely controlled by the powers of the fallen Persian archangel. Instantly, he was possessed and lifted off of the ground in front of the mirror. Satan's ambassador picked up the communion table and elevated it up to Isaleer. Like a puppet, Isaleer threw his left hand down on the table in front of himself, and with a demonic smile reached for the knife with which he had just been cutting himself. He stabbed it hard into the back of his left hand; the blade came through the other side of the table. His left hand began shaking. All of a sudden, Isaleer watched his left arm grow three times its normal size. It began to grow claws and scaly skin. Then with an incredible force, Isaleer ripped the blade out of the table and out of his wounded hand, sending the blade flying across the temple and into the stone wall, where it shattered.

Satan's ambassador was forcing the partial change of Isaleer's body. His body caught on fire, and Isaleer began to scream out in agony. In the ambassador's mind, Isaleer belonged to Satan, and until he could fully transform into the gargoyle, he was no match against Satan's ambassador.

Before Satan's ambassador turned to walk out onto the balcony, he looked back at Isaleer and said, "Thou were never mine enemy. Thou hast always been my prey. I delight in knowing you shall live in agony for eternity as a bastard with no father. May this be a moment that screams out from the fiery pits of hell that I get that which I seek! You already signed for it." In mockery of the church, the fallen Persian archangel walked over to the throne in the temple where the Pope would sit. With a vile persona, he proceeded to sit on the throne and commanded Isaleer to bow down. He began to make demands, using his power to force Isaleer to obey. One of these commands was for Isaleer to kill the Arisen general.

Just then, an eerie scream from an approaching foul creature resonated through the temple.

The fallen Persian archangel said, "Good, my dragons are here. As thy corpse hovers, so let it remain and follow me."

Hovering above the ground, Isaleer followed Satan's ambassador to the balcony. As they reached the outer walls of the temple, Satan's ambassador turned to face Isaleer. He swished his arm, and Isaleer's corpse began dangling over the side of the temple. The ambassador reached for the reigns of his dragon and began to place himself in the saddle. Satan's ambassador's last words to Isaleer were, "Without your father, you shall never solve the riddle. You shall never be a gargoyle by the control of your own mind; therefore, as you clearly see, you shall never defeat me. What shall it be? Shall I toss you over the side of this balcony, or shall you come with me to stand before your father Satan and swear your allegiance?"

He brought Isaleer back to the balcony. The ambassador let go of his demonic hold on Isaleer, and young Isaleer quickly fell to the ground.

Coughing and hacking, Isaleer began to regain his motor skills and then gained full consciousness. He was prepared to be tossed over the ledge to his death. From the darkness near the mirror, Isaleer saw a set of eyes begin to glow as they quietly made their way out of the mirror.

In slow motion, Isaleer saw his gargoyle brother Number Six pounce from the shadows near the mirror onto the fallen Persian archangel and begin pulsing lightning from his palms. Number Six began pumping Satan's ambassador full of electricity. Convulsing from the shock, the ambassador stumbled over himself and fell against his foul creature. The fallen Persian archangel screamed out in terror. "No! How can this be? No! You are not supposed to be able to do this on your own. No! Do you realize what you have done? You think you have won, but now this means war! I shall tell Satan of this matter, and he shall call forth every creature from every element to his side. Your army of gargoyles shall not withstand even the first wave of Lucifer's army. You have doomed the Earth. None shall live until the children of Satan are dead. All those who defend the gargoyles shall die!"

Number Six roared in fury as his eyes rolled into the back of his head, "THOU ARE NOT WELCOME HERE! GO!"

Without hesitation, Satan's ambassador fled on his dragon-like creature, disappearing into the blood red sky.

"Isaleer! Isaleer! Are you ok? My God, dude. You're bleeding pretty badly, bro. Sorry, I don't really carry around boo-boo stickers, bruh. I would patch you up, but I don't have anything to do that with. Hm…I think Awa will fix you up, though. Come on. Let's get out of here."

Number Six began carrying Isaleer through the temple.

Isaleer mumbled, "What's going on?"

Number Six said, "I'm not fully sure anymore, broseph. I do know this, though; we must unite the gargoyle squad. I don't think we can wait any longer. The Illuminati are making a machine that will power up all the mirrors of the world, so people can walk through them to that weird #$& dimension in middle-Earth. The problem is that once they walk through, there is no coming back. People in reality are not ready to fight back. We need to be their defense!"

Isaleer said, "I can't transform like you, can I?"

Number Six said, "Oh yeah, sorry. Here's a vial! You only have to drink it one time. When you were in the laboratory, they controlled your shifting when they would séance over you simply by drugging you with a hallucinogen, so when you shifted you were not able to control it. This vial lets you tap into your father's bloodline and control the beast inside of you. They never wanted you to have this because they knew if you could control it, then you would be a major threat to their armies."

Isaleer said in haste to his brother, "Give me that vial."

Number six said, "Take this vial and drink it! You are a gnarly looking gargoyle. You're white with glowing turquoise blue eyes. You stand about twenty feet tall. I'm not gonna lie; you're kinda shredded."

Number Six carefully sat Isaleer down on the ground inside the temple. Isaleer closed his eyes, pulled the cork off the vial, and then tilted the bottle back. The flavor of the liquid made it difficult to choke down. Nevertheless, for the ability to control his transformations, Isaleer would drink nearly anything.

Both Number Six and Isaleer waited for something to happen. Number Six said, "Oh! I forgot you won't need Awa to mend you up. When you decide to transform into a gargoyle, your body will heal itself."

Isaleer kept waiting for the feeling to kick in, but nothing really happened.

Isaleer asked Number Six, "How do I transform now that I've drunk this?"

Number Six said with a smile, "Let out the feelings Number Seven would have, and quit fighting the feeling. It's going to feel like pure, unmerciful hatred, rage, and aggression at first. You are about to release the demon inside of you. You must learn to harness your hate. During the end times, this is the only way you will survive. Be prepared; when you transform back into your human flesh, you will feel super drained."

Closing his eyes, Isaleer began thinking of all the evil things he would have loved to do to Satan's ambassador.

That must have been the ticket because Isaleer when opened his eyes, he was standing high above the floor. He looked to his left and then to his right and saw his wings. Isaleer ran to the mirror, and just as Number Six had said, he was all white with glowing turquoise blue eyes.

Number Six smiled. He proudly said for the first time, "Hello, my brother!"

Isaleer replied much differently than he would have normally replied. With a much more direct tone of voice, he said, "My brother! We have much to do; rally our family. It is time."

Number Six answered, "You must go and speak to the Arisen elders. They will need you to help them take Lucien Vanderbuilt hostage. He is the one who controls the Illuminati army and will be extremely hard to access. Lucien Vanderbuilt is also the one making the plans to build the mirror portal through which he plans for humanity to walk into the new dimension of Earth. At this point, on Earth, they will begin executing the prisoners in the death camps to make more room for new prisoners. You just saw it yourself: The beast was released. It's about to get ugly really fast."

Isaleer asked when he was allowed to shift into a gargoyle. Number Six explained, "Only in times of battle, at least until we get the Arisen familiar to the gargoyle side of us. Let's try not to freak them out all at once. Eventually, we will be able to go in and out of gargoyle form as we so please. Let's just be slow at first."

Isaleer then proceeded to shift back into his human form. For the first time, Number Six transformed into a human as well.

Isaleer said in surprise, "Number Six?"

Number Six said, "No. My human name is Oxford. Enough talking, though; you need to go talk with the Arisen elders and learn of your history and your mission. Find Awa!"

Isaleer walked out of the throne room after saying his goodbyes and searched for Awa. Fortunately, Awa was just on his way back to the temple to retrieve Isaleer. Awa came with urgent news. "You have a tracking chip in your right hand, and it has been blinking for almost one hour! We need to break that thing quick!"

"They were looking for me," Isaleer said to himself.

Awa took a knife and stabbed Isaleer's right hand. He pulled out the tracking chip and then threw it on the ground, stomping on it until it shattered.

Awa then said, "Take off all your clothes. It's time to put on your new outfit."

He handed Isaleer all-white sandals, an all-white turban, and an all-white robe. Then he prayed and anointed him. As Awa was praying, Isaleer began crying. He was so grateful to the Arisen, but he was even more grateful that God had forgiven him. Awa hugged him and said, "Come on. Let's go meet the elders."

Chapter 14

THE09990SPACE8157776STATION

Click-clack. Click-Clack. Awa's dress shoes clamored down the hallways as Isaleer and Awa made their way through the underground and to the aircraft-loading dock. They were in an extreme hurry; though the sights and sounds were so beautiful and worth stopping to talk about, they didn't stop for a single minute to gaze at the underground scenery. When Isaleer first entered the underground, he entered through the elevator, which led him to RS-7. He now was miles away from the elevator where he first was introduced to the underground, and there were still miles to go. During Isaleer's journey through the underground, he learned of many secret passageways which lead to command stations and other Arisen military locations. This helped keep the underground informed of what was going on at ground-level. It was these underground roads that made the Arisen undetectable by satellite or human tracking. The underground was also home to an elite military base called the Haven. The Haven's soldiers were trained to seek out any lost survivors and bring them to the underground; they were also trained in direct warfare against the armies of the Illuminati. Isaleer wondered who funded all this technology and who the mastermind behind all the architecture throughout the thousands of miles of the underground. How did the Arisen have access to such extensive military weapons? Right now was not the time for questions, however. Isaleer had a mission, and he needed to stay focused.

Isaleer knew way too much about the enemy, so wherever he went inside the underground, as he would pass soldiers, commanders, or any workers, they looked him up and down like he was the enemy. When he had first come to the underground, Isaleer was accepted and welcomed, but then one of the commanders noticed he had a pyramid tattooed on his right hand. The welcome mat was pulled right out from Isaleer's feet. Some even became extremely hostile towards Isaleer. It was clear he was going to have to prove himself. As Isaleer and Awa started getting closer to the aircraft station, it was made clear to Isaleer that what he was about to see was the Arisen's space station. He continued to walk and was then escorted by guards through the long and wide hallways. Thousands of people gathered to form extremely enraged mobs. The guards had to equip their shields and begin pushing people away from Isaleer as he walked closer to the entranceway to the space station. The angry mobs were trying their hardest to harm Isaleer, and he had to do something fast. All he could think to do was what he did when he was a politician alongside Mr. Morgan; he just smiled. They began yelling things like, "You murderer! You killed my family, you with your need to be at the top! I hope you burn in Hell, you traitor!"

Isaleer smiled with confidence as the guards continued to push their way through the angry mob. They gave Isaleer a large bubble in which to walk freely as they progressed towards the space station. He thanked the soldiers for protecting him. Isaleer stopped to pay the soldiers one hundred thousand dollars each, considering they had defended a man they once had fought to defeat. Isaleer wanted them to know he was on their side now, and what easier way to make friends than to give them money? It was one of the perks of being a billionaire! At this point, the dollar bill was still usable, so Isaleer was now the wealthiest man in the Arisen.

Before joining the Arisen, it was nothing new for Isaleer to have to buy his friends, girls, homes, boats, and airplanes. He even had to pay to have laws passed.

As his first major play in politics, Isaleer paid Congress one hundred million dollars to declare martial law in America. Congress knew it wasn't Isaleer who wanted that law passed; however, that didn't stop him from walking up the steps of the House of Representatives and barging his way into Congress, halting the whole meeting by walking right up to the front podium and pushing the man speaking off the microphone. The whole House of Representatives looked at him disgustededly, as if to say with their faces, "Who are you?" He was Mr. Hollywood. The pop star holds no weight in that room. It was rather entertaining for Isaleer to stand up there, knowing how out of place he was. His custom-fitted suit was pressed and polished. His glasses made him look smart. His one-point-two-million-dollar wrist watch gave him the essence of wealth, but it was his Black Forest Order of the Thirteen secret crest ring that entranced everyone in the room. Isaleer realized that they were about to attempt to kick him out of that room; most likely, they'd try to arrest him or have security shoot him. Then Isaleer shot out a Freemason sign, and a thirty-third-degree Mason stood up and said, "Who do you come representing, my brother?"

Isaleer spoke up and said, "Weaving spiders come not here!"

He heard gasps all the way across the room. Isaleer had just broken it off with Evette; he was heartless and ready to grip the reins of power and make the sky fall. Isaleer then went on to say, "Since none of you have the stones to do what needs to be done, I was told to come make myself comfortable in this room. Ladies and gentlemen, America as you know it dies today! Today we begin change. It is time we all chip in. It is time America is given a curfew. You vote 'yes,' on martial law today, or you are fired."

Just then, the conference phone began ringing over the loud speakers. It was a call from the UN.

Isaleer smirked and said, "I mean, I would pick that up if I were you."

With fear in his eyes, the Speaker of the House pressed the little green button. Congress was now being held hostage. They would either comply or be fired and killed by a random heart attack which the witches and warlocks would hex upon them using voodoo dolls. These people had to be killed if they would not comply because they knew too much now. Random heart attacks were how they usually killed people. It was quick and untraceable. A voice came boldly over the speakers. Orders were now being given directly from the Great White Brotherhood. Without beating around the bush for long, they declared martial law, even though Congress felt no need for it.

"That's absurd!" one of the senators yelled out.

Over the intercom, the leader of the Great White Brotherhood said, "Absurd? Ah-ha-ha. Let me make this more clear. You either declare martial law, or else oil will spike to five thousand dollars a barrel."

Five thousand dollars a barrel meant gas all over the country would go up to two hundred fifty dollars a gallon. This would essentially make everyone in the U.S. completely immobile unless they owned a horse. That shut Congress up. Within ten minutes, the President of the United States declared martial law and renounced the alliance with Israel just to show his loyalty to the Illuminati. The president then retired to his office, where he then gave orders to withdraw the American soldiers protecting Israel and send them to Afghanistan to begin training the terrorist soldiers for war against the American people. Now, America was done playing games; they showed the whole world they were the powerhouse on the playground. Isaleer was wiring the House of Congress a generous one hundred million dollars to help boost the economy as a token of his gratitude for their cooperation. Isaleer then flipped his suitcase closed and proceeded out into the hallway, where lobbyists were making deals to make more money by using loopholes to screw with American taxpayer dollars.

Isaleer left the building and was walking down the stairs when a fleet of all-black vehicles drove up next to him. They said, "Thank you for your service to us. Your money will be replenished back to your account tonight as a generous thanks from the Rothlefeller brothers."

What an eye-opening moment for Isaleer to realize the Rothlefeller brothers were in contact with him personally… or at least with his money. That's what happens when one family controls the world's currency. Isaleer mumbled, "I bet even people look like money to them."

Isaleer got into his limo and, with a smile, said to himself, "You just bossed the government of America around like they were children who needed to obey. Yes, sir, Isaleer, you are now officially a superstar! Let's find some beautiful women and some strong drugs and celebrate."

When he got done with his power-high for the day, he arrived at the executive airport. He left the government limo and boarded his personal G6. Isaleer went to the back of the airplane and laid down on his bed. No sooner did he close his eyes than he received a text saying, "Thank you, Mr. Horus, for speaking for us today. As a token of our appreciation, we have replenished your account. We would never make you reach into your own pocket for such a ridiculous act. All one hundred million is now returned to your account. Have a wonderful day. We look forward to seeing you soon. -GWB"

Isaleer was so zoned out on remembering the old days, he had forgotten that he was walking in the underground. As Awa and the security guards were fighting off the mobs of angry people, they had forgotten to keep one side of him guarded. As Isaleer zoned out, he smacked right into a young woman. He was in such a rush to get to the space station to go see the elders, he unknowingly had increased his walking pace. Both Isaleer and this young lady fell to the ground.

Isaleer looked up at her and said, "Oh my gosh. I'm so sorry, sweetheart."

She looked at Isaleer, frantically trying to fix her hair, and said, "You have always been such a marvelous spectacle for the world to love and hate, Mr. Isaleer Horus."

She bit her lip and handed him her card with her name and number on it. Then she put her pinky and thumb to her face and mouthed the words, "Call me."

Isaleer smiled, rolled his eyes, and said, "Stupid girl."

When they finally reached the end of the hallway, two soldiers guarding the door punched in a code, and the blast doors opened. Into the next hallway they went. This hallway was different; it was most certainly a more exclusive experience. No angry mobs were in here. This hallway had gun turrets and mounted cameras so that anyone who wasn't allowed in there would be filled with bullet holes in seconds. Isaleer felt safe. Thank God Isaleer had access because those were some big guns—big enough to light Isaleer up like the Fourth of July.

The doors automatically opened, and there before Isaleer's eyes was a space station. It was huge, the size of a mountain, complete with spaceships. He couldn't believe that space ships were real. Isaleer was a billionaire who had no clue how advanced the world had become. He was a billionaire who had no idea that the world had spaceships. He laughed and said, "Wow! If I had known this world had space ships, I would have bought one."

Isaleer looked at Awa and said, "Like, dude, what is this?"

Awa smirked and said, "This is how we win!"

The Arisen was traveling in space? Psh… If the Illuminati knew about this, they would kill everyone right now. It was clear the Arisen trusted Isaleer, but why?

As Isaleer walked into the huge indoor hangar, he saw that it was not like regular hangars. He slowly took this all in. The hangar was lined with stairwells, catwalks, and indoor control rooms. It was legit. Isaleer asked if he was still underground, and one of the soldiers told him no; they were at ground level within the mountain's reinforced shell. So much technology and so much movement was going on around the space ship, clearing it for take-off.

As Awa walked up, some of the soldiers guarding the ship began mocking him and laughing at him for having to escort Isaleer. They believed that if he would leave the Illuminati, he would switch sides again and sell out the Arisen. In Isaleer's heart, it was not like that. He was grateful to have a full knowledge of Christ and understand what was going on around him. At this point, he now hated the Illuminati.

Just then, one of the men standing guard went to say something to Awa. Randomly, one of the Arisen soldiers walking into the ship jumped down from the side-entry hatch and punched that soldier in the face. He said, "Shut up!" and began giving the Arisen soldier the death-glare.

As Awa and Isaleer boarded the space ship, Isaleer found his seat and sat down. He checked his profile on Myface.com, but he couldn't login to his profile because the WiFi was locked.

All of a sudden, the rear entry ramp that led into the ship began to close.

Isaleer, being the social person he was, walked over to the cockpit and introduced himself to the pilots. While they began preparing for lift off, they instructed him to go sit in his sit and strap in. The roof to the space station opened up, and all the flight deck crew evacuated the flight deck. One of the pilots asked Isaleer if he had ever been in space. Isaleer said, "Yes! One time the Illuminati held a meeting on the space station."

The pilot laughed and said, "No, I mean have you ever been into space?"

Isaleer said, "Well, if the space station orbiting the earth isn't space, then I guess I haven't been in space."

The pilot looked at Isaleer and said, "This is about to be the fastest take-off of your life. We are pressurizing the cabin right now so that no one will die on this take-off."

The floor of the flight deck began to lower, and the space ship began to hover. The pilots were waiting on two things before they began the launch sequence: a pressurized cabin and a clean shot into space with no detection from Illuminati satellites.

Flight control ordered the pilots to be prepared. They were waiting for a satellite to fly over. Then everyone on the space ship was going to shoot right by the Illuminati satellite undetected.

They pressed a button. The chrome-colored ship turned invisible by directing the reflections of the surroundings through prisms that the mirrors formed as the hologram for the LCD paint display on the space ship's exterior.

The ship quickly pressurized, and they were weightless, strapped in their seats, and ready for take-off. The pilots said, "Hold on tight!"

> "If you think looking at the stars by the ocean at night makes you feel small, you should try going into outer space and looking at the universe and how it makes the world look small. All of a sudden you realize that we are the grain of sand on a grain of sand."
>
> —Dexter K. Rockwell

As though someone had pulled a rubber band back and released it, they were gone…

Chapter 15

MAN303ON1333THE1792MOON

When they had passed the vision of the short range satellites, the pilots came over the intercom and gave them all permission to freely move about the ship.

The ship was about the size of a standard cruise ship, so there were going to be plenty of places Isaleer could explore while he was on this journey. One of the places he wanted to visit was the kitchen. There had to be some food somewhere on that thing, right? Isaleer walked into the cockpit and said to the pilots, "It was nice meeting you guys."

The pilots said, "The same goes for you, sir."

Isaleer set off on a journey to find some food, some pizza bagels or pizza squares, ravioli, sushi—anything!

Isaleer stepped out of the cockpit. The inside and outside of this room was covered in system monitors, different computers, and computer screens that projected the analysis and condition of the spacecraft. What caught Isaleer's eyes were all the fun blinking buttons, all safely placed behind a PlexiGlass box that was simply lifted to engage the buttons on the other side. This ship was lit as well as anything Isaleer had ever seen; there was no direct light. Behind the ship's wall were nine-inch light bars that were located all around the ship. At any time, they could be changed to any color in the rainbow. The floors and the walls were a glossy white color, as to accent the colors of the lights being projected. In fact, every monitor and projector was white. It gave the ship an extremely clean feeling. Down the hall from the control room was a huge open room, like an entertainment room. It had a huge TV, couches and video games.

Continuing to walk down the hallway from the cockpit, Isaleer gazed in awe at the way the hall opened up into a huge, open mall-style courtyard which had eight floors of overhangs. Isaleer looked around for Awa, and he found him watching a basketball game on TV. Isaleer had no clue Awa was a basketball fan. Quietly, Isaleer snuck up behind Awa, grabbed his shoulders, and yelled, "Slam dunk!"

Awa spilled his energy drink all over the front of his shirt and then stood up and grabbed Isaleer.

Awa threw Isaleer over the couch and onto the floor, yelling, "Boom, sucker! Haha."

Isaleer laughed so hard. Then he got up, tackled Awa onto the couch, and said, "Dude! What's up? I didn't know you liked basketball, bro!"

Awa said, "Well, if you want to watch it with me, the score is eighty to seventy-two. It's the fourth quarter."

With all this talk of basketball, Isaleer was thinking about joining him. But first…he needed some food.

Awa had about ten minutes left in the basketball game, so that gave Isaleer enough time to nuke something in the microwave and catch the final minutes.

Isaleer asked Awa where the kitchen was, and Awa pointed his finger down the stairs and into the commissary.

Isaleer was like, "Alright, bro. Thanks, dude." Then he dipped out in search of food. Isaleer walked down the stairs, which kind of resembled something from a shopping mall.

Each balcony walkway above the first level had glass floors which allowed one to view the floors beneath. This was a nightmare to walk on for someone who was afraid of heights. It would be terrifying to go to the very top floor and look down at the ground level of the space craft's courtyard. Isaleer was walking down the stairs when he saw the glass elevator.

Isaleer turned back around, walked over to the glass elevator, jumped inside, and pressed the button for the first floor. He had no clue were the commissary was, but being on the seventh floor, he wanted a longer ride in the elevator. As he was descending to the bottom floor, he stopped to appreciate the magnitude of this space ship. This thing had full on homes in it. If one looked all the way up, he saw the Penthouses. All around the ship, there were such fun things to do, like ride a waterslide that led to a pool and surf on artificial waves. The elevator dinged as it reached its destination.

Isaleer saw it; it was Heaven all over again…the Kitchen. He ran over to the doors and made his way to the food. He realized he was not in the commissary; in fact, he was very much in the kitchen area. The chefs were all yelling at each other; meanwhile, others were busy putting ingredients together and preparing dinner for everyone on the ship. Amidst all the commotion, Isaleer made his way over to the fridge and began shuffling through it looking for some food. While everyone was flipping out over the cooking, Isaleer decided to take it upon himself to use the blender and make a gnarly smoothie. In went the bananas, coconuts, strawberries, mangos, blueberries, apples, and watermelons. Then he needed something to put a pep in his step. He reached for an energy drink, but he couldn't decide which one he wanted, so he just grabbed his three favorite and grabbed Awa a couple as well. Then the clouds opened up and the angels sang, "I love you, Isaleer!"

All of a sudden, he opened the freezer and he found it! It was like God said, "You can have it all." Isaleer's eyes filled with all assorted pizza bagels, pizza bites, chicken strips, frozen pizzas, and burritos. He grabbed all the bags and began filling up large mixing bowls with the different foods and then tossing them into the microwave.

After spending about twenty minutes putting bowls into the microwave one after another, Isaleer started walking out. One of the chefs came to him, laughed, and said, "Ew, don't eat that stuff! At least try some gourmet food."

Isaleer defended his "dude food" at all costs, but he was willing to give gourmet food a chance, assuming it was done right.

Isaleer said, "You got any meat or something spicy?"

The chef laughed and said, "How about a twenty-ounce sirloin and gyros with juicy lamb?"

Isaleer replied, "Psh. Well, well, my good sir, if you can make it, I can eat it."

The chef finished and placed the plate before Isaleer. To the chef, this was a masterpiece, and he wanted Isaleer to eat it and marvel at the amazingness of the gourmet food he had just prepared. However, it did not quite work out that way. It was such a beautiful presentation, but Isaleer couldn't have cared less. He said, "Awesome! Good God, great food; let's eat."

Then he tossed the meat and gyros in the bowl with the Bagel Bites, ruining the presentation, and handed the chef back his plate. He said, "You can have this green parsley thing, bro. Green is not my thing. Peace, homie!"

The chef stood heartbroken as Isaleer walked out. He was speechless; Isaleer had just blown his mind.

He headed back up the elevator and back to the entertainment room. Isaleer made his way, ready to devour the steak and gyros, so he could start in on the pizza food. Isaleer made the assumption that Awa was done with the video games when he saw the man sitting and watching National Geographic. This was Isaleer's favorite, so he quickly plopped down and offered food and drinks to Awa. It was a documentary on the Amazon River and the Goliath tiger fish. Isaleer had no idea Awa had such an appetite. The show came to a commercial break.

Isaleer asked Awa, "Where are we going?"

Awa said, "To see the elders."

Isaleer shook his head. "No, I mean like, where are we going?"

Awa smiled and said, "Did you know? Space-X and NASA still haven't made it to the moon. That's where we are going. We have established life on the moon. The elders live on the moon because it's too dangerous on Earth for them."

Isaleer was super excited to see the moon. He had finished half the food. Then he looked at Awa and said, "I feel so tired, bro."

Awa replied, "Yeah, man, space travel does that." He walked Isaleer to his room and explained its functions.

After making sure Isaleer knew how to control the climate and firmness on the king-size bed, it was then safe for Awa to leave. Isaleer's room was the size of an average master bedroom. It was complete with a bathroom and a walk-in closet. The shower was Isaleer's favorite part. When the shower door was shut, one could turn off the cabin pressure and float with the water droplets. Isaleer made a cool game out of it. He pretended he was an action hero hanging from the ceiling. Then he turned the cabin pressure on and descended to the floor with the water droplets. As the water droplets hit the shower floor, it looked like an action scene where the hero had landed on the ground ready to kick someone's face in.

After his shower, he threw on his boxers and then jumped in bed and fell fast asleep.

Chapter 16

I WILL BREAK THY SPELL, OH JEZEBEL!

As Isaleer slept that night, he was taken back into his dreams, back to sunny California, back to the days before he became famous in Hollywood. These were the days when he was just a regular guy who went to high school and had a high school crush, before he was picked up by a major record label and became Isaleer Horus. These were the days when Isaleer was selling grams of bud out of his backpack in the school bathrooms and hallways and making a killing doing it, too. Way before Isaleer was selling out arenas and driving hyper cars, there was a girl who truly loved him.

Her name was Haley Morgan. She had blonde hair and hazel eyes. She was five-foot-one and weighed a hundred twenty-five pounds. Isaleer couldn't stop thinking about how hard they fought to get to each other in the beginning of their relationship. He was on the road all the time being Mr. Hollywood, and Haley was on the road all the time speaking at conferences and expos. They met by chance at a huge rock festival that Isaleer's band was headlining. They were peaking the charts just as metal had begun to take the world by storm.

The distance between them was super gnarly. She lived in West Palm Beach, Florida, and Isaleer originally lived in California on Ocean Avenue.

Isaleer remembers selling bud non-stop that summer to save up enough money to move to Florida. Isaleer actually reflected back on that day he managed to buy a one-bedroom condo and a brand new truck. Actually, Isaleer did so well saving up that the first year's rent was completely covered. Some say selling bud is a horrible way to make money, but Isaleer didn't really care. He was seventeen and driving a thirty-five-thousand-dollar, lifted four-by-four, fully paid for in cash. The neighbors to his left and right were both lawyers from Ivy League schools. In his mind, he was simply working smart, not hard.

Isaleer was easily making five thousand a month selling loud for twenty dollars a gram. His neighbors' children were in their late twenties and killing themselves to go through college in hopes of one day making half of what Isaleer was making. Here he was, seventeen and still in high school, with money to blow and stacks on deck. Regardless of what anyone would say, all Isaleer had to say was, "Show me the money, bruh."

Isaleer could still remember the day he landed in Florida....

Haley was waiting in the terminal with balloons and a gift bag. As soon as she saw him, she abandoned both the balloons and the gift bag, wheeling herself towards him as fast as she could.

He took her hands and got down on his knees. Isaleer wanted to be eye-level with her. He said, "Haley, I freakin' love you! Would you please be my girlfriend? Please!"

In shock, she ripped her hands away from his and quickly covered her mouth. An overwhelming amount of emotions caused her to melt like a popsicle on the Fourth of July.

As she began unsuccessfully trying to hold back the tears, she said, "Aww. Oh my gosh! Of freakin' course! I love you, too, Isaleer, and yes, I will be your girlfriend."

Like all couples who fall in love and fall just a little too hard, the desire to go all the way loomed over their heads deep inside their subconscious in every make-out session. Haley was a virgin, and Isaleer wanted to keep her that way...at least until they got married. Then Isaleer was gonna plow her into the headboard.

A missionary family with morals and standards had raised Isaleer. They had taught him that sex was only for a husband and his wife after they had said their vows to one another in front of a pastor. Then they could freely have sex with one another. This ensured that the emotions and feelings felt by both the man and the woman could be freely expressed without the terror of abandonment or rejection of the love they had for one another. The vows took two individuals and, through mutual agreement, forged them together into one creation.

Both Isaleer and Haley kept these morals intact throughout all of high school. They weren't angels, though. At night, they would cuddle while watching movies on his bed. Things would get heated, and their make-out sessions turned to touching and feeling. She would rip off his pants and tell him to lie back, but Isaleer would smile and begin laughing as he lay back. Just then, he would wrap his arms around her as he began to stand up. Holding her, he whispered in her ear that it was time for an intermission. Then Isaleer would run to the bathroom to take a cold shower and calm down a bit. His love for her caused him to develop a deep passionate respect for her honor. Haley was not a whore who just had fun with her body. No! She always said she loved Isaleer and Isaleer alone. She knew how to make him feel special. In return, Isaleer wanted to do her this honor and cherish her as a princess. Isaleer had multiple dreams in that single slumber. His thoughts of Haley were quickly interrupted by thoughts of Evette. There was no doubt that both girls were extremely attractive, but Evette had something Haley didn't: the desire to go all the way.

Evette was a bad girl with a taste for lust and seduction.

Right in the middle of Isaleer's dream, as he was running his hand up Haley's skirt, waiting for Haley to slap it and say, "Calm down, mister!" Evette appeared. She grabbed Isaleer's hand, pulled it away from Haley, and dragged it up her soft, tan thigh. She said seductively, "She's never going to give you what you want, but I will give you everything you want, master."

Instantly, Evette had Isaleer's attention. Haley was a beautiful girl, but she was a good girl who battled with her prudish ways. At first, this was something Isaleer wanted to treasure. Isaleer was not a virgin, and she was. He wanted to keep her a virgin until they got married. That was fine until repetitious make-out sessions with Haley left Isaleer angry about being sexually frustrated. It went from such a cute, passionate experience to what he felt was her teasing him and then watching him suffer. The other thing Isaleer was beginning to hate about Haley was her modest outfits.

She wasn't too much into wearing heels or dresses that showed off her curves. She had a nice butt and cute boobs. Yeah…the word "cute" really explained Haley; she was cute in an innocent and naïve way.

Isaleer and Haley were both twenty when they finally broke up. They broke up because Isaleer couldn't take how insecure she was about him always being on tour. In her mind, Isaleer was cheating on her with every girl he saw. Of course, she was just insecure. Isaleer was extremely faithful to her; that is, until the night he met Evette.

That night, she was standing at the bar, and she grabbed him by the tie, pulling him into to a private room. As she stripped and had sex with him, Haley was the last thing on his mind. Isaleer broke it off with Haley and advanced from dating his high school crush to dating a professional porn star/model/video vixen. Isaleer loved how she dressed. All she wore were heels and tight clothes. Her boobs were super nice and perky. Her butt was incredible! She was a perfect little plastic Barbie. What Isaleer loved more than anything was that Evette knew how to twerk. Dang, could she drop it low and make it clap!

After Haley and Isaleer broke up, Isaleer never heard from Haley again. A couple months later, Evette and Isaleer got married and became Mr. and Mrs. Hollywood.

Of course, nothing in Hollywood ever lasts. The night Isaleer came home to see Evette shooting porn in his house brought back the thoughts of Haley. How selfish he had been for expecting Haley to be perfect. The fact was that with either girl, Isaleer was miserable. With Haley, the misery was derived from his neglect of sexual activity, so things with Haley hadn't even been explored yet.

Evette was great sex; Isaleer wouldn't deny that. Being that she was a porn star, it had become a scientifically formulated performance for her. Her love was a lustful elixir which he shared with the porn industry. It was a seduction which was never to last. After ditching the love of his life for a fantasy and a fling, Isaleer left himself standing alone with a broken heart and mounds of money to blow.

Seeing Evette on the couch riding some guy really freaked him out. The part that Isaleer never fully got over was how he was so easily able to put a gun to that man's head and blow his brains out without hesitation. Isaleer was blown away that in the corruption of the apocalypse, he was actually able to pay the Hollywood police twenty-five million dollars to file a missing person's report on the dead man he had murdered. Literally, Isaleer got off scot-free of any charges, and all it required was a lump sum of money—not even a court date to question the gun shot. In fact, all they did was feed the body to the sharks out in the harbor. This lifestyle was insane…

Night after night, Evette begged for Isaleer to forgive her. Without him, she was nothing, and she knew it. Isaleer was the superstar. Evette was beautiful, but so were all the women in Hollywood. Evette was proof that looks were not everything. Without a contribution, she was just another face. Isaleer was the one making all the contributions. Isaleer Horus had many titles: member of the Order of the Thirteen, mainstream media mogul, and head of mainstream media, pop culture and fashion.

Repaying Evette for the night she brought a film crew into his home to shoot porn, he began sleeping with more women than he could even slightly remember.

In fact, many in the secret Orders questioned if Isaleer was a reincarnate of Solomon himself with all the concubines he kept.

"Just pieces of meat… Just pieces of meat…" Isaleer would smugly reply, though it probably wouldn't have been like that if he hadn't been cheated on. Every time Evette found out that Isaleer had slept with another girl, it would cause her to have anxiety attacks, and she would begin crying. She had broken Isaleer's heart and lost his trust. She knew she was wrong, but nothing could warm Isaleer's broken heart.

Isaleer woke up in a cold sweat!

He looked through the pocket of his overcoat and found the card, which had been given to him by that girl he had stumbled over in the underground. He couldn't believe his eyes. The card was Barbie pink and with gold writing, and it said "Evette Rockwell." It had her number and her lips puckered in lipstick. He couldn't believe that she had found him in the underground. No one in the Illuminati was to know about the underground. How did she get in? More importantly, why didn't he recognize his ex-wife?

He almost called her, but he thought maybe it was a trap. Instead, he did what any guy who had just come out of such a sexually stimulating dream like that would do: He went on the internet, looked up some porn, and relieved some stress. Even in outer space, the computers had Wi-Fi. Isaleer felt like such a whore for the way he had treated Haley. Even worse, he felt like such a worthless piece of garbage for the way he had had so many girls in his bed and treated them like whores. That night on the space ship, Isaleer cried and begged God to set him free from this sexual immorality. He hated how much he desired sex and how much sex he had just given out. He looked up and said, "God, I want a wife, not just another good time."

Isaleer couldn't sleep, so he pulled out his small pocket journal. This one in particular he carried everywhere with him. It was always located in his left pants pocket.

He began to write down his thoughts. He had forgotten how much he needed to write his personal thoughts. This would be something he would get back into a habit of doing from here on out.

(May 29, 2012)

Dear Journal,

I can't stop lusting. Everywhere I go, beautiful women are trying to tear me away from God by seducing me into their beds. I cry every night because I know it makes God sad. I hate that I hurt my king. I wish I had the strength to say no, though with women, I do not. When I am alone, my sadistic side comes out. I found out my biological father is Satan. When I let the demonic side out, I turn into a gargoyle. When I am a gargoyle, everything gets dark, morbid, and violent. I would rather lie naked with beautiful women in my bed than lie on my stomach under a guillotine, chained down like some animal. Of course, that's just my flesh talking in fear of death. There is nothing for my flesh after death. It is me, the spirit inside of me, that will leave this meat suit and join the Lord Jesus in Heaven forever. I know I want to go to Heaven, but can a man who got wealthy from corrupting the masses be forgiven and enter into Heaven? I can't help but think about what my stepparents would say: Nothing is bigger than the Blood of Jesus. They said that all the time. I sure hope they're right. If, by some chance, God can see what I am writing, I love you, God. Please tell me Jesus came to Earth to die for my sins, too. Lord, can you ever love something as disgusting as me? Lord, you had to know that there would be people who would suck at life, right? I want to be forgiven, but I know I am not strong enough to say no to a woman. If you are willing, please make me strong enough. I want to make you proud.

P.S.

I'm on a space ship on my way to the moon. The space ship has pizza and a glass elevator.

Isaleer finished his journal entry and felt relieved. He noticed his room had speakers built into the walls, so he grabbed his mp3 player, put on some music, and passed out…

Chapter 17

I GUESS THE HONEYMOON IS OVER

When Isaleer woke up, his journal was open and strewn all over the place. He frantically began searching the room for each page, and he placed them back into the spine of the book in chronological order. He noticed something… Pages were missing. He marched out of his room, went to the main lobby, and in the most pissed off voice, he yelled, "Who touched my journal?"

Then he ran over to the nearest wall and began punching and head-butting it. Isaleer was furious.

He ran from room to room, and everyone was asleep. He woke them up, asking them if they had touched his journal. He set off downstairs to the kitchen, but it was empty. Isaleer said to himself, "Who touched my freaking stuff, dude?"

That was all he was concerned about in this moment. As he began walking around in the hallways for clues, he began mumbling to himself, "I thought these doors locked?"

He checked the data entry log. The times and dates showed that Isaleer was the only one who had been in his room since nine o'clock the night before. This let Isaleer know that he must have been sleepwalking or something. Isaleer had to assume that, subconsciously, he hated his journal because of all the secrets and bad memories it held.

Isaleer went to the bathroom to splash water on his face. He looked up, and he noticed a note that was left sitting on the bedroom floor under the corner of the bed. It was from his journal. Isaleer could see his bedroom from the bathroom because of the mirror over the sink. He turned around and walked over to the note. He picked it up and saw that it was from three years ago.

"Learn to control yourself, Number Seven.

You will need every bit of that anger really soon."

God Bless 777,

Oxford

Isaleer was blown away. Oxford was right; he really did know him back then, back in the asylum days. Isaleer stopped to wonder if he had heard anything while he was sleeping. He was a very light sleeper. He didn't remember hearing anything, though. After all his ranting and raving, his hands and head were aching from punching and head-butting the walls. He lay down and tried to relax. As he was lying down, he smiled, dropped all his emotions towards the stupid journal, and fell asleep.

That didn't last long, though! Isaleer woke up to the violent entrance of the Arisen troops who quickly surrounded his bed and began beating him. They quickly subdued and handcuffed him.

They took him to the interrogation chamber on the ship's lower deck. They chained him up from the ceiling, and he dangled on his tiptoes. They tortured and interrogated him. They threw a bucket of ice-cold water on Isaleer's face to shock him after they had knocked him out. Then they said, "No, you don't! Wake up!"

The only thing that came to Isaleer's mind as a proper reply to the Arisen soldiers was, "I guess the honeymoon is over, huh?"

They informed Isaleer that there was a camera watching him in his room at all times. The night his journal went missing, while Isaleer was sleeping, they snuck in the room and tranquilized him with sleeping gas. They looked through his journal for clues of betrayal or any clues to the location of the Illuminati soldiers.

The Arisen soldiers began questioning Isaleer like a prisoner. "Where is Lord Navari?"

Isaleer replied, "He could be anywhere! That's way too vague a question for way too broad an answer."

One of the soldiers came forward, punched Isaleer in the stomach, and then backed away. The next solider stepped up and said, "Who is the leader of the Illuminati? Who is the Dark Lord?"

Isaleer said, "He is not a human man; he is Satan in disguise. That's all I freaking know, man!"

One of the soldiers said, "What is a gargoyle?"

Isaleer said, "They were experimenting one night and captured a thirteen year old virgin girl. They tied her to an altar and summoned a principality to manifest and rape the virgin, consummating his seed in her body. Gargoyles are half-man and half-demon."

The soldier said, "Take him down from the chains and tie him to the table."

Isaleer said, "I thought you guys were my friends!"

One of the soldiers who had made fun of Awa when he was escorting Isaleer onto the space ship stepped up and said, mockingly, "I thought we were, were, were… Shut up! We are soldiers who hate the Illuminati and anyone who is with them. You can say whatever you want, but you will always be one of them to us!"

As Isaleer fell from the ceiling, that same soldier kicked him in the ribs and said, "Your mother was a whore to Satan. What's worse is that you're a demon. We should pull your entrails out and…"

Isaleer's eyes changed colors; enough was enough! These soldiers were unarmed, and Isaleer knew it. He played nice until they made fun of his mother. In a matter of seconds, he felt his vision enhance, and all of a sudden, he could see in the dark. He felt his teeth grow, extending into long saber-tooth fangs. His scalp set on fire as he felt hair and ram's horns begin to extend through his skull. He could feel his wings bursting out through his shoulder blades. His body instantly gained an incredible muscle mass. He stood up and was instantly transformed into a gargoyle. This was the official moment when Isaleer knew he could transform at will.

Isaleer grabbed the soldier by the throat, picked him up, and said, "Say one more thing about my mother. I am trying to live for God and serve him by doing the right thing by controlling myself, but so help me God, say one more thing, and I will punch a hole straight through your body. I'll rip your head off and eat it!"

All the soldiers marveled in fear of the gargoyle. Isaleer towered high above these men who came only to the sides of his knees. As Isaleer held the soldier in the air, he began to piss his pants. He was dangling fifteen feet in the air, high enough to be two stories off the ground. Isaleer slammed the man against the wall and said, "Come on, coward! Say something! A minute ago, I couldn't shut you up!"

The man was speechless and filled with fear. Isaleer spit in the man's face and then transformed back into his human flesh.

Isaleer yelled at all of them in agonizing pain, ending their fun and games. "If I wanted to, I could have sent the Illuminati armies to kill all of you! I am not one of them anymore. Pshh… Scratch that! If I wanted to, I alone could kill everyone on this ship, and none of you could stop me! Don't ever touch me again! Do you understand me? If any of you ever touch me again, with all of my might, I will unmercifully destroy this space craft and everyone in it."

The Arisen commander ran into the room after hearing all the noise and said, "Dear God, what happened here?"

One of the soldiers said, "He's a gargoyle!"

The commander said, "Do you have any idea how much $#@& we are going to be in when we arrive on the moon and the elders see

Isaleer beaten up and bruised? I said to question him. You were not to touch him or hurt him! Take him and clean him up. Now!"

The soldiers involved in the interrogation rushed to grab Isaleer and carry him to the showers. When they got away from the commander, they tossed him in the showers and said, "Clean up, gargoyle!"

They threw the soap at Isaleer and told him to get every bit of blood off his body. The soldiers turned and walked towards the door to wait outside the showers. Isaleer began to put soap all over his body. Luckily, none of his bones were broken, but he was in severe pain. His stomach was in knots from being kicked and punched. Isaleer threw up blood. The only thing he knew to do was somehow get some soap in his mouth and slosh it around, hoping to sanitize the wounds inside his mouth. He then spat out the soapy waster and the blood. After he finished showering, the soldiers carried him to his bed and said, "Sorry, gargoyle—I mean, Isaleer."

It was unlike Isaleer to be forgiving; he believed apologies were for the weak. However, tonight for the first time, he apologized and laughed. "Sorry for almost killing you!"

Isaleer rolled over and kept clearing the blood out of his mouth. After some time, Awa came into the room and said, "Holy crap, man! What happened?"

Isaleer was in such pain he could hardly talk. Awa rushed and found some pain reliever in the medical kit near the nightstand. He said, "Yo, dude! Take these right now, bro."

As Isaleer swallowed the pills, Awa said, "Listen, man, they are going to be severely reprimanded when we land on the moon. They will most likely be charged with hazing and excessive violence, along with disobeying orders."

Awa continued to explain that it was not their place to ask him about the gargoyles. The elders were going to talk to Isaleer about that and get him up to speed with what was really going on. The elders wanted to know if the gargoyles were friends or foes. Awa said to Isaleer, "Get some sleep, man. I'm gonna hang out in here and make sure nothing else happens. I'm sorry it has to be like this. I promise, you will get much better treatment once we land."

Chapter 18

LONG TIME NO SEE

"It's so beautiful," one of the space captains said to the whole crew as they all stood there, feeling so joyful for what their eyes were beholding.

Isaleer couldn't believe it. It was like some moment from a parallel universe; he looked at the Earth rising over the moon.

As they began to pull into the docking station, the commander looked at the boys and said, "Be prepared. When the elders see Isaleer banged and bruised up, you are going to get it!"

The space shuttle's captain came over the loud speaker and said, "Welcome to the Arisen moon command station one. Please take all your personal belongings and exit the space ship through the main hatch. We hope you enjoyed your travel."

Isaleer smiled and said, "Dang! I am so ready to experience this!"

The team was ready to get off and walk around. They waited in front of the blast door to the main hatch as the space craft was locking into the docking station and beginning to pressurize. No one could exit or enter the ship until pressurization had completed. The command tower in the hangar gave them the green light. The blast door to the space ship opened, and they exited the space ship. Luckily, the blast doors and the pressurization made it so that gravity was normal.

The elders halted dead in their tracks when they saw Isaleer all bruised and beaten. They spoke amongst themselves and then ordered the commander to point out who was responsible for this violence. The commander ordered the four main soldiers to come forward and take their charges. The elders were dressed in long, fancy robes, similar to those worn by the Pope, complete with extremely expensive jewelry. They welcomed Isaleer with open arms, but they became furious at the soldiers when they saw Isaleer's face all bruised and battered up. One of the elders said to the soldiers, "Is this how we welcome our honored guests?"

One of the Arisen soldiers spoke out in defense and said, "But, sir, this is one of the Illuminati gargoyles."

The elder looked at the soldier and motioned for him to come close. He began to mock the soldier by saying, "But, but, he, he, he…"

Then with all of his force, he struck the guard down to the ground with his golden scepter and said, "This is why soldiers cannot be leaders; they aren't able to think. As we see here, some are not even able to follow simple directions. So tell me gentlemen what can you do?"

He repeated himself, slamming his scepter on the ground with each word. "What! Can! You! Do!"

He continued, "Your orders were to escort and protect our young Mr. Isaleer Horus and bring him to us, not to chain him up and torture him. This man alone is our only hope for stopping Lucien's army, and you are trying to kill him?"

The soldiers were told to get out of his sight immediately. The elder sincerely apologized for the actions of the soldiers and requested immediate medical assistance. Isaleer had several gashes across his body that were still open and would not close. As they walked to the medical center, the elders asked if there was any food Isaleer was particularly craving. Isaleer spit on the ground and said, "Some sushi, Pizza Rolls, and a tall cherry Slushee sound just about perfect right now."

The elders said, "Of course! Let us see what we can do. Meanwhile, Isaleer, if Awa would be so kind as to continue escorting you to the medical center so that you can get all patched up, that would make us feel much better."

Isaleer walked into the nurse's office, and there poised before him in her wheelchair standing before him was one of the most beautiful blondes he had ever seen. She was wearing an actual nurse's outfit like the ones from World War II. "Wait! Jenna?"

She dropped her tray. "That's a nickname only one guy has ever given me in my life. He called me that because…"

Isaleer finished her sentence. "Because when the sun hit your eyes, you just looked like a Jenna."

Isaleer looked at her and said, "Haley, what happened?"

She ran towards Isaleer and smacked him in the face. "Yeah, Isaleer, what happened?"

Isaleer recovered from being smacked in the face and said, "You were there, and then you left."

Haley smacked Isaleer in the face again and said, "No! You broke up with me on one of your tours, and then I never heard from you again."

Isaleer stood motionless. "I mean, #@!$. I guess I had that one coming, huh?"

Awa heard Haley and Isaleer arguing as he passed the treatment center and followed the voices until he got to Isaleer's patient room. He then knocked on the door and made his way in, asking, "Is everything alright?"

Haley looked away from Isaleer and said to Awa, "Can I get a few minutes alone with him?" She shewed Awa out of the room.

Awa said, "Well, if this is all, I will just go find the elders and get started on making a checklist."

Awa walked away and left Isaleer standing there alone with Haley. As he made his way into the room, the head doctor said, "Haley, if you would just take Mr. Isaleer Horus to the back room and stitch him up, I would greatly appreciate that."

Haley said, "That is perfect. I would greatly appreciate that, too!"

Haley smiled and said to Isaleer, "Come on, tiger. Let's stitch you up!"

Isaleer's eyes got big… This girl was going to get revenge for the way he broke her heart by shoving a needle through his broken skin. For some reason, Isaleer knew this was not going to be pleasant.

They shut the door to the surgical room, and Isaleer sat down on the medical table. Haley began washing her hands and preparing to give Isaleer a numbing shot in the areas that she needed to stitch. She began telling Isaleer the stories his mother had told her about how one day all the Christians would be caught up in the sky. She didn't believe it, but she definitely knew something wasn't right on Earth. The masses were talking about a chip.

Haley's father was a part of the Illuminati. Her father had been a member of Congress, and in order to keep his rank, he had to accept the New World Order. She kept talking, telling Isaleer how one night her father came home from a late night dinner and began drawing a Ouija board on the floor of his office. Then with his fingers and his thumbs he formed a triangle and began running his fingers over the letters, trying his hardest to figure out what he needed to do next.

"Isaleer, he was possessed," she said with such a sure voice.

Isaleer completely knew what she was talking about. He had been to plenty of those late night dinners, but he wasn't going to let on that he knew.

She began rubbing ointment all over Isaleer's cuts and wounds. One of the Arisen soldiers had thought it would be funny to put his cigar out on Isaleer's thigh. Haley reached for the hole and saw it had gone all the way through the pants and into Isaleer's flesh. This required Isaleer to remove his pants. Haley bit her lip and pulled his pants off. She looked at Isaleer and said, "Oh my gosh! Isaleer, that's an infection."

The burnt ashes from the tobacco had built up under a blister. Haley reached for her scalpel, sliced the blister open, and began to squeeze the oozing substance out of his leg.

She smiled and said, "I have to keep going until I see only blood coming out of this sore. Then I will pour in some iodine to kill everything and sanitize the wound."

After she had played doctor to Isaleer's leg wound and had stitched up all his wounds, she began fanning her face, saying, "Whew. Is it hot in here, or what?"

Isaleer laughed and said, "It's actually really nice in here. The temperature is really nice."

Haley said, "Shut up, Isaleer. You know what I mean." She looked all kinds of hot and bothered by finally being reunited with Isaleer.

He smiled and said, "You are definitely way hotter even since college. I remember you being cute, but now you are freaking gorgeous, if I do say so myself!"

Haley turned in her wheelchair, rolled over to the door of the patients room, and locked it. She said, "Wow, ok! You are going to get me in trouble in here, boy."

Isaleer laughed and said, "Ok. Let's go then, girl."

Isaleer and Haley had their moment and knew the feelings were still strong. However, to change the subject, they began talking about the secret societies and how she walked into her father's study one night when he had drunk himself unconscious. She saw a healthcare bill that instated martial law and R.H.I.D. chips which would be required in everyone's right hand or forehead. She said, "In the letter to Daddy, whoever was talking to him said it was mandatory that they find a way to pass this bill!"

This healthcare bill had more than just martial law at its core; it had the whole New World Order agenda inside of it. Little did Haley realize that Isaleer was the one who had marched into the House of Representatives and taken charge by forcefully taking the podium and establishing martial law long enough for the American government to pass the final stages of the healthcare bill. Martial law being instated assured that the American citizens could not stop the politicians' plans from coming to pass.

Again, Isaleer wasn't going to tell her that he was the one who had taken the bill and marched into Congress after her father had worked up the bill's terminology.

Haley continued to explain how Isaleer's mother was the one who single-handedly took Isaleer's trust fund money and used it to build fortresses and safe havens all over the world for the Arisen armies. She started a space program and secretly launched rockets to the moon to begin building the moon's command station. It was Isaleer's money, but it was her mind. All in all, Isaleer realized that all of this was thanks to his family. That was why he got such special treatment from the elders. Isaleer got misty-eyed because although millions of people had gone missing off the face of the Earth, it was a relief to know that they were safe by the works of his hands. These millions of people who just vanished off the face of the Earth in what the mainstream media called "the Rapture" were gone. The Lord Jesus Christ had returned to call his people home— away from the suffering which was to come in the days of The Apocolypse. Although millions had been called up in "The Rapture" there where still billions of people left behind to face the Tribulation and Apocalypse period spoken of in The Book of Revelation. Amidst the chaos, to determine where these Christians had vanished to The Illuminati broadcasted over every news station in the world it had now become mandatory for everyone on the planet to receive The mark of The Beast. Knowing this would happen, Isaleer's mom created an evacuation program for those who were left behind and wanted to hide from The Illuminati. Thus she funded the underground cities and the space program. Without even knowing it Isaleer's money was saving people's lives, during the Tribulation and Apocalypse. They were still very much on the Earth; they were just underground. Isaleer missed his family. For the first time, Isaleer cared about the mission to kill the maker of guillotines. He quickly snapped out of his emotions, collected himself, and said, "Where are the pain pills, Haley?"

She pulled some out of a drawer from the other side of a prescription counter and said, "Take one of these pills every six to eight hours."

Then she escorted him to his sleeping quarters in his own special housing made for the Horus family. It was the penthouse suite of all penthouse suites built on this command station. By the time he laid down, Haley was almost carting him to his bed. As they reached Isaleer's bed, he picked her up out of the wheelchair and fell back onto the bed with her. She smiled and said, "Just like old times, huh? I'll forever be carrying your drugged-out butt to bed, won't I?"

Isaleer, completely drugged-out on pain medicine, lacked the couth to restrain his words. In his intoxication, he said, "I love you, babe."

Haley said, "I love you, too, stupid boy."

Unable to leave his side, Haley curled up next to Isaleer and wrapped herself in his arms. She sighed and said quietly to herself, "I really, really do love you, Isaleer, and I've missed you so much. I missed you holding me and kissing me. I promise I will trust you if you give me a chance again. I promise I won't be clingy this time. I promise."

Isaleer woke up just enough to mumble, "Babe, who are you talking to? Tell them to go away and be quiet, and you come here. Quit talking to people, and cuddle closer to me. Now!"

Haley smiled and said, "I'm all the way up against you, baby. I can't get any closer. That is, unless…you wanna…"

Isaleer began snoring. Clearly, whatever plans Haley had had now been cancelled. She cuddled up as close as she could possibly get to Isaleer and fell asleep in his arms.

Chapter 19

KILL YOURSELF OR DROP DEAD

eanwhile, back on Earth, the United Nations had declared that, instead of having the chip, everyone must have a visible mark on their right hand or forehead. They were gathering people up house by house. If one refused the mark of the beast, he or she was taken to a prison camp.

In fact, Revelation 2:10 says that they will torture Christians with extreme prejudice…

These camps were very similar to the concentration camps used to harbor the Jews during the reign of Hitler. Before executions, generally the same scene was repeated.

"I will not turn away from the ways of God Almighty. I read the Book, and I believe it! If I have to die, then it's my honor to go to my death," one of the prisoners screamed out as he was apprehended from his prison cell by an Illuminati soldier and then drug to his execution…

It was pitch black in the prison cells but for the cracks that leaked in light from atop the prison-style buildings. The atmosphere in the prison was hot and humid from the way the Illuminati soldiers packed everyone in like pigs and cows in a slaughterhouse, waiting to become processed meat.

The prisoners could hear movement as the cells were being opened. Normally, this would spark a sense of freedom in a prisoner's mind. However, this was nothing near normal. The prisoners were Christians of the tribulation.

The guards had been human until Lord Navari and the entire elite society no longer trusted the New World Order to be carried out by human hands.

At that point, Lord Navari gathered all the Illuminati soldiers from across the planet to a desert in the Middle East. Through witchcraft and black sorcery, he caused them all to turn on one another. They fought to the death, all in the name of a war that the globalists had staged to end human armies. Their blood sank deep into that ground and awoke an evil the world hadn't seen since the Old Testament and the serpent in the Garden with Adam and Eve.

Out of the dry desert ground, demons arose. Some took to the sky to control the airways. Some were scouts who alerted the more powerful demons when they spotted something, almost as a hunting dog would alert his master when he had found something to pursue. Others just appeared to be animals that had no particular purpose but to live and kill. Some of these new Illuminati soldiers were warriors. Others were laborers, assassins, and high-ranking kings who took orders from Lucifer as to how to rule their designated kingdoms. The demonic hierarchy worked in accordance with the plans of New World Order; they took orders from the globalists in the Occult Orders, who in turn got their orders from leaders such as Lord Navari. Of course, among all these purposefully driven demonic soldiers, there appeared to be animals that had no particular purpose but to live and act as part of the advancement in the animal kingdom.

In spite of their positions and authority, at the sight of human flesh that was not marked by Satan, they all went mad. They had a hate for the living. It seemed that Lord Navari was the only one who could control them.

As Lord Navari placed his hands upon his wooden staff, a beam of light shot out of it and went deep into the sky. Instantly, the light beaming from the wooden staff turned from a red laser beam to a fog which filled up the air. All of a sudden, out of the sky came serpents, dragons, and principalities. They came and landed amongst the corpses of the Illuminati armies lying dead in the desert sand and began to eat the flesh of the dead humans.

The demons and demonic royalty praised the principalities which came forth. These principalities were the highest-ranking forms of evil other than the Dark Lord himself.

The principalities set forth from all points of the first Heaven and completely other dimensions. Among them were fire-breathers, ice-breathers, gas-breathers, and those who controlled electricity. There were principalities with two heads. The most powerful one came and landed, and all bowed down before him. He had twelve heads. No matter their color or ability, they were dragons. Evil had just been released to roam upon the Earth in carnal bodies.

It felt like middle-Earth had just become reality. The days of old were happening right here in the twenty-first century. They called these beasts flying serpents or fiery Serpents. They brought such a presence with them. Though they did not speak directly with their mouths, they could. Their favorite way to communicate was by getting into their victims' minds, but that goes for all of the evil spirits. The mind is the Devil's playground. In the end times, the voices were much, much louder, and many demonic creatures refused to speak any human tongue. So as they would speak to their victims, they would speak in their many ancient demonic tongues. Though no human could fully decipher their dialect, images would appear in their victims' minds as the demons and principalities would speak. It was all a matter of putting the puzzle pieces together to form a translation.

Lord Navari let down his wooden staff. As he did, an extreme silence filled the desert. Thus forth, the armies of the Illuminati were now controlled by mystical creatures, shape-shifters, wizards, the Occult, and the demonic hierarchy.

Any dragons that had not landed began to make their way to the ground, coming to receive orders from Lord Navari. The hounds of Hell came out of the caves surrounding the desert as well.

When Lord Navari spoke to the armies of Hell, he was not using a human language. In fact, it sounded like he was speaking in a newer, not-so-ancient demonic tongue. His voice carried all throughout the desert, even to the mountains. He began speaking of the plans for Jerusalem and the temple. He spoke of America and its glorious wastelands. He spoke of the overthrowing of European nations and the imprisonment of those who resisted in Europe, Africa, Australia, Russia, all of the Middle East, and all the Asian nations. Lord Navari spoke of the major corporations and public broadcastings from a hidden place in the Black Forest in the Bohemian Grove. The Illuminati would need an international broadcasting xhannel to make their addresses to the world and all its continents.

All of a sudden, Lord Navari spoke of two castles in America. Though both were apparent, they were not to be made known but by one's own understanding. Let those who are wise determine the American castles' whereabouts, for they do exist.

He spoke to the armies and gave them a timeframe for when the Antichrist would come forth to claim his throne in the temple of Jerusalem. Until then, the new demonic Illuminati armies were to hide out of human sight. It was thought that the Antichrist was Satan in the flesh, but at first the spirit of the Devil was not strong enough to take full form on its own. When he would make his first appearance, one of the already chosen globalists would be fully possessed. He would be The Dark Lord's puppet— just like Jesus Christ had submitted himself in his body to the submission and plan of his Father God. The Devil would need a puppet to operate through at first, too. However, when the Beast himself eventually became powerful enough, he would be the serpent of all serpents, bigger than all the other serpents who have ever come and deceived nations.

"Hail Satan!" was shouted in unison and séance from all the mouths of the demonic hierarchy present in the desert.

Lord Navari had to remind them to be patient. First they had to unlock the seals.

THE ABOMINATION SEALS

Step One:
Collect the rebels and anyone who will not obey.

Step Two:
Place a tracking chip in every person on the planet, in case anyone else goes missing.

Step Three:
Bring them all to one continent for easier control.

Step Four:
Make them slaves; make them build monuments to the different deities.

Step Five:
Slaughter those who have remained locked in the prison camps, in public view of the masses.

Step-Six:
Make humans cannibals.

Step Seven:
Forget all rules; just make yourself happy.

Step Eight:
Outlaw clothes.

Step Nine:
Outlaw sobriety.

Step Ten:
Force women to have intercourse with demons.

Step-Eleven:
Make human men obsolete.

Step Twelve:
Continue searching the planet for resisters or terrorists to the New World Order.

Step Thirteen:
Walk through the mirror into the first Heaven when the beast comes forth.

Step Fourteen:
Prepare for the final war against God and his army.

A year and a half into the great tribulation, they had already reached step six.

The Illuminati were outnumbered and outsourced against God Almighty, and they knew it, but their lust for power consumed them, and they didn't care about the odds. The sad part was that they were about to bring the entire human race down with them in their pursuit to control the Heavens—but what were the remaining humans of Earth compared to Occultist billionaires? They had the technology to nuke nations in their pursuit of their illusion of being God. The citizens of the world never fought back against the Illuminati because they were afraid.

The scene continued in the prison cell.

"Prisoners!" one of the demons yelled out, almost joyfully, at the sight of the fear that glossed itself over the prisoner's eyes. He proceeded to say, "This is no longer a game to see how long you can last in refusing the mark of the beast and taking the chip. The prison cells are full, and we are at maximum capacity."

One of the prisoners, nearly in tears, looked at the guard demon and said, "As if it has been a game all this time?"

The demon looked around and said, "Who said that?"

The demon in command ordered the lights to be turned on. There was just enough light to expose the nakedness of the prisoners and the body structure of the demons.

"I did. I am prisoner 727-648a-3271. I once had a name; it was Paula, but now I am a number. I have been in the prison cell for thirty days. You have fed me once a week. You beat me every day. Once this month, you tortured me. You turn the intercoms on and tell us all there is no God through your séances and Occult rituals. You try to put a spell on all of us through hypnosis. Your guards rape me every day. I smell fecal matter throughout this whole prison camp, and you do nothing about it. I have begged for you to kill me and let me go home to my Savior, but no matter how much I beg, you do not listen. Today, I kill myself. May God have mercy on my soul, for I am homesick and only wish to be with my family who have already joined Jesus after you executed them on their arrival to this prison camp."

She then began to smash her head against the wall, screaming and gnashing. With every splash against the wall, her face filled up with blood, and her skull began to crack. She stopped and began to try to hold herself up. The demon knew she could not kill herself, but he enjoyed this sight so much. The demonic Illuminati soldiers thought it would be a good chance to instill fear in everyone else in the prison. She had tried to kill herself three days ago by chewing through her arm. To prevent her from completing her suicide, they had pulled her teeth out. As the prisoner fell to the ground, the other prisoners got quiet and scared.

The demon began laughing and said, "Who needs an executioner when they do it themselves?"

Her body lay wiggling on the ground. The demon started to walk away, and one of the prisoners yelled, "She's alive! Praise Jesus!"

That name sent the demon into a rage. Eyes glowing red, he rampaged towards her cellblock. He ripped open her cell, grabbed her up, and said, "Drop dead!"

The demonic Illuminati soldier slammed prisoner 727-648a-3271 to the ground and stomped her skull in, finishing her death. Then he grabbed up the others in her cell and said, "Off with their heads!"

The demonic Illuminati soldiers forcefully led all those in her cell out the side door and into the courtyard in front of everyone. They said, "Tribulation Christians! Ha! That's what you call yourselves, right? There is no God; if there were, wouldn't he save you? Not one bit of mercy is shown from this God you worship. Why does he not save you? You cry for him like children lost in a shopping center, and nothing happens. Accept it—he doesn't exist, and if he does, he doesn't give a #&*% about you. The leaders of your world have simply asked that you be chipped and marked, yet you act like they are trying to send you to Hell personally. You'll trust fairydust in the sky, but you won't trust the Illuminati? Ok, then, you have done this to yourselves. As you will not join the Earth in New World Order, this is what you get. You are ungrateful to your leaders who are looking out for your best interests."

One by one, the demons threw the prisoners under the guillotine and yelled, "Hail, Satan!"

With tears streaming uncontrollably down his face, one prisoner yelled in absolute terror and horror, "Jesus! I am ready to come home!" The blade fell and severed his head from his body.

When the prisoner said the name of Jesus Christ, it sent chills down the demons' backs. They hated that name.

Death by guillotine was actually instantaneous as long as the victims were lying throat-down because it severed their spines. In this case, the pain was not signaled to the brain, so it was actually about as painless as a bullet to the skull. However, if the throat was facing upwards, it was one of the most painful deaths. The pain of a blade ripping through someone's tendons, throat, and veins would send an unimaginable signal to the brain, and by the time the blade had met the spine, the pain receptors in the brain had already received the signal for all the unimagined pain. It is said by scientists that for eight seconds after being beheaded, a person still has consciousness in reality, though this is only hearsay and cannot be fully proven.

When the executions were finished, hundreds of semis pulled up with large black wooden boxes. They began throwing the corpses of the dead prisoners into the boxes. Each box was about the size of a mini-van. They put six people in each box and then and loaded them back onto the truck to be sent to the slaughterhouse where they processed cattle and livestock be mixed in with the processed meat for food to the masses.

The Illuminati had plans for the strong prisoners who refused the mark of the beast. They were sending them to the Middle East. They were going to be forced to fight to their death against other resisters publicly as entertainment. After the fights, the corpses would then be served to the audience in their dinner that night as a ritual to celebrate the rise of a higher-level thinking society who had welcomed in the New World Order.

As for the desolate continents of America, Europe, Africa, and South America, none of these places were inhabited anymore. After the Twenty-First Century American Civil War, the action had moved to the Middle East. Naturally, so did the major societies. It was all thanks to the Illuminati, who had moved the major populations to the Middle East in preparation for the rise of the Antichrist.

Chapter 20

HUMAN IS ON THE MENU

Many people wondered where the human corpses went after they were executed at the concentration camps. What happened when there was no more life in their bodies?

The answer was dark and simple: They were thrown into coffins, and then they were loaded into semi-trucks and taken to the slaughterhouses to be processed. They were taken to the incinerators in the Black Forest. They were taken to tribes and sold as sacrificial bodies for rituals. The tribes used so many of the Illuminati's executed bodies that it actually developed a strong market to trade bodies for goods; it especially paid off for the Illuminati as most of the tribes preferred gold and diamonds as currency. The Illuminati's thoughts on this were that they would never know the difference. Anyway, periodically, men fell into the meat grinder and came out on the other side in hamburger meat. Just like the cows and pigs, when a human went into the conveyer box and to the meat funnel, there was no saving him. Machine rods punched out the cows' legs and sent them tumbling into a one hundred-by-fifty foot funnel. The cows and pigs screamed out in agony when they were chopped up slowly by human-size blades at the bottom of the funnel. This was how they made the processed meat used in every fast food chain. It was fast, and every bit of the cow was put into the patty. It's kind of gross to think that bone marrow, gizzards, and organs are in a processed hamburger. The sad part wasn't the death, which was by no means was instant, but rather the fact that the cow on the bottom of the funnel had about fifteen cows on top of him, crushing him and suffocating him. The biggest evil was that the factory owners never had to tell the media how they slaughtered their livestock. No pity was given to the meat that was about to be sold for one dollar on a patty at some fast food chain.

The Illuminati made it mandatory to dispose of the human remains in the processed meat because, in their minds, only lower-life humans ate processed meat because it was so bad for them. That is what turned America into a dry wasteland. They started to drill for American oil without asking the Americans, and then they put Americans out of jobs, forcing them to get lower paying jobs. In their minds, they had to eat fast food. When they started secretly putting humans in the meat, people started losing their minds and killing each other over things that made absolutely no sense.

The crazy part came when the chem-trails in the sky had dispersed. Following them were small illnesses that kept everyone sick from the flu. After eating the processed meat, their metabolisms were nowhere near strong enough to fight off even basic illnesses.

Instantly, America was overrun with mindless cannibals. This was a great excuse to get everyone of the higher class to leave America and move to the Middle East.

Those left behind to fight in America would either be killed by the cannibals or would have to kill the cannibals. For the first time in hundreds of years, America was a third-world country with nothing to offer the world but savages and cannibals. America was a barren wasteland filled with gas masks and nomads who bounced from house to house, looking for other survivors and trying to survive themselves. They pillaged from car dealerships, electronic stores, and malls; they survived off the resources the world had left behind. The only places that were still fully functional were the military bases. That was the other thing the survivors had to fight against—military personnel.

The Illuminati set up posts all over the U.S. to search for any survivors and give them a new life in the Middle East if they would take the mark. Anyone who refused was shot on sight.

There were some fully functional cities in America, but people had to have the mark and the chip to be able to function in them. Los Angeles, New York, Orlando, Atlanta, and Washington, D.C. were the mainstays for the Illuminati fortresses.

Meanwhile, the Illuminati and the other secret societies filled the American forests. Like witches casting spells in the forest, the glimmer from their sacrificial fires could be seen from miles away. There were many dark wizards who were considered strong. They were strong enough to cast spells and transform into animals. However, none were as strong as Lord Navari, who alongside the Order of the Thirteen preformed black magic sorcery and Occultist rituals. It was clear by the power he could summon that he was in fact the Antichrist's right-hand man. He could make fire come out of the sky. Lord Navari rode on the back of the largest principality. His dragon was gigantic, about two hundred feet in length, double the size of a blue whale. Most wizards rode on the backs of the hounds of Hell. They were demon dogs the size of horses. They could run almost as fast as cheetahs. At night, these things almost looked like cheetahs or saber- tooth tigers. Their howls sounded very much like war sirens, gradually progressing and then sustaining. Hearing ten of these hounds howl together was bone-chilling.

Thanks to the crash of the American dollar, America was the new Russia. Europe was the new America, and the Middle East gave everyone their authority to do what they did. The Middle East was the center of it all. Dubai had never been busier or more corrupt. Video vixens were treated as queens in the city. Outside of the city, demons patrolled, keeping order and searching out for the Arisen. However, on the inside of the city, principalities ruled with all the might given to them from the beast who was Satan. Both the demons and the principalities used their human bodies unless they were in war, but something about the principalities made their genetics perfect. They were beautiful specimens to behold in their human bodies. They were men who belonged on the cover of the most elite men's magazines. They ruled over politicians and lived like rich, careless playboys. Even emperors wondered at them. They were the only ones allowed to breed with the video vixens. They wanted to create more gargoyles for the army against the Heavens. Those in the cities had no clue what was going on anywhere else in the world, and they really didn't care. As humans who had taken the mark of the beast and the chip, they were so overjoyed to finally have their lives back that they didn't really concern themselves with politics and government anymore. The masses just wanted to be able to shop at upscale stores and eat cuisine again. All the humans who had made it to the Middle East cared about was having fun and enjoying life. They had no more cares, not even for other people. The phrase "Do you and what you want" took over. All people wanted to do was have fun.

Meanwhile, the Illuminati were looking hard for the Arisen fortresses. No matter what tactic the Illuminati tried, they couldn't find them.

Isaleer was only on the moon for a matter of about one week as he recovered from the torture he had received in the interrogation room. In a matter of one week, the world that Isaleer knew had gone from just passing out a chip for healthcare to killing anyone who refused. In Isaleer's mind, he would return to the world, and America would still be waiting. He couldn't wait to visit his mansions and see all of his stuff. Before the big disappearance, his family had been given full access to Isaleer's trust fund. The greatest thing they did was buy up military vehicles and aircraft and hire engineers to build prototypes. Then they started construction on the underground and RS-7. They knew a war was coming, and they began preparing for it. They wanted all the Christians to have a fighting chance. They started buying up non-perishable foods and began stockpiling food for the future starving nation who would so desperately need the Arisen's help.

Currently, the sound of shepherds' flutes filled the air in the city of Jerusalem and made travelers feel welcome in the city of wonders. However, today was like none other. The most valuable executive jet was flying into Israel, carrying Lucien Vanderbuilt, the General of the Antichrist army; Lord Narvari, High Lord Master Sorcerer of the Dark Arts and the High Priest of the Order of the Thirteen; Evette Jaymes, Mistress of darkness and Isaleer's former wife; Colonel Fetelli, Colonel of the Illuminiti army; and Dr. Killjoy, the head of the Science and Weapons Development Division for the Illuminati government.

Last but not least, for the first time, the whole world laid eyes on the Antichrist. Society had no clue he was in fact the human embodiment of Satan; rather, they thought he was just a noble humanitarian who took center-stage to unite all nations during a time of crisis and chaos.

News reporters from all over the world gathered for this foretold moment. Unlike the principalities and demons who were still in their human bodies, the Antichrist resembled a human in every way, but the shapes and structures of his aesthetics were much more chic and exotic. He was so pleasing to the eyes that, combined with his charm, it caused one to obsess over him. He had the eyes of a serpent and the face of a wolf. He was wearing a suit, but no matter the clothes, he was a marvel in every way. He had a charming, beautiful presence that held such a deep, dark, passionate, and lustful desire which would draw one in closer and closer. His charisma was love at first sight. His presence alone could almost give away who he was. Once the age of demons came, he would shed his human flesh and take on appearance of the Dark Lord Satan.

They thought he had had extensive work done surgically, and whispers floated around. Because of how exotic he looked, society thought he was an alien coming to save the world.

Humanity had reached an utter low and was in desperate need of a Savior. Hearing of their desperate cry, the Antichrist arose.

By the control of man's hand, the sky was covered in clouds for this momentous occasion. The secret society caused great lightning bolts to strike the region in which the Eye/Antichrist would give his speech. It was the Antichrist himself who would present Project Blue Beam as a spectacle by which the masses would be amazed. By way of satellite and telecommunication, at the perfect timing the holographic images would shoot across the sky—across the entire globe.

As the masses gathered, they did not realize that the secret magic behind his power was all based off fifty-two satellites in the sky which projected beams of light. All they saw was him lift his hand, turning the whole sky into a telecast, thanks to AARCH, which were high frequency waves that controlled the weather. They could hold off the severe lightning momentarily, long enough to present the biggest spectacle the world had ever seen. The entire sky became a huge projection screen for media transmissions.

The Eye/Antichrist made his way from his armored limo to the podium to make his speech to the world. As he was qeued and in position, the podium floor began to slowly and timely elevate. The Antichrist presented a speech of unity, starting like this, "To those who couldn't attend, you merely have to look to the sky as I begin this evening, saying from satellite beams in the clouds: hello, world!"

Scientists all over the world were using a satellite system that beamed projections and holograms during times of war. This same technology was exercised in Desert Storm, but to use Project Blue Beam to its full magnitude and project a television news feed on the clouds across the world… This had never been done. When the Antichrist took to the podium in the Middle East, they spared no expense in showing off their full capabilities.

The Antichrist continued, "I'm sorry I have taken so long.

The ratings were in the billions. People loved it. He was strange, but so were most of Hollywood's pop stars. These were strange times, and they needed a strange leader. Without hesitation, the whole world bought it. After one single speech, this one single voice now controlled the whole world. It was official…

While Isaleer was on the moon, they had established One World Order. The beast was the sovereign leader of the entire globe. After his speech, he entranced all who watched as he performed signs and wonders alongside the already well-known Lord Navari. Yes—signs and wonders. The beast was only a puppet in which Satan manifested himself so he could operate in the natural world. However, a day would come when all would die and not leave the Earth. Then they would meet Satan…but that was not this day.

Jesus, the Christian's Savior, was God embodied. God found a vessel to deliver forth the great Messiah, Jesus through Mary. He walked on the Earth, presenting great signs and wonders, before he died on the Cross for the sins of the world. Now, everything God does, the Devil does an exact opposite imitation, so to the tribulation Christians, this was no shock. They knew he would come as the imitation Savior. Of course, it didn't help their case when he could perform signs and wonders. However, in the Bible it says that God gave Jesus that ability only momentarily.

Out on the streets of Dubai, famous rappers and pop artists began singing as their stages took flight into the sky. They rose about a hundred feet into the air. A robotic camera flew beside them, and several of them projected images in the sky. They were not as sophisticated as the Antichrist, but symbols contained subliminal messages. It was official; the Antichrist needed no television network. He controlled the sky. The onlookers were so hypnotized by his presentation that they all began a huge one million person orgy in the streets. As the demons and principalities in their human forms escorted the Antichrist and his leaders through the city streets, people bombarded him with praise and adoration.

When they reached one of the buildings, they traveled up the stairwell to the rooftop, where they ascended into the sky in a private helicopter. The Antichrist and his entourage journeyed to Dubai, where people of all nations were awaiting his arrival.

As the people of Dubai saw him and his fleet of military escorts, they began shooting off fireworks. The military flight escort dispersed, and the Antichrist landed at the Buri Al Arab. Instantly, they had complete and full control of the building. They were presented with the finest chambers and accommodations. As the principalities shut the door to the Antichrist's private chambers atop the highest skyscraper in Dubai, the Antichrist asked Dr. Killjoy, "What happened to the gargoyle squad? Why are my children not present?"

Dr. Killjoy stood up from the fifty-foot-long conference table and walked to the glass window overlooking the city of Dubai. He put his face down and said, "They escaped."

The Antichrist stood up, slammed his fist on the table, and said, "What?" The Antichrist began making his way slowly and maliciously toward Dr. Killjoy. "How did this happen?"

Dr. Killjoy replied, still gazing out the window, "Number Six… He was too strong, and the Arisen captured him. We are trying to locate him, but they took the chip out of his body."

The Antichrist said, "Him? You mean Isaleer? He was given everything, and he showed the most promising results. Why did he defect?"

Dr. Killjoy began shaking his head and put his hands on the window. "It was his mother…"

The Antichrist said, "How did he find his mother?"

Dr. Killjoy replied, "No, not his real mother. His adopted mother." With a deep breath, Dr. Killjoy said, "The Christian mother."

Laughing, the Antichrist replied, "The Christian mother? Isaleer is a gargoyle. He signed over his life to the entertainment world. He's Mr. Hollywood. You're telling me Isaleer got a conscience all of a sudden? Did you keep him sedated? Wait, hold on a minute. Isaleer is alone. He's on the run from the Illuminati armies. Without the ability to control his mutations between man and gargoyle, how can he possibly be so difficult to capture? We took away Evette by contacting the adult entertainment company she was signed to and getting them to shoot porn in Isaleer's house just as he was coming home. Remember? When he walked in and saw Evette having sex with another man, he gave his all to darkness and fully took on his title as a member of the Order of the Thirteen and began pushing political bills to bring forth New World Order. He has been involved in the Occult since the day Mr. Morgan discovered him and brought him to the yearly encampment in the Black Forest in the Bohemian Grove. We killed off those two original members just so we could assure a place for Isaleer among us. Dr. Killjoy, he had no knowledge of anything other than money and power. What changed his mind so suddenly?"

Afraid and frustrated, Dr. Killjoy replied, "No, he is not alone. He is with the Arisen. His mother put them together with the money in his trust fund. He is meeting with the elders, and they are going to tell him everything."

The Antichrist, clinching his fists and tightening his arms to his side, said, "Did you leave him the file?"

Teeth gritted and eyes closed, Dr. Killjoy said, "We searched his homes and all his private belongings, and we found nothing. However, if he had found the file, he would be here in the Middle East trying to find us. I'm almost certain he's made contact with at least one of his brothers or sisters."

The Antichrist was now standing alongside Dr. Killjoy, overlooking the city of Dubai. Out of nowhere, he turned the conservation from argumentative to physical when he grabbed Dr. Killjoy with great force and broke the glass of the conference room at the top of the skyscraper. Dangling Dr. Killjoy out of the top floor of the building, he said, "Do you realize what you have done? You let him free! I should kill you for this! I should let go of you and make you to fall to your doom. You had one job, Killjoy; bring me my children. That's it. The weapons manufacturing was just to buy time. Those gargoyles along with Lord Narvari and his demonic Illuminati army were more firepower than we would ever need to control mankind. Now that you have let him out of your sight, he has escaped into the arms of the Arisen. He has found his way onto the other side of the playing field. Do you realize what you have done? If the Arisen get him and his siblings to side with them, they actually stand a fighting chance to overthrow our plans."

Dr. Killjoy, in absolute terror, began screaming for his life. "Please! Please! Please don't kill me. I'm sorry. I'll find him. I'll do whatever it takes! Master, please don't kill me."

The Antichrist threw Dr. Killjoy on the conference table and said "We begin passing out the mark next week publicly. Since so many already have it, I intend to be the one to personally mark everyone as they stand in line waiting for the chance to glorify and worship me and give their lives over to me. I plan to make this a fashion trend to overtake the world, all the while becoming their savior and king. By the end of next week, I will be seated in the temple in Jerusalem. By this time next week, I will be God in the eyes of the entire world. Seven days, Killjoy. You have seven days to find him and all of his siblings. Seven days, Killjoy! I want my children."

Dr. Killjoy said, "What if he is dead from starvation?"

The Antichrist replied, "Then bring me his body as proof, with the understanding that as his fate claimed him, so shall yours claim you."

It was clear at this point what needed to be done. It was also clear that the only way Dr. Killjoy could restore his honor among the elite societies would be to retrieve the entire gargoyle squad and bring them before the Antichrist, alive and unharmed.

The Antichrist, laughing at Dr. Killjoy, said "Dr. Killjoy, I think you pissed your paints. Better clean up."

The Antichrist, thinking he had won, laughed and left the conference room. Walking to his private quarters, he said, "Remember, Killjoy—seven days. Now, enjoy yourself. You're in Dubai."

Chapter 21

HALEY'S GOT A CRUSH

Isaleer had slept the whole night away. This seemed to be what Isaleer did these days. He was recovering from his encounter with the Arisen soldiers on the space craft and was now beginning to function normally. The only thing left to do was be weaned off the pain pills. After a week of being on the moon, Haley began to grow rather accustomed to taking care of Isaleer.

Everything changed one morning. As the pain medicines began to wear off, so did Isaleer's pain. He woke up to the sound of Haley singing to him while he slept. She smiled, smacked him with a pillow, and said, "Wake up. You're such a lazy bum."

Isaleer laughed and said, "Ugh! I'm up. Ok. Ok."

He could smell breakfast in the other room. For a moment, he felt at home again. It was like it was ten in the morning, and his sister Lizzy was buzzing around the kitchen making breakfast: eggs, avocados, steak, ham with honey, bacon, Belgian waffles, hash browns, cinnamon oatmeal, Cream of Wheat, morning tea, monster cookies, and homemade vanilla ice cream.

A tear secretly fell from his eye as he thought of the old days. Isaleer loved his mother. She always had something encouraging to say, and it never mattered what the conversation was about; she could always bring it back to God. At this point, all the memories were just memories now. Isaleer's family was gone, and he was here on the moon, united with his love Haley Morgan. He snapped out of it and realized that this was what he wanted more than anything. To be united with Haley again, Isaleer would do anything. Now that he was here, he needed to enjoy and be present in this moment.

The fact of the matter was that Isaleer was in a space station command center on the moon. He needed to speak to the elders and begin his quest to undo the slaughterhouse chains, but right now he had to get Haley off of him, so he could get out of bed.

They were play-fighting. As it got intense, he grabbed for a cup of water and threw it at her. "Hahahaha!" he laughed.

Shocked and perplexed, Haley smiled and said, "Why, you! I'm gonna kill you."

As Isaleer ran down the hallway and Haley followed wheeling as fast as she could in her wheelchair, the smell of breakfast got stronger in the air. He ran and turned the corner to the kitchen, hiding behind the island near the stove and sink. He said, "Food smells amazing, Haley!" hoping that would get him out of a butt-beating.

She stopped everything and said, "Aw, really?"

Isaleer, caught off-guard, said, "Heck yes."

Thinking she was on the other side of the counter, he stood up and said, "Since day one, you've been amazing at cooking. I almost compare you to mothe…"

SPLAT! Haley fell to the floor laughing as she peed her pants, saying, "Banana crème pie to the face!"

Isaleer laughed and wiped off his face. Then he said, "Haley, catch."

She opened up her arms, and he sprayed her face with the kitchen sink hose. The war began again. As Isaleer began running, Haley chased in her wheelchair around the kitchen, Isaleer said his blessing over the food. "Lord Jesus God, bless this food. In your name, I pray. Amen."

It wasn't quite like his sister Lizzy's breakfast, but the Texas toast and extra marshmallows in the cocoa were pretty close. As he began to eat, he ran around to keep from getting caught by Haley. He grabbed the toast and ran to the living room, with Haley close behind, wheeling in her wheelchair trying to keep up.

Isaleer yelled, "What's your plan?"

Haley yelled, "Shut up! I'll figure something out."

Isaleer yelled, "You got nothing, Haley."

Just then, he looked out the window of his living room and saw the Earth. Haley wheeled over to Isaleer and climbed on his back. With Haley on his back, he held up his right hand as though he was holding up a glass and said, "Here's to you, Earth."

In the elders' chambers, Awa and the elders were busy preparing the room for Isaleer and all the things they would have to tell him.

"I wonder if he's got a green thumb like his mother?" one of the elders asked.

Another elder chimed in, asking, "Is it time for the meeting to begin?"

The Arch Elder spoke with old, wise words, saying, "Soon, soon."

But soon couldn't come quick enough for everyone in the room; the anticipation built. Isaleer had no sooner finished with his breakfast than Awa came to tell him the elders were ready to see him. He became nervous as it was time to face the elders.

Back on Earth, the Arisen was preparing to hijack the FEMA train in New Mexico.

The cry of war sirens began to scream all throughout the space station's command center.

One of the commanders over the moon's space station noticed a gigantic amount of foreign movement on his scanners. It was heading directly towards the moon in battle formation.

The commander said, "They found us! The Illuminati found us!"

Isaleer, the elders, and Haley did not know their space station was about to be under attack by the demonic Illuminati army's fleet of space pilots. They were on the moon and needed to get home, but they didn't even know it yet.

All of a sudden, missiles from the Illuminati space crafts began impaling the Arisen space station.

The sirens for the Arisen's moon command station began to sound. All throughout the facility, the Arisen armies began running to their posts and gearing up for an all-out attack. The Arisen military pilots began dog-fighting in the sky, hoping to bring down the Illuminati and safeguard the moon's space station.

Isaleer knew he needed to get Haley to safety. Survival mode quickly kicked in. Transforming into a gargoyle, Isaleer said to Haley, "I'll explain later, but here, get in my arms, and let's go. I'm not gonna lose you again."

Not even thinking to explain to Haley, he grabbed her up. She was shell shocked, and he threw her on his back. Before he could even think, they were running down the hallway at full throttle.

Security was trying to stop Isaleer because they had never seen him in his Gargoyle form; however, as he got closer, they realized it was in fact him. "The elders' chambers!" Isaleer yelled to the Arisen security guards.

They pointed him in the right direction. Isaleer flew through the ship docks as bullets flew everywhere. The Arisen army were fighting in the sky, but they were outnumbered because Dr. Killjoy had sent every single space craft they had to retrieve Isaleer and his gargoyle siblings. There would be no screw-ups this time; every precaution was taken to assure absolute victory and apprehension.

Isaleer, Haley, and Awa had to get to the evacuation ship quickly. All the evacuation ships were set to auto-pilot back to Earth and into the underground's space station located in the fortress of RS-7.

Isaleer could hear the Illuminati calling to him from the loudspeakers of the Illuminati mothership, which hovered unharmed by the shots being fired at it by the Arisen army. "Isaleer, come out! Make your presence known! You will not be harmed."

The Illuminati kept raining down bombs on the Arisen space station. They wanted Isaleer and would not stop until he was in their possession.

Isaleer barged through the doors to the elders' chambers and said, "What do I do?"

The Arch Elder said, "Do not show yourself. A spy was on the space ship that carried you here…"

He was wrong. A spy was in this room. One of the elders' right hand started blinking. Then all of a sudden, he ripped off his robe and began trying to shoot Isaleer.

The Arch Elder yelled, "Isaleer, kill him!"

Without hesitation and with gruesome force, Isaleer killed him. He leaped towards him in a fifty-foot pounce, grabbed him by his throat, ripped his arms off, and forced him to tell the entire room who had sent him. As the spy began bleeding out, the Arch Elder came next to Isaleer. He said to the spy, who was an elder for the Arisen, "Why? I trusted you."

The spy said, "The Arisen is outnumbered. It's time we quit delaying our fate. They will have our heads or our hands."

Isaleer snarled, squinted his eyes, drew back his right hand, and punched a hole in the spy's head. He then smashed the blinking hand, crushing the chip inside. "That's how they found us, that stupid blinking chip," Isaleer said to the elders.

Isaleer copped out with a cheesy line and said, "It seems that was the wrong answer. That's for trying to shoot me."

The Arch Elder said, "Isaleer, Haley, we need to get to Earth. War has begun. We stand a fighting chance with the gargoyle squad with us. It seems even in the tribulation, God shows mercy. Isaleer, you are a blessing from God."

Before Isaleer could respond, an Arisen commander pilot ran into the room and said, "Good news. They only brought transport ships. We shot down the fighter aircrafts. We can travel faster than them.

This will be our last space travel. Space travel is no longer safe, nor is it an option. We must get to Earth and hold our ground from RS-7 and all the tunnels of the underground."

The pilots waved for the elders, Isaleer, and Haley to follow them quickly to the ship docks. They ran with all their might.

One of the air locks had broken, so they were losing oxygen fast inside the space station. One of the blast doors closed in front of them, preventing all of them from getting to the ship. The elders began beating on the door. The command pilot said, "This is a six-foot-thick door. Beating on it is not going to do anything. Move!" The command pilot began trying to put in codes to open the door.

Isaleer yelled, "Putting in a code when the box is on fire isn't going to help either. You move!" Isaleer, a twenty-foot-tall gargoyle, backed up and ran towards the door. He kicked the door, and it cracked open, but it was not big enough to get through. The fire was building in the room. Haley yelled, "Hurry, Isaleer, hurry!"

Isaleer's eyes began to glow. He drew back his fist in fury. He punched the door off the hinges. After everyone made it through safely, they continued to the space craft.

As soon as one of the pilots saw Isaleer and the elders running through the docking stations, he pressed a button from the cockpit to open the main hatch. Awa was already waiting on the ship, safe and sound.

Isaleer and Haley strapped up for take-off. The Arch Elder said, "Awa, do you have the file?"

Awa said, "Yes." Turning to Isaleer, he said, "This is for you." Awa handed him all the answers to all the questions he had.

The captain said, "Hold on tight."

Just then, the file fell to the ground and out of Isaleer's hands. He had no time to retrieve the file, so he would have to retrieve it after he had gotten into space.

They shot off like a bullet, travelling through space. All Isaleer could think about was what the spy had said: "They will have our heads or have our hands."

It really made Isaleer think and understand. At the end of the day, would he stand against what is wrong and be strong enough to give his life, or in trying times would he agree and go with the flow to live?

A book he read in middle school said, "For me to live, something must die." What must die for him to live? In the Bible, Paul said, "We must die daily to our desires and everyday align ourselves with the voice of God."

Who could be so hungry to never see death that they would sacrifice the safety of those around them or compromise their morals in order to avoid confrontation or death? Would they live in oblivion alone so that they would never die?

> "For me to live, something must die... What is going to live? What is going to die?"
>
> —D. K. Rockwell

Isaleer, Haley, Awa, and the elders reached the orbit of Earth. They frantically sought to reach the underground fortress RS-7 without being discovered. This had ended the age of the great tribulation and had begun the age of the apocalypse. Things from here on out would only get much darker and much more Satanic. Isaleer would have to be strong in order to stand against the forces of evil, which never slept and never stopped searching for him. The Arisen space craft found a way past the Illuminati satellites. As soon as they landed, it would be time to begin building a strategy and uniting the gargoyle squad. Isaleer was allowed to move around freely throughout the Arisen space craft for a period of ten minutes before the ship descended through the Earth's atmosphere and into the Arisen space station located in the underground fortress RS-7. He quickly picked up the file and began looking through the papers.

There, the heading of the front page read, "The Redrum Diaries."

TO BE CONTINUED IN VOL. II

AUTHOR'S ANSWERS TO THE MAJOR THEOLOGICAL QUESTIONS

BIBLICAL EXPLANATION FOR THE MARK OF THE BEAST AND ALL THAT IMPLIES

The mark of the beast is coming in a time known as the apocalypse. Getting the mark of the beast will have eternal consequences. After being given this mark, there will be no turning back. [**Revelations 13**] contains a Bible prophecy that will be fulfilled. It will affect every person on Earth. Satan does not want you to know what the mark of the beast is. Take a few minutes to learn about this important Bible prophecy. *If you worship the beast and receive the mark of the beast, you will receive the complete wrath of God. The book of Revelations in the Bible gives us this strong warning:*

Revelations 14: 9-10

"If anyone worships the beast and his image and receives his mark on the forehead or on the hand, he, too, will drink of the wine of God's fury, which has been poured full strength into the cup of his wrath."

If you get the mark of the beast, God's complete wrath will be poured out on you. You will see the sky blackened, never to shine again. You will live to see a time when all of mankind scatters blood upon the ground. By taking the mark of the beast, you are joining in a demonic séance on an international scale, saying no longer "I," but "we" as a collective whole. By taking this mark and renouncing Jesus Christ, you are taking your name out of the Lamb's Book of Life, subjecting yourself to the punishment and damnation of Satan and all the demonic forces. At this point, you are all thrown in box cars and sent into the age of Warm-wood, the age of dragons and beasts, and the age of fire. Satan and all his army shall be set free as vicious monsters to roam free upon the Earth in the flesh. Everyone upon the face of the earth will seek to hide and flee God's wrath, but nothing will save you. You will die and burn in Hell. You will see no justice in your afterlife. You made your choice. Now, all at once, God will cast you from his sight. You will never know love again. It is worth your death to please God. Forever is a long time. This life is only temporary.

❖ *The mark of the beast will be required.*

Revelations 13:16-17
"He causes all, both small and great, rich and poor, free and slave, to receive a mark on their right hand or on their foreheads, and that no one may buy or sell except one who has the mark or the name of the beast, or the number of his name."

"When you are required by law to get the mark of the beast, and when you can't buy or sell without it, how will you live? You must learn to self-sustain or else parish. You must go into survival mode."

-Dexter Rockwell

❖ *What is the mark of the beast?*

The mark of the beast is a combination of letters and symbols that will be physically and permanently be placed on your forehead or right hand. Most people will consider it an honor to receive the mark. It will be like a key for them that will open doors of acceptance, prosperity, and peace.

> "This mark will have a way of unifying and singling out at the same time."
>
> -Dexter Rockwell

The mark of the beast will be placed on people who worship the beast and choose to receive his mark. There will be severe penalties for refusing the mark and great rewards for accepting it.

The mark of the beast will be enforced. The people who believe in the beast will worship him. The beast will have but to stretch out his hand. He will have no need to demand. You will either say "yes," or you will say "no." Those who take his mark will come to him proudly.

The beast is not a person or a human organization. The beast is Satan himself. When Satan comes as the beast, he will appear in a glorious body. People will not recognize him as the Devil. He will claim to be God, and most people will believe that he is God.

The mark of the beast is an outward physical symbol which shows that the wearer has chosen to worship the beast and receive him as God.

❖ *The mark of the beast is a symbolic union.*

When two people become married, the wife will often take the last name of the husband as her own. The husband and wife will both wear a wedding ring as a symbol of their marriage. Likewise, people will take the name of the beast and will wear his mark as a symbol of their allegiance to him.

There will be six hundred and sixty-six different ways to get the mark. Six hundred and sixty-six comes from Revelations 13 in the Bible. Six hundred and sixty-six is a human number that is connected with the mark of the beast.

❖ *The beast is Satan claiming to be God.*

The beast is Satan in a brilliant, perfect body. He will appear to people as a glorious being, and he will claim to be God. He will have many names, all of which are different names for God. In fact, he will have a total of six hundred and sixty-six names.

Revelations 13:17-18

"No one could buy or sell unless he had the mark, which is the name of the beast or the number of his name. Here is wisdom. Let him who has understanding calculate the number of the beast, for it is the number of a man: His number is 666."

❖ *There are six hundred and sixty-six blasphemous names.*

This verse tells us to calculate or count the number of names the beast has. The beast will have six hundred and sixty-six names. When he first comes to Earth, he will start out with seven blasphemous names, and over the next few months, he will keep adding names until he reaches six hundred and sixty-six blasphemous names. These are blasphemous names because they claim to be God, but they aren't God. When you count up all of his names, there will be six hundred and sixty-six names.

❖ *The mark of the beast is six hundred and sixty-six names.*

The mark of the beast is the name of the beast or any of his six hundred and sixty-six names. In other words, you receive the mark of the beast by taking any one of the beast's six hundred and sixty-six names. So why does he need so many names? He wants to appeal to every person here on Earth. He carefully selects his blasphemous names so that one of his names will appeal to each person on Earth. He will come as Allah or Imam Mahdi to the Muslims, Maitreya Buddha to the Buddhists, Jesus Christ to the Christians, Krishna to the Hindus, Messiah to the Jews, Saoshyant to the Zoroastrians, the Dark Lord to Satanists, and so on through the whole list of six hundred and sixty-six names. His goal is to win the worship and allegiance of every person on earth.

❖ *What does the mark of the beast look like?*

The mark of the beast will be a literal, physical combination of letters and symbols, rather primitive or technological. Thinking it would be permanently and prominently engraved or tattooed on the forehead or right hand of each person who gets the mark of the beast is a little outdated. The mark of the beast will most likely come with a modern day presentation, such as a rice-sized R.F.I.D. chip; a digestible micro-chip; advanced nano-technology tattoo ink; or drinkable nano-technology liquid, etc.

(The list of possibilities can lead up to what would seem as six hundred and sixty-six very possible ways to be administered.)

Include one of the beast's six hundred and sixty-six names. Each of the six hundred and sixty-six names will be a name for God. The beast is Satan, coming to Earth, looking like God and saying that he is God. Each of his names will be blasphemous because he is not God.

❖ *Can the mark of the beast look fashionable?*

The mark of the beast will look attractive and beautiful. It will please the senses and will excite the admiration of those who behold it. Most people who wear it will be proud to have it. It will be something that will allow you to avoid having to self-sustain. The mark will be plainly visible for all to see. Your friends and family will be able to see if you have received the mark. Your employer can look at you and see the mark. When you go shopping, the store clerk will be able to see if you are wearing the mark of the beast.

❖ *Is the "VeriChip" or "R.F.I.D. chip" the mark of the beast?*

The VeriChip is a small radio frequency identification device. It has an identification number, and it is the size of a grain of rice. The VeriChip is implanted in the human body. It is currently used in some countries for medical information.

By itself, the VeriChip is not the mark of the beast. The mark of the beast will only be offered after the beast has come. The beast is Satan coming to earth disguised as God. He will appear in a beautiful body and will require people to worship him and receive his mark.

❖ *The VeriChip or R.H.I.D. chip could be part of the mark of the beast.*

When Satan comes to earth claiming to be God, he will require people to receive the mark of the beast. It is possible that a VeriChip could be implanted in the forehead or right hand as a part of the mark of the beast. This would probably only occur in the more industrialized countries.

Currently, the VeriChip is not the mark of the beast, but at some point in the future it could be part of the physical mark that is put on a person's forehead or right hand.

❖ *The mark of the beast will be forced on everyone.*

Revelations 13:16

"He also forced everyone, small and great, rich and poor, free and slave, to receive a mark on his right hand or on his forehead."

The beast is Satan, but he will appear on earth as a powerful, awesome being. He will claim that he is God. This will happen very soon. A few months after the beast comes to Earth, he will attempt to force every person on Earth to receive the mark of the beast. He will make a law requiring every person to receive the mark of the beast, and there will be stiff penalties to anyone who refuses. This law will apply to every person in every country on Earth.

It won't matter if you are very wealthy or if you are poor. It won't matter if you are the leader of a great country or if no one knows your name. You may be free, or you may be in prison or in debt. You may be old or young, male or female. You may be very religious, or you may not even believe in God. Nothing about you will matter. If you are alive, you will be under great pressure to receive the mark of the beast.

❖ *Who will get the mark of the beast?*

Almost everyone in the world will get the mark of the beast. There are many reasons why people will choose to get the mark:

1. It will be required for everyone.
2. There will be severe penalties for refusing the mark of the beast.
3. There will be great rewards for getting the mark of the beast.
4. People will believe they are honoring God by receiving the mark of the beast.
5. People will be afraid of not getting the mark of the beast.
6. Most other people are getting the mark of the beast.
7. You can't buy or sell without the mark of the beast.

8. People will want to get the mark of the beast because then they will be allowed to buy food, water, medicine and clothes. They will be able to work and get paid.

Humanly speaking, getting the mark of the beast will be the logical, sane, safe, smart thing to do, but spiritually speaking, it is not wise to get the mark of the beast.

Please understand that God will not allow anyone to receive the mark of the beast unless they choose to get it. People will not be physically forced against their will. Most people will choose to worship the beast and to receive his mark.

❖ When will the mark of the beast be required?

It is not possible to get the mark of the beast right now. First of all, the beast does not currently exist, and second of all, the mark is not being offered or required. When he comes, he will bring millions of his demons with him. They will not appear to be demons. Many of his demons will appear as glorious angels who pretend to be from Heaven. Some of his demons will claim to be people who have died and gone to Heaven. They will say that they have come back to Earth to teach and help other people. They will appear in beautiful, perfect bodies.

❖ Two demons will appear to be Moses and Elijah.

There will be two powerful demons who will claim to be the prophets Moses and Elijah. They will come with the beast. The three of them will appear to be God, Moses, and Elijah.

The two demons who pretend to be Moses and Elijah are described as a beast in Revelations 13. They are called the beast with two horns. The two horns represent two beings, one Moses and the other Elijah.

Revelations 13:11-12

"11 Then I saw another beast coming up out of the earth, and he had two horns like a lamb and spoke like a dragon. 12 And he exercises all the authority of the first beast in his presence, and causes the earth and those who dwell in it to worship the first beast, whose deadly wound was healed."

The demons pretending to be Moses and Elijah will be gentle and kind like a lamb, but their words will be the words of Satan. They will have great power and authority. They will tell people to worship the first beast. This first beast is Satan. He appears to be God, and people will adore and worship him.

❖ *There will be fire from Heaven and miracles.*

Revelations 13:13-14

"13 He performs great signs, so that he even makes fire come down from heaven on the earth in the sight of men. 14 And he deceives those who dwell on the earth by those signs which he was granted to do in the sight of the beast."

The demon who is pretending to be Elijah will call down fire from Heaven to prove that the beast is God. The demon who is pretending to be Moses will work miracles to prove that the beast is God.

Revelations 13:16-17

"16 He causes all, both small and great, rich and poor, free and slave, to receive a mark on their right hand or on their foreheads, 17 and that no one may buy or sell except one who has the mark or the name of the beast, or the number of his name."

After Satan and his demons have been on earth for a few months, the two demons pretending to be the prophets Moses and Elijah will force people to receive a mark on their right hand or on their forehead. They will enforce the mark of the beast.

❖ *How do you get the mark of the beast?*

First of all, you can't get the mark of the beast accidentally. You can't get it without meaning to. The mark of the beast is not a disease, and it is not contagious. You will get the mark of the beast by making a conscious choice to receive it. There will be a magnificent, powerful, loving being on earth claiming to be God.

There will be two glorious, powerful prophets with him who claim to be the prophets Moses and Elijah. The three of them will convince almost everyone in the world to worship this beautiful, charismatic being who looks like God. They will convince almost everyone in the world to get his mark. These three beings will offer protection, eternal life, peace, and prosperity to people if they will worship the being claiming to be God and receive his special mark as a symbol of their allegiance. This is the mark of the beast.

Most people will be deceived into believing that they should get the mark of the beast. They will line up to get it. They will feel honored to get it. Please note that this awesome being is not God. You should not worship him. He is the beast. He is Satan. You should avoid his mark at all costs. You will not receive peace, prosperity, or eternal life. All six hundred and sixty-six versions of the mark of the beast are false and dangerous.

❖ *What if you get the mark of the beast?*

Here is a very important point. If you choose to get the mark of the beast, you are choosing to worship the beast and give him your allegiance. You will be worshiping Satan. You will be breaking the first of the Ten Commandments. In the first commandment, God says,

---

Exodus 20:3
"You shall have no other gods before Me."

If you worship the beast, you are placing another god before the true God of heaven.

If you choose one of the beast's six hundred and sixty-six names to be put on your forehead or on your right hand, you are choosing to worship the beast as your god. You will be worshiping a false god and will receive the undiluted wrath of the true God who lives in heaven.

At this point, by accepting the mark of the beast, ultimately you are saying, "I would rather live than die." In the Bible, Jesus says that in order to truly live, you must give your life away. Of course, this is in the manner of obedience; however, he is not only referring to submission in your actions, but also he is saying that it is better to die and live forever than to live and go to Hell. Hell is a real place, and this is where Lucifer is doomed. He does not want to go there. He wants to be seated upon the throne of God. He is coming to Earth to assemble an army to war against the Heavens when God comes to judge him. He wants to try to fight off the judgment; however, he will fail and will be cast into the lake of fire, and anyone who has sworn their allegiance to him will be cast into the lake of fire with him. Forever...

❖ *You will be allowed to buy and sell with the mark of the beast.*

It will seem like a good idea to get the mark of the beast because then you will be able to buy and sell. You can buy food and water. You can buy medicine and clothes for your family. You can continue to work at your job and get paid.

The mark of the beast brings the complete wrath of God. Receiving the mark of the beast has a very serious consequence. The most solemn, fiery threat in the Bible applies to anyone who receives the mark of the beast.

Revelations 14:9-11

"If anyone worships the beast and his image, and receives his mark on his forehead or on his hand, he himself shall also drink of the wine of the wrath of God, which is poured out full strength into the cup of His indignation. He shall be tormented with fire and brimstone in the presence of the holy angels and in the presence of the Lamb. And the smoke of their torment ascends forever and ever; and they have no rest day or night, who worship the beast and his image, and whoever receives the mark of his name."

If you receive the mark of the beast, you will receive the full wrath of God. His wrath will not have any mercy mixed in it.

Everyone who has the mark of the beast will receive seven terrible plagues. The first plague will be terrible, painful sores.

Revelations 16:2

"So the first went and poured out his bowl upon the earth, and a foul and loathsome sore came upon the men who had the mark of the beast and those who worshiped his image."

❖ *Get the mark of the beast, and die eternally.*

Beyond receiving seven plagues of the wrath of God, the people who receive the mark of the beast will lose the opportunity to live forever. They will die eternally instead.

❖ *What if you refuse the mark of the beast?*

If you refuse to get the mark of the beast, you will not be allowed to buy anything or to sell anything. You will not get paid for your work. You will not be able to buy food, medicine, water, fuel, clothes, or anything at all. You will be cut off from support, and most likely you will be killed. You can't buy or sell without the mark of the beast.

❖ *As a Christian, you will be hated and likely killed.*

Matthew 10:21-22
"Now brother will deliver up brother to death, and a father his child; and children will rise up against parents and cause them to be put to death. And you will be hated by all for My name's sake. But he who endures to the end will be saved."

You will be forced to get the mark of the beast. If you refuse the mark of the beast, you will not be allowed to buy or sell anything. You may be put in prison, and you may be killed. So why would anyone refuse the mark of the beast? Refuse the mark of the beast, and live eternally.

Some wise people will refuse to worship the beast and to receive the mark of the beast. They will choose to worship the God of Heaven instead. Many of these people will be killed, but a short time later, they will be raised from the dead, and they will live and reign with Christ for one thousand years.

Revelations 20:4
"Then I saw the souls of those who had been beheaded for their witness to Jesus and for the word of God, who had not worshiped the beast or his image, and had not received his mark on their foreheads or on their hands. And they lived and reigned with Christ for a thousand years."

After the one thousand years is over, the people who refused the mark of the beast will live forever and ever with God. They will be perfectly and eternally happy. Every person will be required to choose between two options. Please carefully consider these two options:

Option One: Get the mark of the beast
– You will be worshiping the beast. The beast is Satan claiming to be God. You will be able to buy and sell. Many people will like you. You

can keep your job and your house. You will soon receive the full wrath of God poured without mercy. You will die forever.

Option Two: Refuse the mark of the beast
– You will not be able to buy or sell. People will hate you. You will lose your job, your house, and most likely your life, but God will have mercy on you. If you believe in Him and worship Him, you will live again, forever.

❖ *Worship God or Satan?*

This is ultimately what all of life's choices come down to. Then there are the people who worship themselves. I assure you that selfishness is a sin. Therefore, if you worship yourself, you are indirectly worshipping the Devil. By allowing yourself to become center-stage, you are becoming your own God. This is blasphemy to the creator. So ultimately it all ties back to the choice: "God or Satan?"

www.ingramcontent.com/pod-product-compliance
Lightning Source LLC
Chambersburg PA
CBHW061022120726
47910CB00006B/2060